D0882167

To Peter Limón

Beloved uncle and incomparable inspiration

The Intriguing Life of Ximena Godoy
by Graciela Limón

© Copyright 2014 Graciela Limón

ISBN   978-1-633930-00-1

All rights reserved. No part of this publication may be reproduced, stored in a retrieval system, or transmitted in any form or by any means – electronic, mechanical, photocopy, recording, or any other – except for brief quotations in printed reviews, without the prior written permission of the author.

This is a work of fiction. The characters are both actual and fictitious. With the exception of verified historical events and persons, all incidents, descriptions, dialogue and opinions expressed are the products of the author's imagination and are not to be construed as real.

Published by

Café con Leche
an imprint of Koehler Books

3 Griffin Hill Court
The Woodlands, TX 77382
281-465-0119
www.cafeconlechebooks.com

📖 bitlit
A **free** eBook edition is available
with the purchase of this print book.

CLEARLY PRINT YOUR NAME ABOVE IN UPPER CASE
Instructions to claim your free eBook edition:
1. Download the BitLit app for Android or iOS
2. Write your name in **UPPER CASE** on the line
3. Use the BitLit app to submit a photo
4. Download your eBook to any device

"The Offended One clings to revenge."

Sor Juana Inés de la Cruz, Writer and Nun,
Seventeenth Century, Mexico

The Beginning

Los Angeles 1950

XIMENA GODOY stood in the empty cocktail lounge, struggling to catch her breath. It was just before daybreak, on an early December morning, She had sprinted up the stairs to glare out the window at the commotion below. After a moment, Ximena opened her fur coat, fumbled to feel the wetness, then jerked her hands away and wrapped the coat tighter to cover the blood. On impulse, she reached for a cigarette and her lighter, but when she flipped the lid, the metallic click was so chilling that her hand shuddered violently. Once the cigarette was lit, she sucked in a long drag, inhaling deeply into her lungs, and waited for the jumpiness to pass.

Ximena tried to shake off the terror gripping her, but her mind slipped and staggered as she relived the moment when Camilo's body had crumpled onto the street. She still felt the impact of falling onto her knees and hunching back on her heels, holding his bleeding head on her lap. Now, trembling, she looked out the window and muttered, "It's done." She took another drag on her cigarette, but the steadying calm she needed from the cigarette still didn't kick in; the earthquake inside her continued—it just would not go away. Again, she glanced out the window and this time saw the coroner's ambulance pull up next to the man's body sprawled on the street.

The nightclub faced Sunset Boulevard, on that half curve

just before it intersected with Alvarado Street, so from her vantage point Ximena could see up and down the street. As she watched, it filled with cops piling out of black-and-white patrol cars, cherry lights whirring, splashing the damp pavement with flickering shadows. Some of the officers were busy writing; others exchanged words about the killing that had happened less than an hour before. On the opposite side of the street, a couple of newspaper reporters haggled over a camera and the pictures they had taken.

Ximena was taking it all in; she wasn't about to miss anything. She watched when the rear panels of the ambulance swung open and two orderlies jumped out to help ease the gurney down next to the corpse. She stared as they paused, took a breath and then heaved the body up onto the stretcher, and just then she took a good look at Camilo's blood-soaked head and shirt. His tie hung limply around his neck, and that sight made her hand shake so hard that the ash from the cigarette flaked onto the front of her coat.

The lounge was dark, lit only by the flickering reflections that bounced up off the street and smeared onto the ceiling. For a moment Ximena looked around at the rows of cocktail tables piled with upside-down chairs. At the end of the room, glittering in strange reddish shadows, was the long bar that had been so jammed with carousing, smoking customers just a few hours before. Nervously looking for an ashtray, Ximena moved closer to the bar, and for an instant she glimpsed her reflection in the darkened mirror behind the rows of colored bottles. She took a hard look and saw an angular face, its sharp features drawn by a startled expression.

It didn't cross her mind that most people thought her looks were very special, even now at fifty. Maybe it was her smooth skin, or that pile of black hair, that made her so attractive; or it could have been the way she strutted on those high-heeled platform shoes; or perhaps the way her shoulders shimmied just a little when she spoke. On the other hand, she was actually more striking than pretty. When she glanced at a man, he got the message right away, and could be enticed to be by her side in a split second. Women, too, responded to her looks. They saw that she had a certain allure, a natural glamour and grace that made her striking. They knew that it came from inside her, and it made her different from other women.

Some people knew that despite her good looks and what they saw on the outside, the real Ximena Godoy was a closed book. Others said all sorts of things about her, especially that she didn't know how to love, and that her life's path was littered with withered love affairs. Well, that might have been so, but who really knew? Maybe it was just that she was reserved and solitary, or maybe the truth was that no one really knew her, and so they had no right to talk.

Ximena's mind was fixed on her mirrored image when the flashing lights suddenly jerked her back to the scene down below. She turned, still searching for an ashtray, but she couldn't find one so she let the ashy butt drop onto the floor and then absentmindedly squashed it with her foot.

"Mrs. Ibarra?"

The detective called out Ximena's name twice before she turned to look, but it took her a moment to make out the man moving toward her. He was dressed in the style of the times: dark flannel suit with a matching tie and vest; a fedora pulled low on his forehead, an unbuttoned raincoat over his suit. In general, the detective cut a heavy-set figure, maybe a little out of shape.

When Ximena didn't answer, he repeated, "Mrs. Ibarra?"

She finally spoke up, "Miss Godoy."

"What? Sorry! I didn't catch what you just said."

"I said, I'm Miss Godoy."

"I thought you were... "

"Married to the dead guy? No. We were partners, not married. My name is Ximena Godoy."

"Right! Well, miss, I'm Detective Poole with Homicide. We need a statement from you. You'll have to come with us to the station."

"Why? Don't you get the picture? There was a holdup and my partner was shot dead. We were robbed. What more do you need?"

"A lot more, Miss..."

"Godoy!"

"Right! You're the only witness. We need to ask you some

questions and get a signed statement from you."

"Now?"

"Yeah!"

"How will I get home?"

"Someone will drive you when we're finished."

Ximena leaned against the bar as she reached for another cigarette, but when she held the lighter to its tip she, realized that her hand was shaking even more than before. She glanced at the detective and caught his sharp eyes taking in her nervousness, so she hid one hand in her pocket and tried to steady the one holding the cigarette.

"All right, let's go."

Once in the vehicle, she crouched into a corner; she was scared, and the dark streets didn't help her get hold of her nerves. It was December in Los Angeles, with one of those drizzles: just enough rain to muddy pavements and cars. Inside the car, the swishing sounds of tires on the pavement and the back-and-forth rhythm of the windshield wipers broke the eerie silence.

The patrol car reached the precinct entrance and pulled up to the curb. When the vehicle stopped, Ximena pulled the collar of her coat high around her neck, stepped out and quickly climbed the steps to the front door. Inside she found Detective Poole waiting and ready to open a door into a small office. Without saying a word, he motioned with his head for her to step in. When she did, he followed and then pointed to a chair facing another man sitting behind a desk. The seated man was wearing a hat but not a jacket; his tie was loosened at the collar, and his face showed signs of serious fatigue.

"Thanks, Poole, and that's it for now." The man turned to Ximena, "Sit there, Ma'am. I'm Detective Tieg, Poole's partner." Then he reached into his shirt pocket for a cigarette, lit it, and Ximena did the same. He spoke with a drawl, as if perhaps he was from Texas, or maybe Oklahoma. He then pushed back his hat, giving her a clear view of his face: lean and craggy with flinty blue eyes.

The room was dim, lit by an overhead fluorescent light that cast a grayish tint on their faces; even Ximena's coffee-toned complexion looked ashy. The bad lighting was made worse by heavy cigarette smoke, so it took her a few minutes to see that over in the corner was another cop sitting behind a typewriter, evidently ready to take down her statement. Tieg slid a form toward Ximena: "Fill this in. We need your full name and address. When you do that much, then we can get to your statement."

Ximena filled in the blanks and then pushed the sheet back toward the detective who was rubbing his face, evidently trying to get new energy. He muttered, "Okay. Let's start at the beginning. About what time did it happen?"

She said, "About three."

"What makes you think that?"

"We usually close the club at two in the morning. We had already done that."

"What happened during the hour between closing time and when the robbery came off?"

"Camilo and I stayed behind to have a nightcap. We do...did that all the time." With that, Ximena turned to look at the man tapping out the questions and answers and wondered how he kept up, but she knew from the clicking and pauses that he was catching every word. Then Tieg asked, "What happened next?"

"As always, we closed the place and headed for the car."

"Where was it parked?"

"Around the corner."

"Where did the robber jump you guys? Were you in front of the club or down the street?"

"We had just come out so we must've been in front of the club."

"Where did he come from? The side? Or maybe from another doorway?"

"I'm not sure. I think he came from behind us."

"Did you see his face?"

"I turned when I heard his voice, but I couldn't see his face because it was covered."

"Covered?"

"Yes. He had a handkerchief tied over his nose down to his chin. And his hat was so low, all I made out were his eyes."

"Is that when he pointed the gun at you?"

"Yes."

"Right or left hand?"

"I didn't notice."

"You said that you heard his voice. Was there anything about it that caught your attention? Anything like a funny accent or drawl?"

"No. All he said was 'Gimme the satchel.' His voice was ordinary. Nothing different about it."

"What about his eyes?"

"What about them?"

"Well, were they slanted, like a chinaman's?"

"No they were regular."

"What does that mean?"

"I mean they were round."

"Was the guy a *metzican* or a negro?"

"He wasn't a negro. If you mean *mexican,* then maybe he was, but then maybe he wasn't."

Tieg made a sour face. "What about his size? Short? Tall? Fat? Skinny?"

"He looked about six feet and he wasn't fat."

"Was he dressed like a bum, or like just another gigolo who might've been in the club dancing and drinking?"

"He wasn't a tramp. He was dressed in a dark suit and overcoat." And after a pause Ximena said, "What do you mean, 'gigolo'?"

"Never mind! Was there anybody else with you and Mr. Ibarra? The barkeep, or maybe a waiter?"

"No."

"Why not?"

"Camilo didn't think he needed anybody tonight."

"Okay, let's go back to when the guy ordered Mr. Ibarra to pass the satchel. What then?"

"Camilo snapped, '*No!*' Then the guy grabbed the bag, but at the same time Camilo tried to rip off his mask."

"Did he rip it off?"

At that point Ximena seemed out of breath. She finally mumbled "No!"

Although he noticed that she was shaky, the detective still pushed for more information. "Go on!"

"They fought over the bag, real hard, going back and forth."

Her voice was rough with strain but she went on. "Then I grabbed the guy from behind, by the collar, and I made him lose his balance. He nearly fell. Then the gun went off."

"Went off? Like, an accident?"

"Maybe. I don't know. There was a shot. That's all I remember."

"And then?"

"And then he pulled the bag from Camilo's hands and ran away."

"In what direction?"

"I don't know. Away from us."

"Then what did you do?"

"The next thing I remember I was on my knees with Camilo's head on my lap. He was shot through the head. He didn't stand a chance." At that point Ximena was finding it hard to breathe so she clammed up. The tapping of the machine stopped. Everything stopped. Even Detective Tieg let up on the questions, but after a while he went on. "I'm sorry, ma'am. I have to ask questions about you and the victim. What was he to you?"

"He was my partner." Her voice was a whisper.

Tieg glared at her and then asked, "What kind of partner?"

"Business," she answered.

"Is that all?"

This time, it was Ximena who glared at him and said, "What do you mean?" Tieg squirmed a little. "I have Mr. Ibarra's driver's license here, and it shows the same address as the one you just gave on this form."

"Yes, we lived together."

"Then I'd say that he was more than a business partner."

"And you want to know if we slept together." Ximena's retort was quick and wrapped in sarcasm.

Tieg countered, "Well, you said it, I didn't, but now that it's out, what about it? Did you or didn't you?"

"Yes, we slept together. What's that got to do with the robbery and Camilo's death?"

Without hesitating he snapped back, "I can't tell right now, maybe later."

"Look, Detective, I'm tired and real upset. I'm going home."

"Just a couple more questions before we finish. How did the

thief know that Mr. Ibarra had money in the bag?"

"I don't know."

"How much was in the satchel?"

"About ten thousand."

Tieg whistled through his long front teeth. "Christ! That's a lot of dough! Was that just one night's work?"

"No. It was money that came in during the week. We kept it in a safe until Sunday when we took it home for Camilo to deposit Monday morning."

"Is that what you always did?"

"Yes."

"Besides you, who else knew your routine?"

"I don't know if Camilo told anyone."

"How about you? Did you ever tell anyone?"

"No."

Tieg stared at Ximena, and she guessed that his eyes were snooping for scraps of information that she might be holding back. When she sensed that he was trying to catch her in a lie she shut up and waited until he spoke. "Okay, ma'am, that's it for now. Don't leave your place in case we have to reach you."

A short time later the patrol car slid through the now-awakening streets off Sunset Boulevard. When the vehicle pulled up to the curb in front of her house, Ximena didn't wait for the driver to come around to the door before she pushed it open, jumped out onto the walkway leading to the front of her house, and in moments she stood facing the front door. "Jesus, why did I let Tieg rattle me? He saw through me, and I let him do it," she muttered until she finally reached into her bag for the key, but because her hand was shaking so hard she fumbled around for a while before she found it.

When she finally made it through the door the house was shrouded in early morning shadows, but Ximena didn't put on a light. Instead she kicked off her shoes, slipped out of the coat, stripped away the bloodied dress and let it fall on the floor. She kicked it aside. The place was cold so she headed to the bedroom to find something to pull on, and there she found the robe she had left on the bed the night before.

Thinking of Camilo, she absentmindedly put on the wrap and waited to warm up. Ximena returned to the front room where she lingered in the long shadows creeping in through the windows. She went to the liquor cabinet, poured a drink, helped herself to a cigarette, lit it, and then she went to the sofa where she sat trying to put things together, all the while smoking and exhaling thick coils of smoke that spiraled up toward the white plaster ceiling. Unmoving, she stared at the shadowy patterns inching across the floor. Daylight was making its way into the room.

Ximena scanned the room: high ceiling, bricked fireplace, polished wood floors, plush woven rugs. She sipped while taking drags on the cigarette, and when it burned down she lit another one, and yet another one. All the while she was lost in thought, reliving the events of the night that ended with Camilo shot through the head. Then, too agitated and nervous to sit, she got to her feet and paced the room while she drank, smoked and thought. *The cops will wise up. They'll track down Chucho Arana, and he'll talk.* The thought of her lover made her stomach churn. *I'll disappear. Just become invisible. Who's to know?* Then, suddenly struck with another thought, she stopped. *Wouldn't that prove that I'm guilty?* With that idea Ximena returned to the couch; she decided to take a chance and stay put.

Ximena felt alone and scared as she sat in the gloomy room staring at nothing, but relieved when after a while she felt herself calming down. Maybe to escape those fears and anxieties bearing down on her, or maybe searching for a way out, she shut her eyes and let her memory take flight back to the beginnings of her life.

PART ONE

Chapter One

Guadalajara 1908

IT WAS the sixth of May, the day of Ximena Godoy's first Holy Communion as well as her eighth birthday. The day began with the little girl standing close to her Auntie Dora while she fixed her hair; in a while it was all done with a white veil and crown. There was a lot of coming and going. Ximena's mother, aunties and cousins, along with chirping canaries and squawking parrots in cages set up on the patio, made a racket that filled the house. Then the time came to leave, and because this was her special day, she was the first to go through the double front doors hand-in-hand with her Papá. Next came her mother, followed by her little brother and sisters, and behind them her aunts ready to join husbands waiting out on the street.

The church was around the corner and up the hill so the family walked the cobblestoned street while neighbors stood at doorways and windows, waving, smiling, and wishing blessings for the Godoy family who were dressed in their finest. Ximena's uncles showed off stylish cravats, Panama hats, and kid gloves to match tailored suits; they held walking sticks for that elegant look. Her aunts followed in graceful long dresses, corseted and bustled just right, with high lace collars for that touch of refinement. They wore their hair piled high and topped by elaborately crafted hats.

Ximena clung to her father's hand as she walked, trying

to miss the dips and cracks between the cobblestones. All the while, her father raised his hat, bowing in all directions, acknowledging his neighbors' good wishes. At the front steps of the church, just before going in, he stopped to squeeze her hand and say something to her. He bent down low enough for her to hear every word, "Remember, daughter, that after you take the blessed host you will be cleansed. You will be as pure as on the day of your birth." She answered, "Yes, Papá, I'll remember."

"Remember also" he went on, "that purity is your most precious gift. Never forget that a woman is like a glass of finest crystal that will always show the slightest sign of being handled. A finger's mark will taint and diminish the value of that crystal. So, until the day that you go from my hands to those of your husband, you must safeguard that purity." When he stopped speaking to gaze up at the bell tower, her eyes followed his to see what had caught his attention, but then he went on speaking. This time his voice was so low that she had to stand on tiptoes to hear him say, "No one, Ximena, must ever touch your body until I choose your husband. Do you understand me?"

Despite not understanding, the girl said "Yes, Papá."

Once inside the church, Ximena joined the line of girls waiting for the signal to begin processing toward the altar, but there was a delay so she stood with a candle in her right hand and a tiny prayer book in her left. She looked nervous and excited as she waited for the nun to motion the girls to move forward. The church glowed with the light of dozens of candles placed on stands, on wall brackets and covering nearly the entire altar. White flowers were everywhere. When Ximena gazed up at the vaulted ceiling, her eyes scanned the faded frescoes she'd loved ever since she could remember. What she liked most of all were the images of saints that lined the walls, some of them in niches, others on pedestals.

She turned her head toward the rear to look at the boys perched up in the choir loft; they were already singing hymns that made her heart beat faster, although they were singing in a language she didn't understand. Then she looked over at the pews filling up fast with mothers, fathers, brothers and sisters, some already grown up, others just fidgety children. From there she glanced over to where the laborers and their families stood huddled against the side archway. They were the *Indios* respectfully standing alongside their women and children, all of them there to witness that important moment in the life of the daughters of their *patrones.*

Ximena stared at those brown men dressed in white rough cotton trousers and loose shirts, the *hacienda* field workers and mule drivers. Their women were dressed in long cotton skirts and blouses once colorful, now washed out and faded. Those *Indias* were the housemaids, nannies, cooks and laundresses. Some girls escaped their mothers' drudgery by taking the only way out and becoming *cantina* girls, but they weren't in the church because they were forbidden from entering.

Still waiting, Ximena's eyes were drawn to one of those *Indios.* He stood on the group's fringe, nervously turning his *sombrero* by its brim, but she noticed that his eyes were riveted on her; they were brighter and wide-open. When he saw that she was looking at him, he smiled vaguely and inclined his head a little, just enough for her to see, but not so much that those around him noticed. The girl did not understand his gesture or the way he was looking at her; she was too young and too innocent to grasp the hunger in those eyes.

Chapter Two

EVERYONE IN the village knew eighteen-year-old Tacho Medina as "El Indio," but what they did not know was that he had fallen blindly in love with Ximena Godoy. Indifferent to the ritual happening at the altar, and deaf to the chanting choir and devotional responses, Tacho's eyes had fixated on the girl whose round face and veil mirrored the angels painted on the walls. No one inside the church imagined that the fire exploding in his groin had hurled him to an unknown place where he held her in his arms, and that from that haven he would never return.

Neither did anyone notice when he moved away to find a corner where he could gaze at Ximena Godoy without attracting attention, where he pasted himself against a wall until the ceremony was over, and the girls began the recessional march. Behind them came parents, brothers and sisters, but Tacho saw only Ximena's face. As she passed close to where he was hiding, he thought that she glanced at him for just an instant, and at that moment Tacho knew that she, too, would one day love him. When the church emptied and the candles were snuffed out, Tacho lingered in the gloom trying to return to his usual calm, but the rapture he had just felt left him wondering how he could ever go back to what he used to be.

The days that followed were a torment for *El Indio.* He couldn't sleep, eat or work without thinking of Ximena Godoy, although he tried. He rose as usual before daybreak, and after washing up, he squatted on the earthen floor of the family hut close to the brazier while his mother patted tortillas and poured coffee into his clay mug, chatting all along about what was to be done that day. All the while Tacho was sullen and lost in his private thoughts. He had nothing to say.

Afterward he joined his brothers at sunrise to herd mules packed with grain and tools to be driven to nearby *pueblos*, and this much Tacho did mechanically without betraying a clue of the storm raging inside him, or so he thought. During those treks he was grateful for the din of braying mules, shrill whistles and loud prodding.

"¡Arre, mula! ¡Epa, mula!"

He found escape in that racket and in the swirls of dust where he abandoned himself to thoughts of Ximena Godoy. Life went on this way for Tacho for a time while he felt safe, thinking that his secret was his alone. But he was wrong because it was not long before his mother took him by the arm one morning and gestured for him to stay behind.

Tacho's mother, Señora Epifania, was a tiny woman with a fearless heart and sharp eyes. She had been left as a young woman to care for four sons when their father was crushed to death by an overturned cart. Being mother and father to those boys, she learned not only to detect signs of sickness, but also when they were sad or frightened. Whatever it was that troubled her sons, she was the first to see it and cure it, so now she said to him, "Your brothers are murmuring."

"About what, Amá?"

"That you're distracted, and that you're not completing your tasks as you should. That you're silent, that you eat very little."

Tacho made a face. "Why do they stick themselves into what I do or don't do?"

"Don't be angry. They're worried. Besides, we must all do our part."

"I do everything that's expected of me. Maybe if my brothers did their part, they wouldn't have time to wonder what I think."

"No one has said anything about what you think," his mother said.

Tacho shut his mouth when he realized that he'd gone

beyond what his mother was saying. He shrank back in silence but she pressed on, hoping to snatch him away from his secret.

"Tacho, your brothers fear that you've been bewitched." When he didn't respond, she went on. "I, too, have seen change come over you, but I don't believe that you've been bewitched. I think it's something else." When still a boy, Tacho had learned that his mother had a way of knowing what was inside him; now she sensed that something serious was happening to him. She said, "It's a woman, isn't it?"

Señora Epifania's words hit Tacho so hard that he felt himself go breathless. He shivered just enough for her to see his shoulders quivering.

"Why are you troubled? You're of age to take a woman and begin a family, just as your older brothers have done. Truthfully, I've expected this of you for some time. Such a desire on your part is good. It shouldn't be a source of worry."

Tacho hunched over, elbows braced on his knees, and he hung his head until it dropped into his hands. He was thinking that she would die if she knew the truth, so he kept quiet. When Señora Epifania saw that he would not respond, she reached out and put her hand on his head, but her gesture only caused him to jerk back, and at that moment she knew that here was something worse than she imagined. When he made a quick move to get to his feet she pulled him back to look closer into his eyes.

"Tacho, name her! Why should she be causing you such anguish?"

He answered, "Amá, leave me alone. You can't help me."

But Epifania didn't let go. Instead, she insisted, "I'm your mother. You must tell me her name."

She pushed him too far; the fire burning inside him erupted. "Ximena Godoy."

It took Señora Epifania moments to grasp what she had heard, and only then did she answer. "What?" She uttered the word in disbelief.

As if a gag had been pulled from his mouth, Tacho went on. "You asked her name, so there it is. Ximena Godoy will be my woman."

Stunned, the old woman muttered, "I don't understand."

And he said, "Yes, you do."

"Tacho, she's a child!"

"She'll soon be a woman!"

'No! It will be years before she becomes a woman. And even when that happens, the Godoys are a family beyond us. They're of another race, and they belong to a different world. They're the owners, the masters. What are you thinking? Are you crazy? If her father heard what you've just said he would have you killed."

"I won't die easy."

"Yes, you will! We all do."

"No! I'll die when my time comes. Not when Ximena's father decides it."

"You are forgetting that you're one of us, a lowly mule driver, an *Indio*, and that no one would even take notice if you were murdered."

"Yes, I'm that, but I'm a man too, and I will have Ximena Godoy. While I'm alive, that is how it will be."

She croaked, "What if she doesn't want you?"

Just as quickly, Tacho spat out, "She will want and love me! I know she will."

"Son, you say that she will soon be a woman, but think! That won't happen until years from now. Your time is now; you can't put off beginning a family. Your brothers were married at a younger age than you are now, and yet you're willing to wait, to lose years. It's a mistake, Tacho."

Instantly he said, "She will be thirteen in five years. I'll wait that long, or more if I have to. That's nothing for me."

To this Epifania countered, "But she will still be a child!"

Tacho was quiet for only a moment, and then he said, "You had your first son at that age."

His words caught the old woman off guard, but because it was a truth she kept quiet. It wasn't until after a while that she was able to say something that at least gained time for her to find a way to pull her son out of the pit into which he'd fallen. "I see that nothing will change your mind. Well, then, at least promise me that while you wait you will never go near her. Swear to me that you won't speak to her, much less touch her. Promise!"

Tacho felt moved by his mother's words, especially by the expression in her eyes. He took her face in his hands and gazed at her wrinkled leathery skin, her narrow eyes and high cheekbones, her white braided hair. He studied the faded blouse and skirt covering a bony body battered by years of overwork, and he filled up with tenderness. "I promise."

After this encounter Señora Epifania was in turmoil because she found little consolation in her son's promise. She knew that from that day onward, danger would sniff at Tacho's heels like a starving dog, and she had no doubt that Don Fulgencio Godoy would have her son murdered if he caught him stealing even a glance at his beloved daughter, Ximena.

Chapter Three

THOSE WHO thought they knew him best sensed there were hidden recesses in Fulgencio Godoy's nature, but because he was withdrawn and secretive, always on guard in case anyone was even tempted to invade his privacy, few people really knew him. No one knew just how fastidious he was, that he had no patience for disorder or for those who forgot their place. Oh, anyone could see that he was punctual, efficient, tidy and exacting in his personal cleanliness, and that he disliked and rejected those who did not live up to his standards. Not so clear was his uncommon possessiveness. Don Fulgencio did not allow anyone to trespass into what he considered his property— not the smallest part of it.

So on the morning of young Ximena Godoy's first communion, not everyone along the way to the church greeted Don Fulgencio with respect and awe. Opinions of how he had achieved wealth and position were mixed; hushed comments were tinged with resentful acknowledgement along with undisguised envy.

"Look! How he struts. Anyone would think he was the king of the world."

Old-timers stood in doorways and along the street gossiping about Don Fulgencio as he sauntered by them, daughter in hand and trailed by in-laws.

"Well, wouldn't you swagger like a cocky rooster if you had

what he has?"

"What? He never worked for it. He just slid into it alongside Doña Pachita Alonso. How much work does it take to do that?"

"C'mon, *compadre*. We're witnesses. We remember."

"What do we remember?"

"We remember almost everything about him. We remember that, yes, he was a Nobody, young and without anything to recommend him. But we also saw that he was hard-working, smart, with a lot of ideas and that he pushed the factory to what it is now. It wasn't just by marrying the *patrón's* daughter."

"*Mierda!* He was a stranger, an opportunist who came from lowdown riff-raff, and now he runs around pretending to have come from the likes of the *patrones*. Just look at him! Prancing and sashaying like a prized colt. He forgets there are still some of us around who remember where he really came from."

The oldest among those old-timers remembered that Fulgencio Godoy had appeared out of nowhere, a young man dressed in a threadbare, ill-fitting suit, claiming a basic education just barely good enough for him to aspire to a beginner's desk job. Beyond passable good looks and smooth manners, there was little else to his credit, but it was good enough to get him a job as an office boy in the Alonso textile factory, the largest in Guadalajara.

Such was the beginning of Fulgencio Godoy's climb upward from meager beginnings, which he did everything to hide. Still, there were a few discerning eyes that caught the signs of his lowly class: the subservient eagerness and the silent presence that avoided drawing attention to his comings and goings. But that was only in the early years; in time, the docile manner vanished and was replaced by an unshakable self-confidence that never went away. It happened after he quietly and patiently caught the eye of the owner's daughter, Pachita. After that, Fulgencio slowly seduced her until she finally married him. After that, his star rose.

Ironically, from early in his climb toward success, he acted as if he had always been part of the privileged few, stubbornly clinging to the image of himself as entitled. It was as if he had wiped clean the page from his life's story that told of how he relentlessly clawed his way upward from nothing into a higher class of people, ignoring that he pulled it off on the shoulders of others.

A well-made marriage, followed by one clever move after another, along with the passage of years, finally put Don Fulgencio in the powerful position he held on the day of his daughter's birthday and first communion. By that time he was already the owner of textile mills as well as land, livestock and dozens of peons who transported his products from town to town, from *hacienda* to *hacienda*. On that day, as he raised his top hat in acceptance of his neighbors' cheering, Don Fulgencio saw himself as nothing less than a self-made man, although the old-timers considered him a unscrupulous climber.

As for Señora Epifania—she was right in fearing for her son, Tacho. Fulgencio would have put him down the instant he suspected that his daughter was the object of the young mule-driver's attention. There was yet an even more powerful reason for Señora Epifania to fear Don Fulgencio: the old man adored Ximena from the moment he first held her in his arms. She was the center of his world, the jewel he guarded jealously. So Señora Epifania was not mistaken to be afraid of him, even though her perception came not from close contact with him, or knowledge of his interior life, but from an uncanny intuition that warned her of certain danger for her son.

Chapter Four

TACHO WAS not himself. He was jumpy, agitated, longing to look at Ximena's face, and although days passed, he could not think of anything else. *Why did I make that promise? What's wrong with just looking at her?* After sleepless nights, Tacho knew that he would break that promise; he could not help it. Without stopping to think that people would wonder what someone like him was up to, he asked them about the girls' school. What time did they go into class? When did they leave their studies? He snooped around until he finally discovered that the nuns took the schoolgirls to daily Mass at dawn; after that, nothing could hold him back.

Since his tasks began at dawn, Tacho planned to wait for just the right moment to break away from the pack to make his way to the church without being noticed. The first time was easy. He waited for the mule train to churn up enough dust to make him invisible, and from there he cut back toward the church undetected. Once he made it to the outskirts of town, like a thief he darted from one dark corner to the other, and from there he slithered along walls until he reached the church. Once inside, he found a spot behind a pillar where he watched the uniformed girls kneeling, side-by-side, devoutly responding to the priest's invocations.

From where he stood the girls looked alike, so it was hard

for him to make out Ximena, but after a while he spotted her. It happened when she turned to the girl next to her and he caught sight of her profile. In that fleeting moment he felt the fire inside him flare up again, this time hotter, more powerful, and he pictured her in his arms, doing to her what he had seen his brothers do to women in dim corners. It was an explosion that made him forget that the mules were getting further away; all he could think of was that he was gazing at the girl who would be his. Tacho could already taste her skin and feel her shoulders.

Tacho was in that daze until the Mass ended. When the girls processed out he pulled himself together, sprinted down a side staircase, and kept running until he caught up with the caravan. When nobody said anything, he convinced himself that no one had noticed, and so Tacho went on taking the same risk almost every day. That is, until one of the nuns grew suspicious of the same *Indio* who appeared mysteriously out of nowhere every day. Mother Bernardine's sharp eyes noticed, too, that he didn't come to pray but to gawk at her girls, so once convinced, she glared at him. When their eyes locked, she jerked out of the pew and darted toward Tacho, but he was quicker than the nun. He bolted down the aisle, out the side portal, leaped down two and three steps at a time, nearly falling once or twice. Panting, *El Indio* ran, not thinking of anything except that he had broken his promise, and snapping at his heels was his punishment.

Tacho didn't slow down until he caught up with the caravan, and there he slid into the thick swirl of dust to wait until he caught his breath.

"*¡Arre! ¡Arre! ¡Mula!*"

He shouted to make sure others saw him hard at work, and when no one mentioned anything or even hinted that something was wrong, Tacho relaxed. He went back to reliving the memory of Ximena's profile and the urges it stirred up in him. Gone was the picture of the intimidating nun, and he did this while caught up in the stench of mules, pesky flies, and dirt.

Tacho's biggest mistake was that he chose not to notice his brothers whispering among themselves, much less did he wonder what it was they were murmuring about. Not only did his brothers whisper, they were also disgusted because everyone they knew was now gossiping about *El Indio's* obsession with early morning Mass. Tacho didn't even see that people hung around street corners, tongues wagging about how he lingered around the church and convent, and there were lewd jokes going around about the hungry look in his eyes. But none of this meant anything to him, and even when the swirl of whispering became open chatter, he was blind to it all, so lost was he in his infatuation.

It wasn't long before the jabbering reached Señora Epifania, and her distress turned to anger that her son had betrayed his promise. On that day she had only to look into his eyes for him to know what was on her mind, and although he wanted to run, Tacho crouched down onto his rump and waited, eyes pasted on the ground.

His mother said, "You betrayed your promise."

"I can't help it. I must at least look at her face."

Epifania was trying to control her voice but her words came out dry, filled with feeling. "Her father will have you killed. Can't you understand?"

He answered, "He won't know. All I do is look at her. What's wrong with that?"

"You're a fool! What are you thinking? He won't know, you say? Everyone knows! How can you ask what's wrong with looking at the girl? What's wrong is that you're doing what's forbidden! Don't you have ears to hear so many tongues already wagging, telling of how you linger around those girls? Señora Teresita came to tell me that even the nuns have noticed you hiding behind the statues. If they know, it's only a short time before they run to Don Fulgencio. You know what will happen then, don't you?"

Tacho's jaw stiffened. He couldn't answer. Epifania waited, and when he kept quiet she took hold of one of his wrists. "I asked you a question. You know what *el Patrón* will do, don't you?" When Tacho still would not answer, she pulled at his wrist and murmured in a harsh voice, "Don't you?"

"Yes! Yes!" He answered. "I know!"

"What good will you be to any of us if you're dead?" Señora Epifania got close enough to her son to wrap an arm around his shoulders. "I understand your feeling, but it's for the wrong one. Look for a woman among our own. Son, are you listening to me?"

"Yes."

After that no more was said. Instead, mother and son ate in silence, each lost in thoughts of Ximena Godoy, but Tacho hardly slept that night. His mind reeled with doubts about himself, about his brothers, his mother, and about every village *Indio*. He was an ignorant mule driver. This he admitted. He didn't even know how to read writing posted on walls, much less sign his name. He laid in the gloom, thinking that if his tongue were to be cut out, he would be powerless to even say who he was, much less write the letters of his own name. What he did know was how to load and drive mules from sunrise to sunset, but that was all he could do. The few *pesos* he earned went to help keep himself and his mother alive, and even then his family was forced to go into debt just to buy tortillas and maize.

Tacho cursed his destiny. *I'm worthless. Everyone knows it, but does it mean death at the hands of old man Godoy just because of my worthlessness? Why does Amá fear this so much? Isn't it true that a man dies only when his time comes?* He looked hard into himself, but found little to make himself worthy of Ximena Godoy. Hours passed until he was finally overcome by sleep.

Chapter Five

LIKE ANY young man, Tacho Medina thought that death was still a long way off for him. His body was strong enough to tire out mules, and he ran faster than most of his fellow *peons*. Tacho's arms and legs were muscular, his belly hard, his teeth white and even and his eyesight matched that of a jaguar trailing its prey. No, it would take ten Fulgencio Godoys to put him down, and although *El Indio* could neither read nor write, his strength alone would be enough to win Ximena; this much he decided after that sleepless night. But it was too late, because his obsessive stalking of Ximena had gotten out of hand; too many people were talking about it.

The villagers knew that it would not be long before somebody plucked up enough nerve to approach Don Fulgencio, hoping to ingratiate himself and maybe even get a little something out of it. When it finally happened, the Informer, hat in hand, and so nervous that he had a hard time keeping his knees from knocking, went to *el Jefe* in his study. When the old man looked up, one quick glance told him that something serious must have compelled this raggedy *peon* to come near him. Nonetheless, Don Fulgencio was unruffled, and with his usual haughty expression, intentionally gave the man the impression that, although he was busy, he would listen.

"All right! Talk! But think before you do, and be quick!"

Don Fulgencio's warning filled the man with yet more apprehension and he shivered, hardly able to speak.

"*Jefe*, I am thinking."

The old man, now more curious than out of sorts, waited for the worker to settle down, but when the agitation would not stop he became impatient and snapped, "Has someone stolen a mule?"

"No, *Jefe*, that's not it."

"Then speak up or get out! You're wasting my time."

"Jefe, the truth is that we're afraid that Niña Ximena is in danger."

Don Fulgencio jerked forward in the chair and his hand stiffened so that the fountain pen he held dropped from his fingers. He glared at the Snitch who appeared to be even more nervous now and stood picking at his hat with shaky fingers, wobbling from one leg to the other.

"My daughter is in danger? Of what?"

"*El Indio* Tacho Medina looks at your daughter with hungry eyes."

The Snitch blurted out the words so rapidly that it took the old man time to separate one from the other to decipher their meaning, but when he did understand that a man was looking at Ximena with lewd intentions, it stunned and sickened him. Don Fulgencio took time to regain his composure.

Maybe it's a filthy lie. Maybe this fool is making up the whole thing just to get something from me.

Doubts flashed through his mind, yet Fulgencio was a man of the world. He knew that men even older than he did obscene things to little girls, that they paid money to lay their hands on those tender bodies. It happened in the *cantinas* and alleys not far from where he sat. But that Ximena should be the target of such monstrous desires sickened him. He rose to his feet and got close enough to the Snitch to make him shiver even more.

"Where did you hear this filth?" His voice was a hiss.

"Everywhere, *Jefe*."

"That's not good enough. I'm asking who told you this? I want names!"

"*Ay, Jefe*, for God's sake! So many people are talking about it that... "

"Who? Tell who those people are!" Fulgencio's voice was a croak. The old man's eyes were filled with so much fury that the Snitch babbled out what first came to him.

"My wife and her sisters do the convent wash, and they overheard the nuns talking about Tacho Medina."

"Talking about my daughter? What did they say?" Fulgencio interrupted the Snitch. He found it unbearable to hear that Ximena's name was dragged through stinking underwear and dirty water.

"How do I know this is the truth?"

"Ask others, *Jefe*. People know it's the truth."

"What's in this for you? What do you expect from me?"

"Nothing, *Jefe!* I swear it on my mother's tomb."

Stunned, the old man returned to the desk. "Who is this Tacho Medina you've named?"

"One of your mule drivers."

"Describe him! What does he look like?"

"He's one of four brothers, sons of a widow named Señora Epifania. He's no more than twenty years old, his mustache is yet thin, and..."

Don Fulgencio held up his hand, palm stretched out as if to cover the man's mouth, silencing him. He realized that he was hearing the description of any one of his workers. If he was to know the man's identity, the informer would have to point him out.

"Take me to him."

"Now, *Jefe?*"

"Now!"

Don Fulgencio's heart was pounding as he got to his feet. His hands shook so hard that he could barely take hold of his hat, but when he did it, he waved roughly toward the door for the man to step out and head toward where the horses were stabled. When his horse was brought, he mounted it, and at the same time he waved the Snitch to trot ahead to where Tacho Medina was to be found.

It was nearly sunset by the time Don Fulgencio made it to the corral where his tired workers gathered at the end of the day, but his unexpected appearance stunned them into forgetting their fatigue. They stood stiff and at attention as they removed their *sombreros*.

"Which one of you is Tacho Medina?"

Don Fulgencio's voice came across controlled and steady, although his body pitched and rolled in rhythm with his horse that pounded the earth with one of its forelegs. As if gagged, the men gawked at *el Patrón* until the old man repeated the question, this time with anger.

Tacho Medina stepped forward. "*Jefe*, I'm Tacho Medina."

Don Fulgencio glared down at Tacho. Then the old man gestured for *El Indio* to come closer, away from the others. When Tacho did as he was ordered and stood alone, Don Fulgencio walked his horse around him several times. The sun had dipped behind the horizon, and the dusky air was filled with silence except for the snorting of the horse and the soft thuds of its hooves on the powdery earth. The drivers stood stiff with fear, expecting Don Fulgencio to do something to Tacho, maybe whip him, or worse, kill him. But the old man did nothing. Instead he reined in the horse, turned it around, and trotted back toward the main house, leaving dust and confusion behind him.

Don Fulgencio always acted the same way when trapped: He retreated into the innermost recesses of his mind, into the solitude where he might find the way to punish the man who had shamelessly looked at Ximena. There was a moment when Fulgencio appeared to be hesitating. Perhaps it was because he could not be certain of what he had been told. Whatever his thought was, he shook it off to allow rage to take possession of him. He did not rant, throw or break things. Instead he sat still, gripped in the paralysis of unspeakable anger and desire to take revenge.

Chapter Six

THE THUGS who snatched Tacho Medina were faceless, their features erased by swirling yellow dust. No one saw them creep up on him as he trotted alongside the agitated mules; no one heard anything above the braying animals and the high-pitched whistles of edgy drivers. Tacho was alone when he fought to free himself from the four attackers who grabbed him. He struggled, kicked, and even bit to free himself, but nothing kept them from dragging him further away from where anyone might have helped him. They gagged and blindfolded him, tied his hands and feet, and then hoisted him onto the back of a mule.

The trek lasted hours until the secluded ravine was reached. Once there, rough hands pulled him off the animal and forced him to kneel on the rocky slope. Then came the most brutal beating of young Tacho's life. At first they all pounded on him in well-timed, synchronized movements, showing no mercy. Then, when each bully gave in to fatigue, they took turns delivering blows. On and on they kicked, pummeled and gouged until they saw him sink to the ground like a rag doll. Only when the hired thugs thought they had bashed out his last breath did they walk away from him.

When the villagers realized that Tacho Medina had disappeared, they knew who was behind it, but no one dared speak out the forbidden name. All they could do was regret having been part of *El Indio's* end. They whispered that he was probably dead, and they mourned just as if they had witnessed his murder with their own eyes. So too did Señora Epifania grieve. She covered her head with a black *rebozo* and refused to leave her hut, so that, one by one, people came to express condolences, vowing they had nothing to do with the false accusations against her son. They huddled, weeping and praying, by the side of the inconsolable mother whose heart was broken because Tacho was gone, and because his body was nowhere to be found, despite so many searches.

Days passed until an old woman appeared at Señora Epifania's hut. It was Señora Isabel, a woman who sometimes drifted into the village with her *burro* loaded with odds and ends to barter for a kilo of maize or beans. That day she headed straight for Epifania's hut, and when she was close enough she called out, but no one responded. So she stuck her head into the hut, waiting to adjust her eyes to its dim interior.

"Epifania, are you there? Are you there, *Comadre*? I have something to tell you."

"I'm here. Who is asking for me?" Epifania responded.

"It's me, Isabel. I've come from Zapopan with something to tell you about your son, Tacho."

The old woman's voice was thin; it rasped like a dry leaf rustling in the wind. "Your son isn't dead. He's hurt, but he's alive."

At first Epifania was silent, but then she answered, "Are you telling me the truth?"

"Yes, *Comadre*, I swear it's the truth. I found him at the foot of the ravine behind my hut where he dragged himself. You see, he was severely beaten, and the guilty ones left him for dead, yet there was still breath in him. I bound his wounds, and prayed over him, but it wasn't until a few days ago that he began to eat and speak a little. He wants to see you."

"Why did you wait until today to come to me?"

"Because I was afraid."

"Afraid of what?"

"I was afraid for myself, but also I did not want to leave him alone."

Epifania got on her feet, gathered a jug of water and a

handful of tortillas. She also retrieved a heavy shawl. Without saying anything, she emerged from her hut and motioned Señora Isabel to lead the way. The sun had dipped toward the mountain ridge in the west, but there was enough daylight to make headway toward the outskirts of Zapopan. Isabel, also without uttering a word, tugged at her *burro* and led the way north.

Bystanders who saw the women making their way toward the *sierra* understood what was happening, so they filed behind them. At first they were a handful of men and women, but soon, more trickled out from behind sheds and huts until their numbers grew. Señora Epifania was not alone; she was trailed by a procession of dusky villagers who hoped to find *El Indio* alive. *Rebozos* were tightly wrapped around the women's heads and shoulders; the men had *sombreros* pulled low over their foreheads; the cortege moved sometimes in single file, other times in small clusters, with only the scraping sound of *huaraches* to break the trek's quietness. By the time Epifania and her companions reached the ravine, they had only the moon and stars to light their path, but as soon as the two women disappeared into Isabel's hut, campfires sprouted against the boulders and *maguey cactus*; there, Epifania's guardians prepared to spend the night in vigil.

Epifania found Tacho stretched out on the ground with only a mat separating his body from the earth. She got down on her haunches to crouch closer to him. Even in the hut's darkness, she saw his wounds and right away, she knew that many were so severe that he would be scarred for the rest of his life. She pulled the thin cover from his naked body for a better view. Her eyes slowly moved from his feet, up to his legs, thighs, groin, belly, chest, neck and finally to his face—still so battered that, although he was conscious, Tacho could not open his eyes because they were swollen shut, as were his lacerated lips. Despite his mahogany-colored skin, his mother detected purple bruises covering most of Tacho's body; smears of blood still crusted around his joints and fingernails. The sight of her son's battered body caused a sharp pain deep in her stomach, but after some minutes she stooped over and took him in her arms.

"Son, you must leave." Her voice was soft but steady as she held him close to her breast. After moments she went on. "The old man tried to destroy you but he failed. The next time, he will get his way."

Tacho listened and after a while he murmured, "I'll leave this place, but I'll come back for you, and for Ximena Godoy. I promise."

Perhaps Epifania was thinking at that moment that her son's obsession with the girl would bring even more calamity, not only for him but also for them all. However, it was too late to question Tacho's path in life; now it was for him to live, and if he was brave enough to defy Don Fulgencio and his sort, then she too must stir up that same courage. That night she kept vigil by her son's side.

It took many days, but after he recovered his strength, *El Indio* Tacho left his mother to join the gathering forces up north. On that day, Señora Epifania blessed him, and then she and her guardians made their way back to their village on the outskirts of Guadalajara where they waited for the revolution.

Chapter Seven

MEXICO ROILED with rumors of revolution until 1910 when the upheaval finally broke out. From north to south, from coast to coast, people ended their workday caught up in stories circulating through villages and along mule trails. In the beginning those voices were merely whispers, but then in time the volume escalated. Chatter built on chatter—sometimes it was true, other times half-truths—but much of it was idle talk inflated as it moved from these lips to those ears.

The truth was that few people really knew what was happening. Here someone said *Porfirio Díaz is down! The strong man is dead!* Over there the answer, *I tell you he's not dead! I heard that he and Doña Carmelita packed up and bolted to the other side.* Much of the swirl of words was met with disbelief: *Escaped to hide out with the gringos? It can't be! I heard that he got on a boat and sailed away.*

Talk of the fall of Porfirio Díaz, *el gran Presidente*, could have been wishful thinking; nothing to be believed, and this was because only a few could remember a time when the tyrant had not been in charge. For most people, he was *el Jefe* of a lifetime, and even the elders had just a dim memory of life without the strongman's iron hand.

Then news came that finally convinced people the end of Don Porfirio Díaz was near. They heard tales of skirmishes and actual armed clashes. The underdogs had dared to fight! Government soldiers struggled to put down spontaneous village uprisings so filled with rage they were hard to suppress. What most stood out about those events was that they gave undeniable evidence of an uprising. It was happening all over Mexico, not just here or there. It was not a rumor. It was real!

Chapter Eight

Guadalajara, 1914

FOURTEEN-YEAR-OLD XIMENA Godoy peered into the mirror to better check out the pimple at the base of her nose. She got closer to her reflection and saw that the growth was plump and tinged red with a yellow speck at its center. She picked at the thing, at first carefully, but then she squeezed it hard until a blob spurted onto the mirror. She wiped it off with her finger to look at it up close.

"¡Fuchi!"

Ximena turned away from the mirror wondering what was happening to her, then twisted back to gaze again at her reflection; it was undeniable, she was changing. Until recently she had been a plump little girl, but all of that chubbiness was melting away from her cheeks and hands; her waist was thinning, her breasts filling, and she had grown tall. But the real change began back before her eleventh birthday, when she bled for the first time. When that happened she didn't know if she had fallen or hit herself on something, and she panicked at the sight of her underpants blotched with blood; Ximena thought she was dying. She had not been told that this was a normal occurrence for women because, you see, Ximena was on her own; she had no one to tell her of those things. There was nobody to prepare her, not even her mother who had run away with a stranger months before.

In time, the girl got used to the bloody spots, mostly because they came each month and since nothing happened to her, she grew accustomed to it. Still, she was tormented regarding these changes, but even more about the powerful urges and inexplicable sensations she experienced. If she didn't throb up here, she tingled down there, and she often woke up with her fingers stuck deep between her legs where, mysteriously, hair grew thicker each day.

Curiosity about other people hounded her. *What did others look like underneath their clothes?* Ximena knew what her body looked like, so she imagined that other girls were similar. However, she had never seen a naked man, so she had no idea of how their bodies were shaped. She had only seen her little brother when he was bathing. *Did papá look like him?* Ximena wondered most of all about her mother and father. She overheard other girls whispering about how a man slipped in between a woman's legs, and after that came babies, but that was all she knew. *Had mamá and papá done that?* She was intrigued by this question since she never saw anything; they didn't even share a bedroom when *mamá* was still with them. Did her father slip into her mother's bed after dark? Did her mother feel the same burning sensations as she? Perhaps. *Could this be the reason why mamá ran away with that other man? Did mamá allow that stranger to touch her? Was she going to have more babies?*

Questions plagued Ximena's mind, tormenting her without letup, and the day came when she longed to run away—maybe then she would find the answers. Why shouldn't she escape? Masses of people abandoned *haciendas* and cities every day. She thought about this constantly until she became obsessed with the idea of becoming like just another *India,* ready to follow her man to do battle alongside him: *una soldadera!* She dreamed of becoming a camp follower, to abandon herself to a man, and find out about those mysterious things a man did to a girl at night. *Then I'd know,* she told herself. But more than anything, Ximena dreamed of being someone special, different from everyone else.

Her imagination was vivid, filled with images of her mixing in with women who flaunted themselves in town. She wanted to be like those women, but, even more, she yearned to be like the rebels themselves. Ximena felt awe for those camp women because they were free, uninhibited, and she wanted to be like them so much that in her daydreams she pictured herself armed with a carbine, *bandoliers* crisscrossing her breast, and her face shaded by a huge rebel *sombrero*. These fantasies, along with Ximena's intensifying puberty, kept her awake at night, battering her until dawn brought sleep.

It was on one of those nights that an unexpected sound startled Ximena out of her half-dreams. It was like that of a pebble hitting the windowpane. She went to the window when the noise kept up, and although the street was dark, she made out the figure of a man she knew right away to be a rebel soldier. The man was dressed that way, he stood that way, but what caught her attention was how he stared at her window. Even in the dark, she made out his eyes that looked so intensely in her direction. She couldn't help but feel a strange sensation come over her, so she opened the window just enough to call out. He answered, and then came close to her.

They talked—she with questions, he with words of love—and when they finished he left, but *El Indio's* image and words stayed with Ximena all through the night until dawn. She knew that she liked everything about him, even the scar that crossed his cheek from nose to ear. The feeling had been instant, and she returned to her bed agitated by the powerful attraction she felt for the stranger. Ximena did not know what had caused that pull, but the man fascinated her, and when he disappeared she felt sad. Ximena yearned for him to return, but more than anything she wanted to go find him and be with him in his world. Then the thought struck her: *He's been waiting for me.* She could tell that from the way he stared at her with hungry eyes that she had seen before, but she could not remember where or when.

Chapter Nine

AS HE promised, Tacho Medina returned for Ximena. Night after night, wrapped in a battle-frayed *sarape, sombrero* pulled low over his brow, he kept watch outside her bedroom window like a sentinel, confident that the power of his desire would sooner or later draw her out. During those hours Tacho's thoughts often drifted back to his near-death encounter at the hands of Don Fulgencio's thugs. Most of the scars were fading except for the one on his cheek; the blow had gone too deep for its rawness to disappear. This memory mixed with recollections of his ordeal crossing the *sierras*, and then of wandering the northern desert to finally find his place among the Villista insurgency, clung vividly. In the beginning, *el General* did not know him, but in time Tacho's skill with horses and mules caught *el Jefe's* attention. *El Indio's* confidence in the saddle made those in charge take a second look at him, and soon he moved up the ranks to ride with the cavalry.

Ciudad Juárez, Tierra Blanca, Chihuahua and Torreón: Bloody hits and painful battles drifted into Tacho's mind while he waited for Ximena to appear. He thought of the men he had killed, of how he had destroyed their possessions, and how that brutality had left its mark on him: he was forever changed, and he knew it. Tacho was a different man now. He was a soldier who had endured wounds, smelled the stench of blood on dirt, and heard the screams of dying men and animals, but those terrible experiences weren't the worst; the scars singed deepest in him were those inflicted at Fulgencio Godoy's orders. *¡Cabrón! One day I'll settle that score with you!* Tacho repeated the vow he made when he nearly died.

This night he knew that his transformation went deeper than the scars on his face; it was beyond what he saw when he looked in a mirror. *Ximena, will you love what's left of me?* Suddenly, that doubt made him shudder. He pulled his wrap closer to help against the chill, but his shakiness persisted. Time dragged as the night's darkness deepened, and all the while he felt himself growing more restless outside Ximena's window.

After hours of waiting, the urge to throw pebbles at the window gnawed at him. *"I can't wait any longer!"* Mumbling under his breath, Tacho let the *sarape* slip off his shoulders and he picked up a handful of stones, waiting after each one hit its mark, but then the clicking sound soon unnerved him. He imagined everyone in the house heard what was going on and he almost lost his nerve. But just as he was turning away, one of the panels creaked open and Ximena appeared. Tacho froze. What he had dreamed of for years was happening, but he couldn't move or speak. *"¡Pendejo!"* he cursed himself under his breath.

"Who is it?" Ximena's voice was hushed but it reached Tacho, touching him, wrapping itself around him. After a few moments she moved away from the window as if to close it, but then she opened it again, wider this time. "Who's out there?"

Suddenly encouraged, he murmured, "It's me, Tacho Medina." His voice was hoarse, choked, but hearing it helped him recover. His legs filled with strength, and he moved closer to the open window until he was close to her. "You don't know me, Niña Ximena, but I've been close to you for a long time."

Tacho wanted to tell her of the powerful feelings, yearning, love and desperation that had clung to him for years, but instead he was stammering stupid words. He longed to say *I've loved you for years,* yet nothing came out of his mouth except what he had already blurted out, and he clamped his eyes shut as if waiting for a blow to come crashing down on him. He was certain that she would wake up the house with screams or some other alarm. *I'll run like a scared rabbit,* he thought, but when he opened his eyes Ximena was still standing at the window. Much to his surprise, she had not moved. Instead, she blinked and squinted her eyes trying to focus on his face.

"What do you want?"

By now, Tacho had made his way so close to the window that only its wooden bars separated him from Ximena. He reached out and wrapped his fingers around those barriers, and there he clung as if to prevent himself from being swept away. Tacho was so close to Ximena that he could have reached in and taken hold of her, but instead he whispered, "I want you to come with me. I want you to be with me for the rest of my life. I've always loved you."

Ximena shrank away from him, but she did not run; instead, she stood gaping at him. Tacho held his breath, hoping that she would stay, not move, just go on looking at him. Despite the dimness he could see that she was thinking, wondering, unsure of what to make of him. *She thinks I'm ugly. I know it. She hates the scars on my face. One day I'll tell her who put them there.* His mind filled up with reasons why he was detestable, but as she stared at him he felt himself gaining confidence. All the while, he looked even harder and closer at her. He stared down and made out her bare feet and the long nightgown; slowly his eyes moved up to her hair hanging loose over her shoulders. He could even make out the swell of her small breasts, and in that moment he loved her as never before.

She finally spoke up, "You're crazy!"

"Yes, Niña Ximena, but it's for you that I am how I am. Come with me! Now!"

Ximena was captivated by Tacho's words. No one had ever spoken to her that way. Even more than his words, it was their tone, their softness, their warmth—and everything in her yearned to slip out through the window to follow him. Years later, she would understand that such a feeling happens only to some people, and that the same deep stirring inside her would never transpire again.

"I can't."

"Why not?"

Tacho's question stunned Ximena because there were so many reasons for not going with him, yet she couldn't name one.

Not the thought of her brother or sisters, not even her father; nothing existed except *El Indio's* passionate desire to spend his life with her, and her own strange longing to stay by his side. She whispered, "Maybe tomorrow."

"No, Niña! Now! Come with me to fight."

"Fight what?"

"Together we'll fight for the revolution, and we can be free."

Not understanding what he was talking about, she said "tomorrow", slammed shut the window, and watched through the glass until she saw him disappear into the night. When Ximena returned to her bed, it was to think of the man who had so mysteriously captivated her to the point that she knew she would go with him wherever he took her. All he had to do was ask again. These thoughts filled Ximena's mind despite her knowledge that if she ran away she would disgrace her family and suffer her father's unforgiving anger. She was, however, too young to let caution drag her away from desire.

Chapter Ten

ONE NIGHT, Ximena waited for Tacho in the dark. Every night he had returned to whisper, "Will you come with me?" Each time she answered, "Maybe tomorrow." But now she had decided, and she waited by the window, listening for the muffled hooves of his horse. When she heard the sound getting closer Ximena stiffened, but she tensed up even more when she made out Tacho's silhouette slide out of the saddle and move toward her window. She watched him as he crept closer, gingerly taking each step, careful not to make a sound. When he got close, Tacho again murmured, "Will you come with me?"

This time she answered, "Yes."

Ximena grabbed the knapsack she had packed and silently slipped out of her father's house, where she had been born, and would never again return. When she met Tacho outside, he didn't say anything except to put his arms around her shoulders and draw her so close that she felt his breath upon her cheeks. He held her for a long time. After that Tacho hoisted her onto the saddle and leaped up behind her, wrapped his arms around her, and nudged the horse toward the rebel encampment. It was early May, and Ximena had just turned fourteen.

The trek over the *sierra* was long and rough, but all along neither Ximena nor Tacho uttered a word. Finally he asked, "Are you tired?" He did not wait for her answer. Tacho just reined in the horse and dismounted to help her down. She slipped off the saddle into his arms where he held her for a long time, nestling his mouth on her neck. When Ximena felt the pressure of Tacho's arms she was thinking *this is the way it will always be. I'll stay here by his side forever. I'm afraid but I want to be free, to be more than the others. I want to be better.*

The sun was rising when he spread his *sarape* on a grassy place and they lay together. It was then that she realized that her nighttime fantasies had not prepared her for when Tacho climbed between her legs and entered her. At first it hurt and frightened her, but the sensation passed and soon faded when she felt his tenderness and caresses. No one had ever shown her so much love.

Chapter Eleven

HOW TONGUES wagged when the news broke out that Ximena had run off with *el Indio* Tacho Medina! The jabbering intensified even more when it got out that old man Godoy, so shamed by what his daughter had done, at first declared that she had been kidnapped, but when he realized that no one believed it, he changed his story. Desperate to cover up his humiliation, he made up the tale that she had been kidnapped and killed, and her body had been found. He even ordered a *novena* of rosaries, followed by a funeral mass and burial. A crowd attended the services to pay their respects to Don Fulgencio, all the while suspecting it was an empty coffin they accompanied to the cemetery.

When the whispering died down, word got around that Don Fulgencio had shut himself up in his bedroom, hardly leaving it even for meals or other needs. When this went on for a time, worried for his children, their aunts took them in, packed their belongings and put them on a train to *el Norte*. After that, very little was heard of Don Fulgencio Godoy, or of Ximena's little sisters and brother.

Chapter Twelve

THAT DAWN Ximena sat behind Tacho, clinging to his waist as they came onto the rebel encampment of General Pancho Villa. She held *el Indio* even closer as the horse trekked down a pathway between piles of gear and stacked provisions, its hooves clopping softly on the loose dirt. This was one of General Villa's largest concentrations of *La Division del Norte*, his revolutionaries called *Los Dorados*, a force coming together those days for the attack on Guadalajara. It was a huge camp; it sprawled haphazardly up slopes, spilling over hills and along gulches. At its center was a rail track equipped with trains that worked day and night bringing in goods, horses, ammunition, and reinforcement of troops.

As Ximena and Tacho made their way, she had a hard time focusing on what was around her because the air was thick with smoke and churned-up dust. She did see some people already stirring and setting up campfires. Up closer she saw mules and horses tethered to carts and wagons. Blinking hard, she made out shelters slapped together with old planks and corrugated metal sheets, raggedy tents, and even broken-down carriages, anything that provided cover for the rebels and their women. Ximena hugged Tacho hard and murmured, "Are we going to live like this?" She waited for his answer, but he kept quiet.

Although she caught sight of one woman stoking a fire

and struggling with an iron hot plate, Ximena saw that most people were still sleeping by burnt-out campfires. "Why are so many still sleeping?" This time she tugged at Tacho's waist until he chuckled.

"Ximena, our *muchachos* face death in battle all the time, so at night we have a good time."

She kept quiet, but then asked, "Are you like them?"

He answered, "Don't be such a *niña*."

What Ximena still did not know was that General Villa's *muchachos* had fought so many bloody conflicts that they binged every night, because nobody knew if they would live to see beyond the next sunrise. Neither could she imagine this was also true of their women, the renowned *Adelitas*, who fought alongside their men, unafraid of getting into the thick of battle. It was natural for those insurgents and their women to say,

"*¡Qué carajo! Let's break out la marijuana, tequila, guitarras and accordiones, and let's get pisto! Like the corrido says, 'If I'm going to die tomorrow, then let it happen today.' Now pass the bottle, por favor!*"

So the rebels drank, danced and fornicated all night long, and then snored until late morning.

As she and Tacho made their way, Ximena took in signs of the night's carousing: carelessly scattered empty or nearly empty bottles, a lopsided guitar buried under tattered *sombreros*, and everywhere she looked there were carbines and cartridge belts hanging here and there. The sight of sleeping women and men lying locked together, legs and arms still entangled after lovemaking, riveted her. That sight really gripped Ximena! Their nakedness and total abandonment shocked her, forgetting that she did the same with Tacho. When she remembered that much, Ximena made herself feel good with one thought: *At least we don't do it in front of everybody.*

Camp life now began to stir. Women especially seemed to be coming out of hovels and from underneath lean-to shelters, and seeing so many of them made Ximena feel more of an outsider, more afraid, so she leaned her head against Tacho's back trying to feel safe. He must have known what she was feeling, because he took one of her hands and murmured, "*¡Calma, Ximena, calma!*" But her nervousness kept on growing, especially when she saw that some of those women stared hard at her. *Their eyes are like daggers. They hate me.* But Ximena stared right back, letting them know what she thought of them. *They're in rags. Look at those faded skirts. ¡Dios mió! What filthy hair and skin!* What she was gawking at was braided hair that hung straggly and flecked with trash, hanging over brown skin made yet darker and leathery by sun and desert winds. It disgusted her.

Ximena didn't even try to hide her contempt. Perhaps this was because none of those women were anything like her fantasies of what she would be like as a female rebel soldier. Yet they were as young as she, some maybe a little older, but others even younger, and if Ximena gawked at those *soldaderas* with wide-open curiosity, they glared right back with defiant eyes. They stood with feet planted wide apart, fists propped on hips, and chins stuck out, a gutsy expression on their faces. Those women, although young, were quick to see that Ximena was not of their sort. No, she belonged in a convent school, or in the dining room of a *patrón's hacienda* where they were allowed only to serve meals or scrub floors.

Those *Adelitas* knew right away that Ximena was intruding into their world, their new upside-down domain where it was now their turn to be on top, and they resented her. Those women gaped at Ximena until she and her man disappeared down the smoky pathway, and then they returned to their chores, all along poking fun at her.

"¡Epa, cabrona! Let's see how long you last!"

Chapter Thirteen

DURING THOSE first months of living among the rebels, Ximena knew that the camp women laughed at her for being Fulgencio Godoy's daughter, and it angered her; this much she could not deny. All Ximena wanted was to be like them, to be a part of them. On the other hand, there was a voice inside her that said, *So, what if I'm not their sort? There's nothing I can do about it, is there? Anyway, who wants to be a part of that pack of putas?*

What Ximena really craved was freedom, and for that she had Tacho who found ways to break away from the intense training and drilling just to be with her. On those breaks, he and Ximena disappeared into the *sierra* where there was no one to stare at them, to jeer or criticize. In that isolation they were utterly free to race, wrestle, roll in the hot dirt, shout, laugh, and usually end their romps naked, anxious to have sex, not once but over and over again.

Tacho discovered that when it came to making love, Ximena was as unquenchable as the desert, and he loved her for it, coming onto her as much as she desired. After each encounter he asked, "Ximena, do you love me?" Her answer would always be "Yes!" Not satisfied with that one-word answer, he pressed her for more expressions of love. "But do you love me like I love you?" She never answered that question; at least he could not remember a time when she did.

Tacho did more than pamper Ximena when they were on their own. He taught her how to be a *soldadera*, how to be a part of an assault on the enemy, and it was not long before she picked up those skills, becoming so good that the other *Adelitas* were forced to show their respect, although Ximena was never complimented directly. Their silence said it all, and she was satisfied.

At night Ximena, arm-in-arm with Tacho, joined the others to sing *corridos* or soft love ballads, and to dance the wild polkas the *norteños* loved so much. When she took her first shot of tequila, it was a turning point in her place among those *soldaderas,* though she didn't know it yet. That night, Ximena put on a big show of confidence and gulped down a shooter just like a *veterana*, but no sooner had the burning liquid gone down when she began to cough and choke up. That was all that was needed; everyone broke out with loud hoots and jeers.

"*¡Ay, Dios!* Somebody give *la catrina* a cup of the burro piss she drank in the convent." From another direction came fake tones of sympathy. "Poor little thing! Her gullet is too delicate! Give her some *atolito con azúcar!*"

However, Ximena wasn't going to take those insults, and for days she mumbled *¡Cabronas! Next time you'll know who your mamacita is!* So she drank shot after shot every night, and it didn't matter to her that she got so drunk each time that Tacho had to carry her to their shack, and that she couldn't remember the next day what had happened. What really mattered to her was that with practice she learned to hold that tequila. Then Ximena became *la mamacita*, and it happened sooner than anyone thought possible. After that there were no more hoots or jeers—just dirty looks.

When Ximena had conquered tequila, she looked around for the next thing, and she discovered marijuana, something she enjoyed even more. From that time on she dominated that pack of jealous women, and soon she blended in; she was by now one of them, at least on the outside. She walked like one, talked like one, dressed like one, and not only that, even her face had changed. Where there had been roundness, there were sharp lines. Where there used to be softness, there was hardness.

Her skin, olive-toned before, was now burned brown by the sun. Her breasts were fuller; her waist slimmer, and her hips rounded. When anyone looked at her they saw that she had transformed from the convent girl into a crafty *cucaracha*.

But this was her exterior, because what she really loved was the freedom of camp life —not the ideals of the Revolution, or its training and talk of liberty for the underdogs. She didn't share the tension felt deeply by the followers of General Villa; she didn't even fear the battle that was about to happen. It was what went on at night when guitars and accordions got going. Her nightlife triggered lustiness inside her, and she guzzled tequila because it filled her with energy to dance around the fire with as many of the *muchachos* that could keep up with her. She stomped and kicked her feet like none other, and she didn't care that everyone could see her legs all the way up to her crotch. She shook her *nalgas* and shimmied her *chichis* with wild abandonment, much to the chagrin of the other women in the camp. She did it with Tacho and the other *pelones* until she tired them out. Only then did she flop down on the ground to swig more tequila, panting, catching her breath, all the time flirting with those big eyes of hers while the other *comadres* hated her for trying to take away their men.

All of this taught Ximena that she did not need anyone except Tacho, though as she got more confident, even he began to fade in and out of her thoughts, and she gave other *muchachos* the eye with more provocation. Ximena was a flirt and she laughed, remembering what her father had urged when she was a little girl.

Chapter Fourteen

SUMMER PASSED and the year slipped into November. Cold northern winds swept through the camp, and no matter how tightly the *sarapes* were wrapped around shoulders, the insurgent camp shivered. But despite the cold there was action everywhere; everyone was in motion now that it was nearly time for General Villa and his *Dorados* to attack Guadalajara.

Train after train rumbled into the encampment, each one loaded with artillery, horses, ammunition, and more *soldados* and *soldaderas*, all of them clinging to the train's roof or hanging out of windows like monkeys. The women arrived, most of them young and Indian, each loaded down with bundles and *mochilas*, backpacks stuffed with meager possessions. Some appeared to be relaxed and experienced, but most of them looked scared and disoriented. Some clung to their man, others were on their own, at least for the time being. Most of the women arrived equipped with heavy cartridge belts crisscrossed over breasts, some with a pistol belt slung around the waist; all of them wore the long ruffled dress that showed them off as *Adelitas*.

When the train slowed down, the lucky ones who rode inside a coach were the first to leap off, unlike the ones riding on the train's roof who struggled to climb down, bags and gear dangling off shoulders. Bad falls happened in the rush to stake out a campsite, a hard thing to do since the best spots were already taken. Fights broke out in the middle of the pushing and tugging, and dirty language was so loud that it reached to where the others were perched. In no time, those brawls spread until they became a sea of bobbing *sombreros* and flapping braids.

As for noise, there was a deafening racket on every side: shouting, cursing, clanging, neighing, braying, squeaking, and even singing and praying. Yet, that action and agitation did not mean that those men and women were unafraid, because it was undeniable that the bitter taste left by the still vivid *Zacatecas* battle was on everyone's tongue. The same calamity could happen again and everyone admitted it. That din and commotion was only on the surface, and not enough to cover up the sounds of fear that battered those hearts —the upcoming battle could be even bloodier.

The day for the taking of Guadalajara finally dawned when General Villa finalized the strategy with his lieutenants. Artillery and cavalry positions were mapped out; hordes of insurgent fighters were put into place. Then the General took time to ride from one side of the camp to the other to personally reach out to as many of his *Dorados* as he could. There was backslapping and joking as he laughed through those big teeth of his, all the time relaxed and confident, with his *sombrero* pushed back on his head — everyone saw the steady look in his eyes as he mixed in with the cheering, elbowing throng of rebels.

"*Muchachos*, we'll split their balls! Just stick with me! Those *carrancistas* are cowards!" Then the shouting exploded,

"¡Qué viva mi *General Villa!*" "¡Qué viva el *Tigre!*" "¡Qué viva la *Revolución!*"

The breakout began when the signal sounded. Everything was ready. The artillery lined up with the cavalry at its head, followed by *los Dorados* and *las Adelitas*. General Villa positioned his horse in the lead, and then came the shrill blast of dozens of *cornetas* signaling the launch of the march toward Guadalajara.

The distance between the encampment and the city was steadily covered, and by the time the sun began to set that day, the General rose in his stirrups, flashed the order, and the thunderous charge broke loose. The stampede of horses, cannons, rushing cavalry, men and women screaming out curses, was stunning. There was a blur of weapons held high in clenched fists, and clouds of dust churned up by horses billowed upward until just the cone tops of *sombreros* were visible.

Ximena was lost in the charging throng that strangely did not last; something unexpected happened at the city's entrance. The first attackers slowed down and then bunched up, forcing those behind to rein in their frantic horses. No gunfire was heard, and then all of a sudden it was all over. *Los carrancistas* did not take a stand; instead, they made a run for it out the other end of town. Like chickens with wings fluttering, beaks hanging open, scrawny legs scrambling, they ran for their lives, and they did not stop until they reached Ciudad Guzmán. Guadalajara surrendered to General Villa and his *Dorados* without a shot fired.

It took time for the word to spread and for the revolutionaries to begin their parade through the city. It was then that every church bell rang out as if gone crazy, and *los Tapatíos*, the natives of Guadalajara, went wild with joy—they had been waiting for General Pancho Villa for years. Hanging out of windows, from rooftops, from trees and lampposts, people waved rags, ribbons, *sombreros*, aprons, anything to show how happy they were. There, on the corner in front of the cathedral, stood Señora Epifania, older now and more stooped, yet proud to know that somewhere in that mass of grinning, dusty insurgents her son Tacho Medina rode.

Endless rows of mounted rebels in their thousands pranced their horses into the heart of Guadalajara, marching side by side, so crowded that their knees practically touched, the brims of their huge cone-tipped sombreros nearly grazing. The uproar was thunderous, and the dust was so thick that it darkened the air.

Then at last, Ximena Godoy appeared in the middle of those ranks. The rebel *sombrero* sat low on her forehead, dirty sweat smeared her face and neck, *bandoliers* crisscrossed her chest, a carbine was cradled on her lap, a revolver hung on her belt, and the long skirt of her dress draped the hindquarters of her palomino. She rode by Tacho's side, and she looked proud.

Chapter Fifteen

FIGHT! *PLEITO!* Shrieks, whistles and shrill catcalls yanked everyone away from whatever they were doing to run to the brawl that had broken out. A pack of *soldaderas* crowded around two women fighting on the ground in a blur of fists, clawing fingers and pulling hair, their legs kicking, arms yanking and pummeling. Goaded by the shouting mob, Ximena and *la Malvada* grunted, groaned and cursed as they pounded one another.

"¡La Malvada contra la Ximena!"

"¡Puta madre!"

"¡Se van a matar!"

"¡Ay, hija de la chingada!"

The onlookers shoved, hooted and yelled out filthy words, mostly in support of their meanest and toughest, the woman who was so bad that she was known as *la Malvada*. Their screeching egged her on to pull Ximena's hair, to bite her arms, neck, anywhere; to get up and kick her in her ass. *"¡Dale en las meras nalgas!"* The shouting and cursing got louder as the two women rolled on the ground, churning up dust, inciting the onlookers to become wilder with each blow; they were all rooting for *la Malvada*.

"¡Dale en la madre! ¡Pártele la madre!"

Ximena's opponent was five years older and a veteran,

hardened by the experience of war, sex and tequila. By the time Ximena showed up in the rebel camp, *la Malvada* had already been partner to several of the top captains, sleeping with each one until she tired of them and moved on to the next one. She was beautiful but aloof and remote; no one came near her except if she wanted it. The males coveted her, and the females envied and feared her, knowing that she was a jealous one, always on the lookout for any woman who might rival her beauty and supremacy.

It wasn't only under the blanket that *la Malvada* proved to be matchless; she had also shown that she was any man's equal in battle, as evidenced at the bloody encounter at *Zacatecas* where she single-handedly blasted away a machine gun nest of *Pelones*. She did it even as her *compadre* rebels shrank back, and in the end, it was General Villa who invited her to sleep with him as her reward. When word got around that she had slept with *el General* at his invitation, the whole camp saw it as the highest tribute. "Who wants a medal when you sleep with *el Mero Mero*?" After that, *la Malvada's* reputation was unassailable—until Ximena came along and the picture changed. Ximena was on the way to proving herself a hardened *cucaracha*, not only under the blanket but also out in the field.

So now it was up to this fight to show everybody who was who, and the gang hollered for *la Malvada* to trounce the convent girl. But as the fight went on, *la Malvada's* strength and gutsiness were not working as her *comadres* thought it would. It could have been because Ximena was younger, or maybe because she did not know better, but the truth was that *la Malvada* was caving in. Her blows were less powerful; it could even be said that some of them were feeble. When she tried to land a good one she missed more than once. When she chomped down with her big teeth, the bite she received in return was deeper and more painful. Toward the end, all she could do was yelp and take wild swings while blood gushed out of her nose and ears.

This is not to say that Ximena wasn't taking a beating—she was. She just happened to be more resilient, her body more flexible, less quick to give up. Each time *la Malvada* managed to get on top of her, somehow Ximena wiggled until she toppled her, all the time punching and shrieking so ferociously that it unnerved nearly everybody. If *la Malvada* poured out curses, Ximena's obscenities outmatched anything the other one spat out.

Then suddenly, without explanation, the two women gave up the struggle. *La Malvada* flopped to one side, and Ximena rolled backward to the opposite side. Both women lay flat on the ground with legs spread, bellies heaving, wide-open mouths panting and gasping for air, each woman trying to hide that she was crying because it hurt so much, and because she had not won the fight.

The screeching mob just as suddenly shut up; no one knew what had made the fighters stop their battle so abruptly. Honestly, *las comadres* felt cheated. They wanted more grunting and curses, more blood and tears; they wanted their *Malvada* to be the clear winner, but now there was nothing. When it was certain the fight was over, mumbling broke out and gossiping got started.

"Why were they fighting?" one of the *adelitas* asked.

"What else, *Comadre*, except for a man? *La Malvada* caught *la Ximena* under the blanket with Teniente Sosa." The woman winked wickedly and shimmied her shoulders as she answered.

"Isn't that *la Malvada's* man?" yet another woman asked as she pushed her way closer to the fight.

"Yes!"

"And she caught them under a blanket?"

"Yes! Doing you-know-what!"

"¡Ay, Ximena Godoy!" The astounded *adelita* muttered, "Wait until Teniente Medina hears. You're going to pay with more than just your front teeth."

Chapter Sixteen

THE FIGHT with *La Malvada* was a turning point for Ximena because afterward, no one gossiped of anything else except that she had betrayed Tacho Medina. Even though it was not unusual for a woman to sleep now with this rebel, and then with another, nonetheless word spread, and when news of the rumble finally got to him, Tacho couldn't believe it.

For a while he dealt with the ugly rumor by convincing himself that it was a pack of lies. However, because he was uncertain of the whole thing, he confronted his *compadres* about it. But they played dumb and pretended not to know anything; no one had the nerve to spill the truth. They knew that his woman slept with Teniente Sosa when Tacho was out on mission, but they were afraid of what he would do if he knew, so they kept their mouths shut.

Sensing he was being made out a fool, and that Ximena was indeed betraying him whenever he turned his back, Tacho was finally forced to accept the truth, which shattered him into many pieces. Ximena's betrayal caught him utterly unawares; he had failed to see the signs, much less suspect that Ximena was capable of betraying him—and maybe this was why it hurt him so deeply.

His first reaction was to disappear into the desert to think, to try to come up with a plan that would make sense. But no matter how much he tried, Ximena's and his lovemaking crowded into his mind. Vivid images of her naked body badgered him, even though he tried to reject them.

Tacho isolated himself for days hoping that something would come to him to prove that it was all talk and lies. He wept and raged, but there was nothing to contradict what was being said all over the encampment. After days of this torment, he knew that the only thing left for him to do was face Ximena. Tacho returned to camp but everywhere he turned he caught looks filled with pity, and he hated that his *compañeros* felt sorry for him. He was devastated by their sympathy, but more than anything he was humiliated, and he found his shame unbearable.

That public disgrace told him he had to deal with Teniente Sosa even before Ximena, if he was to hang on to his pride, but killing a comrade was not easy for Tacho Medina. He was a soldier, not a murderer, so he decided instead to confront Ximena to give her a chance to tell the truth. After days of searching for the right time and place, he faced her.

Although taken by surprise, she kept calm when it happened. She even appeared indifferent; at least that was how Tacho saw her. In that instant, his heart sank because she seemed more beautiful, as if she had taken a secret potion that made her face, her breasts, and her whole body more radiant than before. He was struck by the thought that maybe by surrendering her body to that other man it had become more beautiful, but when this disgusting idea hit him it nearly choked him with jealousy.

"Ximena, why have you betrayed me?"

"I haven't betrayed you. I never promised to be yours forever."

"When you held me and let me hold you, wasn't that a promise?"

"No!"

"When you let me get between your legs, when you let me kiss and touch you, wasn't that a promise?

"No!"

"Then what was it if not a promise to be my woman forever?"

"I loved you Tacho, but not like you loved me. I can't love you that way."

Tacho was disarmed by the way she spoke; so natural and

without guile. The expression on her face was like that of a child telling the truth as she saw it, without cunning or pretense, or desire to please or displease. That look threw Tacho off-balance, and he didn't know what to do.

"Why, Ximena? Why?"

Ximena shut her mouth and refused to say any more. Frustrated, he glared at her, detesting that this was happening, hating her for what she had said, and cursing himself for his stupid confusion. In that empty silence, memory of his mother's warnings came back to him. *She belongs to another people, a different race. Find one of your own.*

He touched the scar on his cheek, and remembered her father's hatred, and that despite his loathing, the old man had been powerless to crush Tacho's love for the girl he first saw in church, or his vow to wait for her. And now, despite all of that, Ximena was saying that she could not love him as he loved her.

"Ximena, you've made a fool of me. Aren't you ashamed?" But still she would not speak. She neither denied nor apologized, and her silence made him want to kill her. He screamed, "Speak to me! Explain yourself, *Cabrona!*" But when she still would not speak, he turned away from her, took a few steps, then stopped and pivoted back to face her. He grabbed her by the collar and pulled her toward him, yanked his revolver from its holster and pressed the barrel hard on her forehead.

Seconds dragged by. Ximena squeezed shut her eyes but stayed mute as he pressed the gun harder against her head, but then, with his finger curled around the trigger, Tacho realized that he couldn't pull it. Maybe he loved her too much. Maybe he didn't have the courage. Whatever the reason, Tacho lowered the gun, and with his free hand grabbed a fistful of her hair and jerked her against the ground with such force that, when she hit the ground, the painful slap of flesh smashing on rock rang out.

When Ximena began to moan, Tacho knew that he had seriously hurt her, but instead of feeling satisfied he was terribly shaken and unsure of what to do. He glared helplessly at her for a few moments and then walked away, vanishing from that place as well as from the encampment.

Years later, when Ximena Godoy was already living in Los Angeles, *barrio* gossip had it that after his disappearance, Tacho

Medina joined up with the southern forces of General Emiliano Zapata, and that he had moved up in rank to become one of that General's lieutenants. It was said that he was part of the troop lured by the traitor Guajardo into *Hacienda de San Juan* at *Chinameca*, and it was there that he and his fellow *Zapatistas* were ambushed and wiped out in cold blood. It happened on a cloudy day in April of 1919. When that volley of bullets slammed into him, *el Indio* Tacho Medina went down with two regrets: That Ximena Godoy had not loved him as he loved her, and he never got the chance to settle the score with her father.

Chapter Seventeen

XIMENA GODOY was alone. Time after Tacho's disappearance was bleak for her because she missed the uninhibited romps with him as well as his reassurances of her beauty and importance. Without Tacho, Ximena melted into the mass of unwashed, tough, foul-mouthed *soldaderas*; she was just one of the horde, and she hated it. Above all, she missed Tacho, the gentle, considerate man. She yearned for the joy he showed after they made love, and she longed for the steadiness in everything he did, and how other men barely reached his strength. She missed Tacho, and wished that she had not betrayed him, but she had; nothing could change it.

Ximena had been careless in her ways with her *compañeras*, and now that indifference caught up with her, too. More than once someone mumbled, *"Quien siembra vientos recoge tempestades"*. Those words were clearly aimed at Ximena, who was now paying for behavior considered bad even among those women of few rules. Her puffed-up ways had come around to haunt her just as sure as chickens return to the roost at sundown.

Now that Ximena was alone, *las comadres* shunned her, and they did it with a lot of satisfaction. They were not about to forgive the way she looked at them, from one side of her nose, and that she did it since the first day she made her way into the camp, riding like a queen on Tacho's horse. Those women gossiped about Ximena all the time because she strutted and shimmied in and out of the camp with her man. *¡Cabrona!* How about the way she flirted with their men, out in the open, in front of everyone? *¡Sin verguenza!* Not one *Adelita* forgot that Ximena rubbed it in that she was better than anyone at shooting, riding, drinking and dancing. So what if she was better? Why show off? On top of this, not far from anyone's lips was that she had played a dirty trick on Tacho Medina, one of their best. Now they had lost him, thanks to her! Around the campfire at night those women mumbled, "It was good that Tacho beat the shit out of her!"

But if anyone asked the real reason why Ximena got the cold shoulder, it was because she was never accepted as one of their own class in the first place. It was that simple! Now that she found herself stranded, she tried to make friends; she even approached *la Malvada* to apologize, but it was no use; it was too late. Everywhere Ximena turned she found nasty looks and grumbling as soon as she turned her back, and even Teniente Sosa cut away in the opposite direction when he saw her coming. Although she wanted it, she was shut out of the shared chores that brought those women together to gossip and joke around. Her exclusion from the night *fiestas* probably hurt her most of all, because she still craved the dancing and carousing; instead, she was left to hang around the fringes of all the good times.

Not only was Ximena alone and hungering for company; now she discovered that she was pregnant. She was not an innocent girl anymore; she had been around long enough by now to recognize the signs: throwing up, gagging, hating the smell of food and feeling miserable most of the time. This part of what was happening she knew well enough, but what she did not know was who had planted the seed, Tacho or Sosa. She hated thinking of this, but she couldn't help it now that she was this way, with her belly bloating up; at night she lay sleepless, thinking about the lump of flesh that grew bigger every day.

Does it have a face, a heart? How does it survive swimming around in what I swallow? Will it hate the day it first sees light? Will I hate it, this piece of me that's come, even when I don't want it?

Ximena tried to put on a brave face despite all the bad feelings around her, but she was afraid. She had watched girls even younger than her turn up with bloated bellies that soon popped out little ones. She saw how the lives of those girls changed, how they were pushed to the edges of the camp to nurse the little things, with nothing to do but hang around, relying on whatever scraps were thrown their way. Then the question remained, what about the lover who stuck the seed in the girl in the first place? Well, he just moved on to his next conquest. Ximena was scared; she cried, she even cursed the path she had taken, but nothing helped. In the end, there was nothing she could do to change her situation. She had to face it.

Chapter Eighteen

IT WAS the coldest night yet. Up close to a small campfire she had put together, Ximena huddled with her knees clasped against her chest, all the time feeling the bulge in her belly. She wrapped the woolen *rebozo* tightly around her head and shoulders, hoping to ward off some of the chill, but it wasn't enough. So she hunched over and stuck her nose into the shawl's folds. That helped a little. The night was clear, and from time to time she glanced up at the stars, trying to enjoy them for at least a few seconds. The crackle of burning branches filled the quiet while her mind swirled in a circle from one thought to the other: *Where will I go? Who will help me?* Then the spiral started over again.

"*¡Epa Amiga!* Can I sit here by the fire?"

The unfamiliar voice startled Ximena, lost in her go-round thoughts. She pulled her nose out of the warm shawl to look at the woman who had already squatted next to the fire; her face was barely visible because her *rebozo* hung so low. Ximena looked hard at her but didn't recognize her.

Grateful for the woman's company, Ximena nodded while keeping her eyes on her. But when the woman's shawl slipped away from her head and part of her body, Ximena saw that the she was maybe just a few years older. She had a round, dark-skinned face with a little mole, right there between one side of her nose and the corner of her lip. When she smiled, her eyes brightened and Ximena liked her right away.

"*Hermana*, my name is Concha Urrutia." Her voice was soft and relaxed, as if she already knew Ximena, who after a few moments murmured, "I'm Ximena Godoy." The woman squirmed on her ample rump looking for a more comfortable spot on the pebbly ground, and then she readjusted her shawl, trying to keep its warmth tucked in. When the wiggling and fussing was over, she said with a touch of sarcasm in her voice, "I know who you are."

"You know who I am?" Ximena, taken by surprise, focused harder on the woman's face. *Maybe I know her from when I first got here. Maybe it was when we marched into Guadalajara. Is she a friend? Or is she one of the camp comadres?*

Concha Urrutia stared back at Ximena, but held her tongue until a grin appeared, then that smile changed, and she made a face as if trying to hold in a big laugh. She saw that Ximena was baffled and did not know what to make of the woman sitting in front of her, and this seemed to tickle Concha. So after holding in her laughter, she broke out in loud cackles, and her round face got even rounder as her cheeks puffed up with snorts that squeezed out through her nose. Concha shook until she lost her balance and wobbled from side to side, all the while grabbing her belly. Suddenly she stopped; the joke was over.

"Godoy, I'm not laughing at you. It's that you know my cousin, Flavia Manrique. That's why I'm laughing."

Put on edge by the woman's crazy behavior, but mostly because she didn't get what was so funny, Ximena snapped back, "I don't know any *cucaracha* by that name. You're mixing me up with somebody else."

"Well, that's because you know my cousin by another name. Around here, she's called *la Malvada*."

That did it for Ximena. She went on alert right away because now she was sure about Concha. *She's one of the others.*

"No, Godoy, don't look at me that way. She's my cousin, but that's it! She doesn't mean anything to me, and I'm glad you kicked her ass. She deserves it!"

"I kicked her ass but I didn't win. Neither one of us won."

"*La Flavia* fights dirty. To come out of a fight with her, and live to dance that night, is the same as kicking the shit out of her. Believe me, you won! Everybody knows it."

Then Concha got back the big grin on her face, and her eyes were brighter than before. "I'll bet that it was over a *Pelón*. Right? That one, she just can't keep her legs closed. Her fights are always over a *Pelón*."

Loud cackling started all over again, but then as before, she suddenly became serious. "As for myself, I'm on my own, just passing the night here waiting for the train that's leaving tomorrow with part of *la tropa*. They're headed for Juárez, and so am I."

There was something about Concha that captivated Ximena despite her suspicions, so she gawked at the woman as if caught in a spell. She saw a lot that she liked in her: she was alone but not afraid; she laughed without caring what anybody thought, but at the same time she could be serious, too. Concha seemed to know that *las Adelitas* hated Ximena, yet she did not care, much less was she afraid; and she was headed to *el norte* without knowing what was waiting for her. All of this made Ximena like her. She broke the silence, "Why?"

"Why what?"

"Why are you going to Juárez?"

"Oh, I don't know. Mostly, I'm leaving because the Revolution is finished here in Jalisco. These *Tapatíos* don't have the *huevos* to fight, and there's no place for me. Up there is where a *gorda* like me can make a life. There're so many *muchachos* and *cantinas* in that town that all the women in the world aren't enough to cover them. A *cucaracha* can tend bar, cook, wash dishes, make beds or even play cards with *la tropa*, and beat them while she's at it. In other words, Godoy, somebody like me can make a good life for herself in Juárez, or if that doesn't work out, there's El Paso."

"You mean working as a *puta*?"

"Well, you use your word, I'll use mine."

Ximena's liking for Concha grew as she listened to her way of talking, her way of planning. For the first time since Tacho left her, a light went on inside her, something that swept away the worn-out, dreary thoughts that had assaulted her. *Maybe,* she thought, *maybe that's the way for me.* She reached for the satchel where she had a few tortillas and cooked beans, and she shared the food with her new friend. Neither one said much more. Instead, they munched, mumbled a few words, stoked the fire, and then each woman curled up and slept, despite the cold wind that cut through those thin *rebozos*. A new idea had been planted in Ximena's mind that gave her a way out, and she slept more deeply than she had in a long time. When first daylight awakened her, she found that Concha Urrutia was gone, but something told Ximena that their paths would cross again some day.

Chapter Nineteen

EARLY NEXT day, Ximena made a bundle of a few pieces of clothing, food and water, and set out to find her father or Señora Epifania. The trek was long and hard. It was winter; the *sierra* was bleak and filled with wandering, lost, uprooted people harassed by marauding bands of bandits and thugs. Along the way she saw the devastation caused by the war that she and her *compañeros* had waged. Some villages had come out of it unscathed, but others were damaged beyond recognition, but the sight that hit her hardest were the countless dead bodies hanging by the neck from trees and telegraph poles, row after row. Some corpses had notes pinned on them: "Here is a traitor to the *Revolución*!" Others said the opposite: "Here is a *chingón* who betrayed Don Porfirio!" Each rotting corpse made her stomach turn and her mind sink. *Whichever side you were on, now you're rotting, just like the other ones.*

Ximena's condition made her journey bleaker and more painful. Every day her ankles and knees became more swollen as her belly distended, but despite intense pain and her feelings of remorse, Ximena pushed on. Eventually she reached Magdalena and Tala, two towns that had somehow come out of the conflict nearly intact. When she drifted into Etzatlán, however, she was distressed to see so many burnt-out homes and buildings. *Where did the people go? Are they still alive?* Thinking like this weighed her down so much that it almost squashed her drive to go on, but she forced herself to keep on the move.

Along the way, Ximena survived only because people felt sorry for her, sharing food with her if they had it. Others let her spend a night under a lean-to, or in a stable where she could fall asleep, hunger always gnawing at her belly. But despite these hardships, she pushed on, hoping to reach Zapopan; once there, she knew she was close to her father and Señora Epifania. On the road, she asked whoever would listen: "Do you know Don Fulgencio Godoy?" Sometimes kindhearted people listened, pretending to remember something, even a little scrap of information, but most often people would turn away with a shake of the head. Once she stopped a man on horseback. "Do you know the Godoy family?" His answer was "I've never heard of them." Those words frightened her more than anything: it was as if her father, her little brother and sisters did not exist, and she found the thought intolerable.

Memories and images came at night to torment her; her sisters and brother appeared. They looked dreary, unhappy, skinny and dirty, as if they had been locked up somewhere, and they looked at her with accusing eyes. *You abandoned us. Just like mamá, you left us for that Indio.* Ximena's heart ached with these thoughts. *Why are they coming to me now? Why not before?* She had been gone for two years, maybe more, but never had she even thought of her family during that time. *Why?* But then each morning, when the awful night ended, Ximena tried to shake off her depression as she picked up her things and pushed ahead. She did this day after day, until she reached the outskirts of Guadalajara. To her relief, she found the city more or less unscathed, as if the revolution had not happened: Ximena had truly expected to find her birthplace destroyed.

She wandered down streets toward *la plaza*, looking in every direction, focusing especially on the people she passed on the way. They looked healthy, with something to do, somewhere to go. *Someone's probably waiting for you,* she whispered as she passed a young woman. As she walked, Ximena gazed up at undamaged walls, and when she reached the cathedral she found its twin towers intact, just as she remembered them. Once at *la plaza*, she sat under a *jacaranda* tree to look at women selling fruits and vegetables, their children playing. Ximena pictured the day General Villa's troops marched through this *plaza*, and she had been in that march. What happened to the revolution? But then she remembered Concha Urrutia's words. *These Tapatíos don't have the heart to fight.* Was this the reason for Guadalajara's escape from the devastation of the conflict? Maybe.

Although she felt unsteady on her feet, Ximena could not put off making her way to her family's home not far from *la plaza*. When she reached it she was overcome by a curious feeling. Unlike her impression of the other parts of the city, Ximena found her street different, although she could not tell exactly what made it so. There was something about the windows, the doorways and the overhanging roof tiles that seemed to tell of gloomy happenings, of unhappy people. She stood across the street from the house for a while, and flashes of the day of her first communion came to her. But more vivid were memories of Tacho. She glanced down at her feet. *This is where he stood. It's from here that he threw pebbles at that window.* She shook her head to shoo away those images, and then crossed the street to reach that front door, once so familiar to her. She rapped the heavy doorknocker and waited for a servant to open the door, but nothing happened. She banged again and again, and still no one responded.

"What do you want?" A woman's voice cried out, startling Ximena, and she looked around trying to see where it had come from. She glanced to the right and left, and even behind her. "What do you want?" The voice sounded out again, but now Ximena realized that it was coming from above. She looked up to see a woman leaning over the balcony of the neighboring house. The woman repeated, "What do you want?"

Ximena did not recognize the woman; she was a stranger, not the neighbor she remembered. "I'm looking for Don Fulgencio Godoy."

The woman stared down at Ximena with an expression of suspicion, and she took a while to respond, but finally spoke up. "Who's looking for him?"

"I'm Ximena Godoy, his daughter."

"Ah! Well, I don't know where he is. No one does. All we

know is that he disappeared when the *carrancistas* ran off."

"*Carrancistas?*"

"Yes, the losers."

Ximena lowered her face, not only because her neck was aching from looking up, but mostly because she knew exactly what the woman was saying, and she felt her heart sink. Her father must have been among those who ran off on the day of the taking of the city. The thought flashed through her mind that, as she and Tacho marched with Villa's *Dorados*, her father was hurtling toward an unknown escape, and now there was no way of knowing what happened to him. Nearly overcome by the dizziness, Ximena pressed her forehead against the door, waiting for the nausea to pass.

From a distance she heard, "*Muchacha*, are you sick? Answer me, are you sick?" But Ximena couldn't open her mouth because it was flooding with saliva. By the time she finally controlled the awful slime in her mouth, she felt a hand on her shoulder.

"Poor thing! I didn't see your condition. Come! A *cafecito* will settle your stomach. Come! You'll feel better in my kitchen."

Ximena wanted to turn down the woman's offer but she did not have the strength to go on, so she followed her into the house, down a long corridor, past the patio and into the dark kitchen, lit only by a window cut high up in the old wall. The woman pointed to a chair next to a wooden table, and then turned to the stove where she kindled a fire to put on a clay coffee pot. Once that was done, she joined Ximena at the table.

"My name is Milagros Aceves. First of all, let me tell you that because my family and I haven't lived here long, there isn't much I can tell you about your father. Most of what I know is gossip, so if that's what you want to hear, I'll tell you all I know."

Milagros got to her feet when the pot began to boil over, reached for the coffee can, added several spoonfuls to the boiling water, stirred it, and stood by waiting for the coffee to brew. She did all of this in silence while Ximena looked on. In a few minutes she filled two clay mugs and brought them over to the table. "Sugar?"

Ximena nodded, happy to have the woman sweeten the coffee and stir it. Milagros then sat back to take in Ximena from top to bottom. The only sound was that of the clinking spoon.

When she was satisfied that she had seen all there was to see, the older woman broke the silence. "I see that you stepped on the bad weed."

Ximena took a long slurp of coffee before she answered. "I don't understand." The coffee tasted so good she didn't want to talk, but she knew that was to be the price for the woman's kindness.

"When we women open our legs and let a *muchacho* get in there, the result is always as if we had stepped on a poisonous weed."

"Yes. I did it." But Ximena did not want to talk of stupid things, so she pushed ahead on what she really needed to know. "You say that no one knows what happened to Don Fulgencio?"

"That's right. The only thing that people know is that he abandoned his house and disappeared with the other *Pelones*."

"Who lives in the house these days?"

"No one, it's abandoned. I heard that after he disappeared, the place was taken over by *Villistas*. But I'm not sure about that because the place is shut up and empty now."

"What about his children?"

"There were children? There's never been any talk of kids. I'm sorry."

"Why do you say that?" Ximena felt her heart beating faster.

"What part don't you understand?"

"You said you were sorry. Why are you sorry?"

"Oh! I said that because it sounds to me that if there were children, and no one knows anything about them, then it must be that they're dead."

"No, *Señora* Milagros! It doesn't mean that! It could be that they left my father before the war came to this city. Maybe he sent them away. No! They're not dead! I feel it here." Ximena put her hand over her heart, and there were tears in her eyes and voice as well.

Milagros scratched her head when she saw that Ximena was distressed, but she did not want to add to her pain so she offered her a bed for the night. "Please stay here for the night. There's room for you next to the patio. Tomorrow will be another day, and when the sun comes out maybe you will see things in a better way. What do you say?"

"I say thank you. I know where to go to find this baby's grandmother," Ximena patted her belly, "but I'm not strong enough today. I'll sleep and feel better tomorrow."

"Eat something before you sleep." Milagros then brought tortillas and fresh cheese that Ximena gulped down. Afterward she followed the woman to a small alcove where she was given blankets, a pillow and a chamber pot.

Without undressing, Ximena sprawled out on the mattress, covered herself, shut her eyes and fell into a fitful sleep that sucked her into a black sea of guilt and anxiety. She had run away with Tacho and forgotten her family, and now she hated herself.

Chapter Twenty

IT WASN'T hard to find Señora Epifania's hut. Tacho had described the place, how to reach the village, and even the distance between it and Ximena's home. It was all just as he had told her. But although the small cluster of huts was not far, it took her time to reach it—long enough to fill her with more nerves and jittery feelings. Questions assailed her: *Does his mother know that Tacho left me? No, I don't think so. How could she know if he's so far away? But...what if she does know?* But whether Señora Epifania knew or didn't know, Ximena desperately needed help, so she had no choice but to turn to her. When she finally located the hut, Ximena stood, shaky and uncertain, in front of its low entrance, and after a long time, she called out. "¡Señora Epifania!"

She called out more than once, but there was no response. After waiting, she slid down onto the ground, resolved to keep waiting no matter how long it took. Weighed down by fatigue, she dozed off.

"What do you want?"

The voice startled Ximena out of the stupor that had overcome her, and in a few moments she struggled to her feet to find a tiny, wiry old woman with flinty eyes standing in front of her. Ximena was so unnerved that she could hardly speak; when she did speak, she stuttered badly: "I'm...

I'm...Ximena Godoy."

"I know who you are. What do you want?"

Epifania's voice was icy, letting Ximena know that she was clearly not wanted. But Ximena had come this far; she had faced too much danger, too many hurdles, for her to turn around and disappear.

"Señora Epifania, I need your help."

Stiff and hardly blinking, Ximena endured the old woman's eyes as they crept slowly up and down her body, pausing when they landed on that belly, now heavily pregnant. "I want to know where I can find Tacho. Please tell me."

Epifania snorted, then abruptly turned her back on Ximena and disappeared into the hut. After a while she spoke out from inside the hut.

"You've come to the wrong place, Ximena Godoy. Go away! Return to your own people. There's nothing here for you."

Hearing the old woman's voice but not seeing her unsettled Ximena even more. "Señora, you _are_ my people. This child inside me is Tacho's. It's your grandchild."

"_¡Mentirosa!_ You tell lies! The child isn't Tacho's. I know the truth; don't try to fool me. You're a cheap _puta_ trying to stick the child on my son, but I won't believe you. Godoy, I'm telling you to leave and never return."

She has heard from Tacho! The thought struck Ximena with such force that her legs wobbled and she slid to the ground again. _How did Tacho contact her? A letter? No! A messenger? Maybe. ¡Ay! What does it matter? The old woman knows!_ Ximena crouched against the hut's rickety wall with her knees clasped against her bulging middle, and she buried her face between them. _The child is Tacho's, it must be!_ But the truth was that Ximena could not be sure, and it was this uncertainty that would continue to haunt her.

She could hear Señora Epifania moving inside the hut, set on ignoring her, but Ximena stayed stuck to the ground, knowing that she would not go away because she could not; there was nowhere else for her to go. So she stayed there, crumpled and hungry, too exhausted to move.

It was early May, the edge of the rainy season, what Señora Epifania's people called _el tiempo de aguas_. It was a time when, out of nowhere, fat black clouds rushed across the sky to unload torrents of rain that lasted days; a time when thunder and lightning shook the earth with such force that even people used to those storms cried out and prayed in dread.

The first of those storms found Ximena squatting by the side of Señora Epifania's hut, yet even the downpour did not drive her away, and she held on for days, drenched and covered in mud, moving only to nearby bushes to relieve herself. All that time she was kept alive with food and drink that kind-hearted passersby gave her, but still Señora Epifania would not break her resolve to keep out the one who had shamed her son.

Days and nights passed, but despite the rain, cold and darkness, Ximena clung to that muddy wall. At times she cried out, "Señora, forgive me for hurting your son, but this child is his. If I die, it too will die."

Yet the old woman would not respond, even when her other sons came to visit and huddle around her brazier. Every night those three men came, stopped to stare at the hunched figure, and then went in to talk about the shameful thing that was happening outside. Each time they asked, "What are we going to do with that woman clinging to your hut? *Amá*, people are talking."

As usual, Señora Epifania's eyes drooped to slits, and she responded, "What are they saying?"

"Some think you're too cruel to the Godoy woman. So what if the woman did slip? Is Tacho a saint?"

"Your brother is a good man and everybody knows it. Besides, people have long tongues, and they talk because they don't have a knife twisting in their heart like we do. What else do they say?"

"Our friends understand our anger, but they, too, ask questions. What does it matter who the father of the child is? Is it the child's fault? Why should the little one be punished? This is what some people are asking, but we think that in their hearts they just hope she leaves because it's too hard to watch her suffer."

"What about *our* sufferings?" Epifania was quick to react. "What if they had a *puta* wanting to slip into their hut?"

These talks went on every night without a resolution, but

village whispering grew every day, and Tacho's brothers became more agitated, especially because their meetings went in circles, without resolution. Sometimes those talks were calm and persuasive, other times they bordered on angry quarrels and shouting—until the night when they finally understood that a decision had to be made.

"I say give her a good whipping and send her packing!"

"And who will do the whipping? How will we force her to leave?"

"Tie her on a mule, or put her on a cart. How can she fight back?'

"¡Ay, Brother! Will it be you to do that?"

"Stop all of this craziness! Why do we have to make her leave? I'm fed up with this stupid mess. Do this! Do that! It's all pure shit! Anyway, doesn't the baby make Ximena Godoy part of our family?" One of the brothers blurted out this unexpected way of thinking, but another one was quick to answer.

"Not if the child isn't Tacho's."

"But what if it *is* Tacho's? How can we know for sure?"

"We can't! Nobody can be sure."

"Well, I'm tired of it all. I say take her in and be finished with it."

Señora Epifania had kept out of the dispute, but the truth was that she was right in the middle of it. If she kept her own counsel, it was because she was profoundly conflicted, and she had chosen to listen to her sons' talk hoping to discover the resolution.

A part of her was outraged that Ximena Godoy had betrayed Tacho who loved her, who sacrificed so much for her, even risked his life. But Epifania was a woman, and she could not help feeling Ximena's disgrace. More than anything, the old woman wanted to understand the frailty that had driven Ximena to her downfall, so she began to have thoughts: *Maybe I would have done the same thing if I had been in her place.*

Eventually, Epifania relented on her impulses to hate Ximena. She had felt the girl's distress, especially at night when she hardly slept, knowing that Ximena was outside desperately clinging to the hut, as well as to life. By day, the old woman's heart shrank as she heard the scratching and sighing, and sometimes she became so disturbed that she shouted, "Godoy, save yourself. Go away!" This happened every day, causing the old woman to get weary and unsure of what she was doing. The day came when she finally emerged from her hut to stand by Ximena's side to say: "Godoy, swear one thing."

When Epifania spoke to her, Ximena did not get to her feet—she was too weak. Covered in mud and dead grass, she was by now almost beyond recognition. Her face, arms, hands, and whatever part of her body showed, were bones wrapped in dirty skin, and she looked frightening. But she answered, "What is it?"

"Swear that the child is Tacho's."

Without hesitation Ximena answered, "I swear that the baby is Tacho's, and that it's your grandchild. With all my soul I swear it."

Hearing herself speak jolted Ximena, for she was in fact unsure of who had planted the baby, and that she probably swore to a lie. On the other hand, in the secret recesses of her mind she thought, *It's not important who fathered the child.*

Chapter Twenty-One

Jalisco, 1916

THE FIRST day of Ximena Godoy's new life began when Señora Epifania pulled her out of the mud and said, "Come into my hut and live here with me." On that day, Ximena followed the old woman into the dim interior, although neither one imagined that this step was a turning point in the path of their lives. Ximena lived each day feeling the growth of the child, as well as a deep rancor for the woman who had made her suffer so much. In turn Epifania, in her silent way, bided her time until the arrival of the child that would fill the last years of her life.

Epifania allowed Ximena to rest, eat, and sleep during that waiting period. There was little talk between the two women; they seemed to communicate with thoughts that crossed the hut's empty space from one mind to the other. This silence, however, had one constant exception: Twice a day Epifania reminded Ximena, "After the birth you will work to earn your tortillas and the child's milk." As if afraid that Ximena would forget, Epifania repeated these words daily, always at sunrise and again at sunset. They became a refrain so predictable that Ximena also mouthed those words, thinking, *Yes, old woman, I'll work harder than anyone you know.*

The wait was not long. The baby came one morning before dawn, just as the sun rose over the *sierra*; it was a day in May soon after Ximena's sixteenth birthday. On that day, Epifania rose from her mat and went about firing up the brazier. Then something made her look toward the corner where Ximena slept. Out of the shadows, two small shiny spheres caught the old woman's attention; they were bright as stars. She put down the clay pot, and got closer. What Epifania saw were the eyes of an infant who looked at the old grandmother as if to say, *I've come! I'm here!* Mouth hanging open, Señora Epifania gawked at the baby wrapped in a faded threadbare *rebozo,* cradled in Ximena's arms.

Its eyes are those of an elder, they belong to someone who has lived a long life. This thought cut into the old woman's baffled mind as she became enchanted by the child, and she was so astonished that she lost her breath for a few seconds; she even felt frightened. *Maybe this little creature is a spirit from another world.* The thought made her reel backwards, away from Ximena and the child, and then she began searching for signs of birthing: soiled cloths, rumpled coverings, bloodied water and other evidence, but there was nothing.

The old woman could not be blamed for being shocked because it was the first time in her life that such a thing had happened. When she stared at Ximena and found her calm, holding the child as if she had done this all her life, Epifania was even more puzzled. At a loss for words, she babbled, "When did this happen?" Nothing else came out of her mouth, although there was much more she could not understand.

"Last night."

"By yourself?"

"Yes."

"The pain...?"

"It came and went."

Epifania slipped down to her knees and sat back on her heels. It was not supposed to be this way; she had never heard of a woman having a child alone, without the grunts and groans and especially screams. Señora Isabel, the healer, had been put on alert to come when called to make sure the birth went right, to see that the proper herbs and ointments were at hand, and that Ximena was brought through the treacherous ordeal of bringing the child into light.

"Is it a boy or a girl?"

"I have a daughter, and you have a granddaughter."

"What of the cord?"

Ximena handed Epifania a bloodied bundle that she had by her side. "This is for you to do as you wish. It belongs to you." Ximena knew that the umbilical cord had to be buried to connect the child with her ancestral roots, and to mark the place to which she would always return if she ever strayed. *I'll give you this part of her,* thought Ximena, *but the rest of her will be mine. And her name will be Ximenita.*

Señora Epifania, now back on her feet, held the bundle in her hands but still did not know what to say. The only thing that occurred to her was that Ximena needed nourishment. "A *cafecito* will do you good. Wait a while. I'll bring it to you."

The child had not come into the world by magic as Señora Epifania suspected, but on the back of unspeakable pain that Ximena bore on her own, and she did it that way because it was her choice. That night, when shooting pain tore through the lower part of her belly and streaked up through her ribs, Ximena pulled herself away from her mat and crawled out of the hut silently. Epifania, who had the hearing of a *sierra* lynx, heard not a thing and slept soundly through Ximena's ordeal. Once outside, Ximena made her way to the place where she had wallowed in the mud, and there waited for the child to tear its way out. Only by spitting out foul oaths and curses was Ximena able to bear the intolerable pain. When it became so unbearable that she could not keep from screaming, she frantically tore off her gown, ripped it to shreds and stuffed it into her mouth. Gagged, her moans and screeches were muffled against anyone's hearing; and this went on spasm after spasm until the end.

The early morning stars were so close to the earth that Ximena believed they were eyes looking down on her; witnesses to her pain, just as they had been to her ecstasy. When the child popped out from between her thighs, she snapped its cord with her teeth. Naked, bloody and shivering, she held the baby to her breast, grateful that up there behind the stars there was a God not vengeful after all, and that she had been spared.

Ximena wiped the slime and blood off herself and the child, then made her way back into the hut without knowing how much time had passed from the beginning to the end of the birth. She had lost track of time, of light and darkness; all she knew was that Ximenita was now in her arms, and never again would she face such an ordeal.

Chapter Twenty-Two

SUNSET COULD not come soon enough for Ximena. At the end of the day she was so tired she could barely keep her eyelids from drooping, and not even the rough jostling of the cart kept her from dozing off.

"*¡Epa!* Move over! You're all over me!" The woman squeezed in next to her shoved at Ximena.

"Sorry! I was falling asleep." Ximena shook her head, blinked, and focused on where they were. She hated being so tired, and it did not matter that two years had passed since her daughter's birth and she had been working in the fields since then. She simply could not get used to the fatigue brought on by intense heat, swarming bugs, and lugging heavy sacks of maize from dawn to the end of day.

As she and the other laborers swayed along with the cart's movement, Ximena looked toward the horizon where the lavender and gold shadows of sunset spilled over the hills. She looked up at the sky's pale light. *The days are shorter now that it's September.* She thought that she was speaking to one of the girls, but she wasn't. It was all in her mind. Ximena was thinking. The harvest was at its end. It was time for her and the others to move on to the next season's work, husking corn. She was part of the army of women who worked from daybreak to dusk. Now, even before the season began, Ximena felt frustration just thinking of the piles of harvested corn she and the others faced every morning. *We pluck kernels off hundreds, thousands—who knows, maybe millions—of corn.* She looked at her calloused hands and thought how those fingers became even stubbier and more swollen during the plucking season. *But Ximenita and I have to eat, don't we?* This time she was thinking out loud, and the girl next to her blurted at her, "Yes! We all get hungry, and when that happens, we have to eat, and so we work."

"*Amiga,* do you dream of escaping from here?" Ximena was eager to hear what others thought.

"No!" With that blunt answer the girl turned away and went back to her own thoughts.

Ximena, however, did dream of escaping the squalor of Epifania's hut and its dirt floor, of being free from its dingy brazier and grimy clay bowls. She felt there was something special waiting for her somewhere else, that she was not destined to be buried in the relentless toil of harvesting and tending fields. She dreamed of one day living in a city, in a nice home with fine furniture for herself and her daughter, and she pictured herself making important decisions in her life. Ximena felt a hunger for something special, a compulsion to do better than others, and above all, to *be* special.

The cart came to a stop. The man holding the reins turned to Ximena when he saw that she was not moving. "Godoy, this is where you get off!" Ximena sprang to her feet, jumped over the railing, and waved to the others as the cart creaked forward. They, just as exhausted as she was, cracked weak smiles and managed to wave good-bye.

Ximena made her way toward Señora Epifania's hut, but slowly: it was the hour when the old woman and her sons huddled around the brazier for their daily ritual of coffee and stories; sometimes it was important talk, at other times it was empty gossip. However, it was a special time for that family, and Ximena didn't like showing up just then because she knew that she was intruding. Epifania and her sons had long ago made it clear that Ximena was an outsider. So when she got to the hut, she sat outside, hoping they would end their talk early. *Why should I go in there now? Just to see long faces? No, thank you!*

Dusk was closing in. Ximena sat with eyes closed, listening

to the last sounds of day, but it was not long before echoes of a past encounter sprang into her memory, a confrontation so bitter that thinking of it still unsettled her, although it had happened soon after Ximenita was born.

On that day, out of nowhere, Señora Epifania abruptly confronted Ximena, her body and arms tensed as if ready to strike her. It happened so suddenly and without warning that Ximena flinched and put her arms up to shield her face, unaware of what had triggered the old woman's hostility.

"Don't forget that you're just someone who happens to be passing through," the old woman hissed. "You're not of this family. You're here only because of the child."

This sudden and unprovoked outburst caught Ximena so much off guard that she could not think of what to say or answer except, "Señora, what are you saying?"

"I'm saying what you heard! You're an outsider, a cheap *puta*, and you're not welcome here."

"Why are you saying this to me now? What's happened?"

"That's for me to know!"

The truth was that, although Ximena had suspected Epifania's sentiments since the beginning, actually hearing those poisonous words intimidated and frightened her. However, when she regained her composure she was able to stand up to the old woman, even if it was with a trembling voice. "I don't ever forget that I'm not part of this family, but I want you to know that as soon as I can make my own life, Ximenita and I will be on our way."

"No! The child belongs to us." The old woman was incensed in a way that Ximena had never seen before. "She's our blood and she stays here to wait for her father's return." Epifania broke off what she was saying to lick her dry, cracked lips. Then she went on. "And there's something else just as important for you to remember."

Ximena remembered the horror the old woman's words caused in her. As if the threat of losing her daughter was not enough to fill her with anxiety, she heard Epifania babbling more crazy talk. Ximena remained speechless. *What else do you want me to remember, you foolish, foolish old woman? What else can be just as important?*

"What I'm saying is that you must never go near my other sons." Further emboldened by Ximena's silence, Epifania went on nagging. "And I forbid you to even ask their names, even as I've forbidden others to talk to you about them or our family."

Hearing those words, Ximena's first impulse was to laugh in the old woman's face because her demand was so ridiculous. But she was too enraged to laugh, so she glared at her and fought off the urge to get close enough to ram her fist into that long, droopy nose. Ximena wanted to smash that wrinkled face, and she yearned to punch in that toothless mouth that was uttering such stupid things. In that instant, she realized that she was not a coward to be shoved and pushed, and the proof of this was that she dared defy this old woman. She blurted out the forbidden word: "Why?"

Not used to having her decisions questioned, Señora Epifania was thrown off balance, and she hesitated; her face crinkled and even her hands twitched before she recovered. "It's *not* for you to ask why, but to obey. This is all I'll ever say to you about this matter. If you go against my wishes, you will suffer. I promise you."

That bitter rant had happened nearly two years earlier, but it was still so vivid in Ximena's memory that hardly a day passed without it returning to her And she never found out the reason for the old woman's outburst. Now, not yet wanting to go into the hut, Ximena sat on the ground in the growing darkness, exhausted, frustrated and disgusted. *Why do I let this woman treat me this way? Foolish, superstitious old fool! Does she really believe that I don't know the names of her ugly sons? Does she really believe that people don't talk, that they don't gossip? I've known their names and about their simple-minded wives all along. Stupid old woman!*

Dusk turned into night, and still Señora Epifania and her sons talked, but it had grown so dark and cold outside that Ximena half-heartedly got to her feet and went into the hut.

"*Buenas noches,*" she murmured. Only Señora Epifania mumbled in response, "*Buenas.*" Her sons nodded and went on sipping coffee, then fell into a stiff silence.

As usual, Ximena ignored their indifference and looked around for her daughter, and found her napping on Epifania's lap. When she heard her mother's voice, the little girl woke up, wiggled out of Epifania's arms and scrambled toward Ximena.

"¡Mamá!" The girl's voice broke through the stiffness. *Like little bells,* thought Ximena as she caught up the child and went to sit apart in her corner where she rested with Ximenita in her arms, chatting with her as if she, too, were a child. Now and then she felt the brothers glare at her. *Dumb like burros,* she said to herself.

Then, for the first time, one of the brothers spoke to her. "Tacho is with General Zapata." That he actually spoke to her was so unexpected it startled Ximena, but what he said unsettled her even more—she had not heard anything of Tacho or his whereabouts. She tensed up, wanting to hear more, but instead the brother returned to his coffee. In moments, however, he looked at Ximena again, obviously about to say something else, but just then the brother sitting next to him shoved a knee into him, stifling whatever it was he was going to say.

Ximena moved away from Ximenita to get closer to the tight circle around the brazier. "This means that Tacho is in the south, doesn't it?" No one answered, as if they were deaf, so she repeated her words. Again they kept quiet, and she understood that the brother who spoke up had blundered, and there was no way he would do it again. Impatient and incensed by their unfairness she said, "All of you know, don't you, that I'll go to look for him, even if you don't tell me more. Others will tell me even if you don't. You can't hold me here against my will."

Ximena's words worked like a prod to make the brothers squirm on their butts; one of them opened his mouth to say something, but his mother interrupted.

"Ximena, you're free to leave whenever you want. Remember, however, that the girl will remain here where she belongs."

In that instant, Ximena snapped back. "She belongs with her father and with me. I am her mother. You have no right to keep her."

"I told you in the beginning that the child belongs to this family where she will stay until Tacho comes for her. So now be silent! Let no one speak more about this matter."

The brothers got on their feet and vanished into the night. Ximena crouched in the corner holding the child, waiting to calm down, but all along she glared at the old woman who sat like a stiff idol on her heels by the brazier. At that moment, Ximena realized for the first time that hatred was swift, and that when it struck it did so with intensity. She knew that she hated the old fool, and yearned to murder her.

But Señora Epifania was not a fool; to the contrary, age had given her wisdom enough to discern Ximena's hatred. That night she looked hard at Ximena and saw that despite meager food and unspeakably heavy work, the young woman had grown more beautiful. The old woman knew that men looked at her with longing, and that Ximena returned that desire in her own glances.

That Ximena was desirable was obvious to Señora Epifania, but she could not look into her soul. If the old woman had been able to do that, she would have seen that Ximena burned with desire, that memories of love haunted her, and that she lusted, especially at night as she lay on her mat listening to the soft sighing of the wind as it surrendered to the mating calls of the male cicadas.

These thoughts troubled Señora Epifania, who had sharp eyes as well as a possessive heart. Her fear of Ximena's seductive powers could have been the unspoken reason for that bitter argument of two years before. It could even have been that by chance the old woman caught one of her sons looking lustfully at Ximena.

Chapter Twenty-Three

Jalisco, 1919 – The Great Influenza

THE BITTERNESS between Ximena and the old woman did not relent until calamity struck. It came in the form of a swift and unexpected death that gripped nearly the entire world. If there ever was anything that could have bridged the rancor between the two women, it was that appalling terror that hit their village with a vengeance.

It was not only their village that was assaulted; the horror stalked even beyond to Tala, Etzatlán, Magdalena and other surrounding towns. Word spread that in Guadalajara, at the foot of the cathedral, people folded over purple-faced, gasping for breath, and within minutes they were dead on the spot. Everyone understood that the invisible terror respected no one: rich, poor, *mestizos*, *indios*, old, young, fragile, and robust. Hardly anyone escaped the deadly embrace of the illness people called *la Española*, or yet more commonly, *la Pesadilla*.

First came weakness in legs and arms; then bloody mucus flowed from nose and ears; and finally a struggle to breathe ended with a painful death by suffocation. All of this happened in a matter of hours; with some poor devils, it happened in minutes. Soon there were too many victims for the living to bury, so bodies were hastily piled into common graves and covered over, along with a few mumbled prayers.

Disoriented people roamed looking with disbelief on so

much misery, but there was nothing that could be done. The living tried to help the dying, to console the grief-stricken, but there was too much death to keep up with. What had once been valued turned to trash, and dwellings were abandoned, fields left unattended; life had turned into hell, and those who tried to turn away collapsed, struggling to breathe.

Señora Epifania was one of the first to be afflicted, after one of her sons fell ill.

"Epifania, come quickly!" On that day, a neighbor woman called as she rushed to the old woman who huddled deep inside her hut with Ximenita in her arms. The caller held her *rebozo* to her nose and mouth like a mask, and kept her distance from Epifania, who finally responded, "No! I won't leave. Here, *la niña* and I are safe."

Her neighbor murmured, "Where is her mother?"

"She left for the fields this morning but hasn't returned."

"Maybe she's dead!"

"¡Diós *Santo!* Don't say such a thing! Why are you here? What do you want?"

"It's one of your sons, Epifania! He's dying. You must come quickly or you'll not find him alive."

At that moment, Ximena barged into the hut, out of breath and fearing the worst for her child, but when she saw that the child looked as always, she sank to her knees, partly from exhaustion, but mostly from relief in seeing that Ximenita was well. When she recovered her breath, Ximena realized there was a neighbor woman hunched over at the other side of the hut. When she finally focused on her face, she saw fear stamped in those eyes, and in the tight grip of the visitor's hand over her masked mouth.

"Who...?" On the verge of asking who had died, Ximena shut her mouth, fearing the answer.

"Epifania! Come with me now! The child can stay with her mother."

The neighbor was nearly out of the hut by the time she mumbled those words through her rigid fingers holding its covering in place. Señora Epifania struggled to her feet, and just as her neighbor was doing, she wrapped her *rebozo* around her nose and mouth. She turned to Ximena, "It's one of my sons. I'll return sooner or later."

Stunned at how quickly the disaster was moving, Ximena sat trying to think: *What should I do? How can I protect Ximenita?* But her mind seemed paralyzed; there were no answers. Suddenly realizing that she might be carrying the infection, Ximena moved away from her daughter and tied her shawl around the lower part of her own face. She then ripped a cloth into long strips, and tied one around Ximenita's mouth and nose, but the child tugged at the rag, all the time kicking and crying, until she finally relaxed and let the mask stay in place. Ximena took the child in her arms to rock her to sleep as she hummed the girl's favorite little songs, hoping to soothe her.

"*¡Chitón, mijita! ¡Chitón!* Sleep like a little angel."

Day turned into night but Señora Epifania was still missing. During those hours, Ximena felt neither hunger nor sleepiness but wondered about Ximenita who slept so deeply, making her fear that she was sick. *Why isn't she hungry? Why doesn't she want to play? Is she asleep, or dying? Where is Epifania? Please, please let her come soon.*

Ximena had never experienced such terror, not even when preparing for battle, or witnessing the countless wounded and dead dragged back into camp after combat. Not all the howling and groaning, cursing and praying of dying men and women struck her heart with the fear she now felt as she held her child in her arms, afraid that each breath would be her last.

The first rays of sunlight were creeping through the hut when Señora Epifania finally returned. Without saying anything, she crawled to her mat and sat there clasping her knees against her chest. Ximena understood right away: The old woman's son was dead. So she kept quiet, and stayed that way for hours until Ximenita stirred, woke up, and told her mother that she was hungry. When Ximena brought the child a tortilla, beans, and a jug of *café con leche*, Epifania finally spoke.

"He's dead. That leaves me only two sons."

"You still have Tacho. You have three sons," Ximena reminded the old woman.

"Perhaps. This one died in great pain trying to breathe. His face got black until his soul finally separated from his body and slipped out through his mouth. When that happened, I felt his spirit fluttering above my head whispering his final thoughts to me, and that went on until he departed to find his way to the other side of the *sierra*."

"*Señora*, I'm sorry for your loss."

"Don't be sorry. My son's *anima* is free from pain and has returned from where it came." Then she fell into melancholy silence for a while, but shortly returned to what she was saying. "We couldn't dig a grave, so we carried the body to a ravine where we piled large stones on him. The body is safe. Not even hungry animals will reach it." She stopped speaking, but then abruptly turned to Ximena. "You and I must now plan on how to save Ximenita. We have to think of everything, and do it quickly, because *la Pesadilla* will soon come for her if we don't move fast."

Ximena, shaken by the sudden death of Epifania's son, realized that Ximenita *was* in danger, and that she, too, could become ill and die without warning, so she turned to listen carefully to what the old woman was saying.

"I know of a cave in the *sierra*, not far from here, yet separate and isolated. There the child can be taken away from the infection. So far, you and I are free of it, so we're the only ones who can shield her."

Ximena murmured, "Yes! I'll take her there right now and we'll stay until this curse passes."

But Señora Epifania shot back, "No! I'll be the one to do that. You will be the one to bring us water and food for as long as it takes for the death to pass."

"What? I'm her mother! I'm the one who must be by her side. Why you?"

"It must be me because I know more than you do. Now, no more talking, we can't waste time. Help me bundle mats and covers, and whatever food and water we can carry. After that, it's up to you to bring us whatever is necessary." Señora Epifania paused for a moment to stare hard at Ximena. "There are two things you must not do. The first is that you must not have contact with anyone. And the second is that you cannot let others know what you're doing or where you're going, otherwise they will follow. Now, enough talk! Let us move!"

Resentful but unable to defy the old woman, Ximena helped

put things together. Epifania strapped rolled up mats and covers onto her back, and whatever food she found she put into her *morralito*. Ximena wrapped up the child in a *rebozo* and lashed her onto her own back, and then crammed as much food into her pockets as she could. The trio then began the trek up toward the *sierra,* with Señora Epifania leading the way.

Although she had said that the cave was not far, hours passed while the day faded into dusk and they had not yet reached the place. They made their way, gingerly stepping over shifting rocks and sliding earth, all along climbing and wrapped in silence. Ximena and Señora Epifania were no longer flesh and blood but stark figures in a painting etched against the darkening sky. They became silhouettes bent low under their load, breathing heavily, and struggling not to fall. The mystery of the night, its stars and rising moon shrouded them, but it was an indifferent beauty, oblivious to the horror threatening to erase those three lives along with the rest of their world.

Ximena, under the weight of her daughter, accompanying Señora Epifania, finally reached the cave. The days that followed revealed Ximena Godoy's persistence as gathering food for her child and Señora Epifania became an obsession. But this task turned out to be unexpectedly easy, because huts and sheds were abandoned and animals ran unattended. Ximena latched on to a roaming cow that provided milk for Ximenita, and a lost *burro* to transport supplies up the *sierra*. She scoured fields to capture chickens, and raided bins for stored beans and maize that she cooked to feed herself and take up to the cave to share with Epifania.

If this is stealing, well then, I'm a thief: I'm guilty. Ximena muttered those words dozens of times, but they didn't mean a thing since there was no one to catch her, much less accuse her of snatching what was not hers.

She scoured abandoned huts, furtively turning away from the few villagers still around—she was as afraid of them as they of her. She grew to fear the desolation, too, as if the world had come to an end, and it got even worse at night when blackness shrouded everything. Ximena's heart was heavy during those terrible days and nights. If foraging for food was not difficult, then living was, because she was always afraid and the feeling of isolation, of being the only human being left on that bleak land, filled her with terror.

Her worst suffering was caused by distrust and fear of contamination, forcing her to shun the few villagers still around. She felt compelled to avoid anyone who might come near her. Yet, she longed for companionship, if only to hear a voice, or a body's movement to let her know that the end of the world had not come, after all. Fear and yearning tore at her as the days passed, and it was this conflict that caused her unbearable loneliness.

Ximena tried to put aside the turmoil assailing her, and concentrated only on the hunt for food; it became her fixation. She neither bathed nor washed, and her hair became matted and infested with lice, and gradually she became covered in grime. Her hands and fingernails were filthy, and her arms, ears and neck were streaked with crusted dirt that stuck to her skin because of unwashed sweat. Worse still, Ximena went without changing her clothes, and soon a sour stink oozed from her pores. But none of this mattered to her as she climbed and tugged the loaded *burro* to the cave twice, and sometimes three times a week. When she arrived, she shouted to let the old woman know that she was there.

"I'm here."

"Leave everything by the opening." The voice that echoed from deep inside the cave always sounded the same, and said the same thing.

"How is my daughter?"

"She's well and not sick.'

"I need to see her. At least let her come to the front of the cave where I can see her."

"Fine, but don't call out to her. And don't come near her."

Each time the girl appeared out of the cave's darkness, Ximena feasted her eyes on her, seeing that she was healthy, that her skin was clear and that she rubbed her eyes just as she always had done since her first days. Ximena looked on from far away, and then she turned away, grabbed the *burro* by the rein and made her way down the *sierra* to Señora Epifania's hut, to nights of desolation.

Weeks passed until the deaths subsided and then gradually

disappeared, just as mysteriously as it had appeared. In Guadalajara, as in most cities, the disease's presence had been so prevalent that most people had perished. Homes were left empty, some with doors still open, by the fleeing grievers. Schools and stores were empty, churches lost their priests and congregations, streets and *plazas,* once bustling with people, were desolate. However, when the curse passed life began anew.

There was no explanation as to how, or from where, that disaster had come, leaving more dead in its wake than even the revolution, but people are people. Their task is to live, so life staggered forward to a new beginning. When Ximena understood that her life had been spared, she climbed up to the cave and called out to Señora Epifania.

"The death has passed. You can come out now. You and the child are safe. We're all safe."

The old woman limped out holding Ximenita by the hand. Both looked dirty and haggard, yet healthy, as they blinked in the daylight, happy to breathe new air. Without losing time, Señora Epifania and Ximena bundled up their belongings along with the child and began the hike back to their village, now severely decimated and mostly abandoned. Those two women and the child had wrestled with death and prevailed, leaving all three with a renewed desire to live.

Chapter Twenty-Four

Jalisco, 1923

XIMENA FOUND it impossible to rid herself of the memory of death, and as she thought of how easy it was to die, time slipped through her fingers. Although some things were different after the great influenza, her life of drudgery had returned, and the times of planting and harvesting were her only markers of change. The sun rose late and faded early, but eventually the days gradually elongated until mid-summer, when the cycle of decline began all over again. *My life is like the unending days of the week; they come and go, repeating, never changing.* As she toiled in the fields, no one imagined her inner turmoil; no one suspected that on the inside, Ximena was a wasteland of unhappiness.

Sometimes Ximena blamed the old woman for the depression that tore through her mind and guts, but in the end she had to admit that the fault was her own. *One bad step after the other,* she mumbled in self-accusation, hundreds of times as she worked, walked, or tried to sleep. Ximena knew all too well that she was in a snare of her own making, but no matter how much she thought and devised, she just could not see a way out. She felt the isolation from the days of the plague had taken root in her heart and was growing every day, and this feeling of aloneness overwhelmed her. Her thoughts often returned to memories of Tacho and the carefree life he had shown her, and she longed for those days but they were gone, and it was she who had thrown it all away.

Ximena asked herself what was it that kept her trapped in that pathetic place alongside people who showed what they wanted was for her to disappear. She wondered why she stayed in a place where she, in turn, detested everyone and everything around her. Ximena asked these and even more questions, despite knowing it was her daughter that held her just as if clamped into a vise. Oh, there had been times when she plotted to run away with the child, but then she realized that it would be folly since Señora Epifania was certain to somehow keep her promise to hold on to the child. There were other considerations, too, that rankled Ximena's mind.

What if I do manage to escape with Ximenita, what then? I can look after myself, but her? Do I have the right to expose her to hunger, to thirst, to brutal criminals who roam the sierras?

These thoughts forced Ximena to admit that she feared exposing the girl to the dangers of the unknown even more than she hated her life in that village. On the other hand, Ximena longed to provide her daughter with the same home and education she had received, with books to read, pens and paper to write on. She remembered the days when she listened to a nun reciting a poem, or she sat at a piano reading, note by note, the magic written on those ruled pages.

Why shouldn't Ximenita have the same thing? The day will come, my darling muchacha, when I'll give you what I had, and even more.

What Ximena truly feared was that her daughter would become a repetition of Señora Epifania and the other village women. There was something else that bore down on Ximena with such force that it nearly suffocated her. It did not escape her that Señora Epifania adored and pampered Ximenita, and even more upsetting for Ximena was that the girl returned that affection; that she preferred her *abuela*.

It was to the old woman's arms that the child ran, it was for her that she cried out when she woke up from a bad dream. As their attachment grew, Ximena felt a deepening resentment which she tried to fight off, if only because she knew it led her nowhere. The truth was that she was jealous, and she admitted it. But what could she do except try to get rid of that awful feeling? Ximena struggled to wipe out that bitterness until an unexpected thought came to her, a thought that helped erase the envy she felt.

Maybe Ximenita really belongs more to the old woman than to me. Maybe that's the way it should be. Wasn't it she who thought of how to save the girl's life?

At first, thinking this way baffled Ximena, but because the thought recurred, she held it close and continued to turn it over in her mind. In the meantime, her life slipped by while she wrestled with discontent, or with devising and abandoning impossible plans of escape; but mostly she bided her time, waiting for the way out to manifest itself.

Ximena thought of Tacho, but because she knew nothing of his whereabouts, she became convinced that he was dead. Yet he might still be alive, she told herself. What she could not know was what he would think of Ximenita belonging to Epifania. Would he demand that Ximena stop thinking that way?

What's the difference? He's not here, and that's that! Anyway, if I leave Ximenita in her abuela's hands, it will be for a short time only, not forever.

During those years, she tried to distract herself from that turmoil by searching for her family. She did it little by little, gathering bits of information here and there. The information did not amount to much, but she did piece together that her sisters and brother had been packed away to *el norte* before the revolution broke out, and that her father perished in the stampede out of Guadalajara before its fall to General Villa. Despite this trickle of information, Ximena never lost hope of one day finding them, especially because searching gave her a much needed distraction.

Another turning point in Ximena's life happened about this time: there came reports that General Pancho Villa had been assassinated. In that instant her world was turned upside down. The news hit at the end of July when summer was turning into the Dog Days of August.

El Jefe is dead! El Centauro's been gunned down in the street like a dog!

In the city, people went wild and ran from house to

house with the terrible news. They spilled out onto streets, hoping that what was being shouted was nothing but another empty rumor. But it was true, and if the city exploded with anxiety, the surrounding villages were grief-stricken; those *Indios* and *Indias* had believed that General Villa was indestructible.

Ximena was one of the first to feel the energy unleashed by the death of the general: she saw it everywhere. It was in the air, in the way people scurried aimlessly and gossiped, in the sudden appearance of strangers on the move, and in how almost overnight, masses of people pressed to leave the land. Yet, she knew that the General's death alone could not have caused so many people to pull up roots and move.

Trying to get an answer, Ximena listened; she even lingered at the train station, captivated by waves of migrations that appeared so suddenly. She asked people where they were going and why, and sometimes some of them resentfully turned away from her. But she still went on asking because she felt that somehow she, too, was involved, and some of the answers awakened something that had fallen asleep in her.

Ximena sensed this was the moment she had been waiting for. Although she didn't know what direction to follow, or even how to do it, she felt that now was the time to turn her back on that life of stifling weariness and loneliness. She had to find the way to get a better life for Ximenita and herself, and maybe this was her only chance.

It all reminded Ximena of the days of the revolution: the overloaded trains, the pushing, cursing, crying; people hanging like monkeys onto roofs and sidings of train coaches. The same thing was happening all over again, and as terrifying as it was, Ximena knew that soon she would join that mass of fleeing people. So she began to plot her escape.

On the hunt for answers, Ximena stayed away from the hut for hours and when she returned, most times late at night, she found Ximenita asleep and Señora Epifania talking with her sons, as usual. But Ximena no longer even tried to be likeable so she usually just mumbled *Buenas noches*, ate, and prepared to sleep.

She followed this routine until she sensed a difference in the old woman, something she could not explain. Finally Ximena caught on that Epifania was spying on her when she was in the hut; that she kept an eye on her with quick, furtive peeks out of the corner of her flinty eyes.

The old woman had said nothing and her wrinkled face showed no expression, but she did not have to say anything because Ximena realized that Epifania had guessed what she was planning, almost as if she had heard or read her innermost thoughts. The spying went on for days, each time more out in the open, until one night, Señora Epifania spoke up after sending her sons away.

"Come sit by my side. I want to speak to you."

Ximena knew what was on the old woman's mind; she even knew the words that were about to come out of her mouth. However, she did as Señora Epifania asked and squatted next to her, waiting.

"You're leaving, aren't you?"

"Yes." This was all Ximena, said and the old woman, apparently expecting more of an explanation, let a long time pass before speaking again. The silence was heavy between the two women, with only the sounds of birds and rustling bushes to fill it.

"You think that you're the same as the worthless vagabonds that pass us every day?"

"Yes." Ximena forced herself not to snap back in defense of the many travelers she had spoken to: those people had lost loved ones, land, and had even faced torture and death. She overcame the impulse to defend them, and kept quiet.

Again the old woman slouched back into silence. Ximena knew that what she wanted was to hear her speak up and tell of her plans, so Epifania could mock her, or more likely, tear her plans apart.

"You have no money."

"No. I give you the few pesos I get for my work in the fields."

Ximena had thought of this, but she had made her way without money before. Surely she could do it again. A few tortillas were enough to keep her until she reached Juárez where she aimed to stay. As for making it onto the train, *well, I'll squeeze in somehow.*

"How do you expect to make your way even to the next *pueblo*?"

"I'll find a way."

"Is there a man?"

There it was again! The same suspicion that had driven a wedge between them from the beginning now showed itself again. Oh, how Ximena yearned to let the old woman know that, yes, she had faced temptation when men offered her the moon and stars in return for just one night of unbridled passion. She ached to admit that she had given in to powerful desires, and it had happened in the dark shade of cornrows and behind sheds. She longed to rub that much in Epifania's face, but she did not—for the sake of the child who had to stay with the old woman. "There is no man!"

"You've forgotten Tacho, haven't you?"

"Tacho is dead! You know that."

Even if Ximena had slapped Epifania, as she yearned to, the old woman would not have recoiled in such obvious pain. Her reaction surprised Ximena. She had believed for years that Señora Epifania had accepted Tacho's death, but now she saw that she had unknowingly landed a painful blow, and it made her feel good.

After a while the old woman seemed to pull herself together, but then again fell into silence; this time because she was shocked. *The old woman doesn't want to think that Tacho is dead. She wants to think that he's still alive, but he's dead and she can't live with it.*

"Ximenita stays here." Señora Epifania returned to her point.

"Yes, but I'll return for her."

"When?"

"When I can provide for her."

Ximena's words clearly relieved Epifania, as if it was all she wanted to hear, as if she had been waiting years for Ximena to leave, but to do it without the child. Powerless to go on stifling what she was thinking, Ximena blurted out, "*Ay, Vieja!* What you want belongs to me. You think that I'll never be able to provide for Ximenita, and that she'll be yours forever. Well, we'll see about that."

Those words put an abrupt end to their painful confrontation. Señora Epifania crawled to her mat, wrapped herself in a blanket and went to sleep; or so she pretended. Ximena, as if in a trance, stared at the brazier's dying embers. She was thinking, *Now is the time to leave. Why should I linger?* After a while she went to where Ximenita was sleeping and took the girl in her arms, hoping to sleep at least a little.

The angry encounter between Ximena and Señora Epifania put a final end to any connection the women had. Ximena had chosen to leave, so what more could be said? Unable to sleep, she waited for cockcrow, and with the first light of dawn she packed a *mochila* to keep her until she reached Juárez.

As she made her way out of the hut, her daughter followed her. They walked to the end of the pathway that turned onto the road heading toward Guadalajara. There, Ximena cupped the girl's face in her hands, caressed her cheeks and kissed her. Then she turned away, walked a few steps and stopped to gaze back. She whispered, "*Adiós,* Ximenita. I'll be back for you. I promise."

Chapter Twenty-Five

IT WAS a time of turmoil for everyone, and Ximena was merely a speck in the midst of so many others on the move northward. The train station swarmed with people dragging children, bags, or just hanging on to one another. Some had tickets in hand; they were the ones who waited anxiously to be let onto the coaches to grab a seat. Those travelers without a pass stood by for the right time to crawl onto empty cargo wagons or climb the train up to the roof.

Ximena was one of those, and when the chance came, she crept up the siding rung-by-rung, not letting herself think that if she slipped the injury would be serious. Like a lizard she slithered up, kicking, pushing, and clawing at other people equally desperate to grab a little space to cling onto the top. Once she made the climb successfully, Ximena hunkered down, gritted her teeth and pulled her shawl tight over her head and nose, all along staring at the ragtag crowd squeezed in around her: gaunt faces stamped with despair, fear, and suspicion. *What a miserable bunch we are,* she thought.

With a blast of its whistle, the train lurched forward, first at a creeping, sputtering pace, and then moving faster until it gained full speed. God only knew what kept Ximena and the others from slipping over the side onto the rocky ground that blurred with the train's movement. She thought that maybe it was the force of the wind coupled with the train's swaying that glued all those rumps to the rooftop.

Whatever it was, she and the rest of that human cargo stuck onto the train as it sped under bridges, past hills, *maguey*-covered ravines and an endless desert studded with tiny villages. The worst part was the relentless din of clanging and clicking of wheels on rails, but the hot dust that caked her face and clogged her nose was almost as bad. It was hard, but that's how Ximena's journey started; that's how she made her new beginning.

When fatigue got too much for her, she leaned her head on her folded arms and closed her eyes, but she spent those hours sleepless. From time to time she glanced around, expressionless, her face so changed from just a few years ago. Ximena had grown skinny and angular; her skin was spotted with dark purplish blotches, drawn tight over high cheekbones. Her shoulders poked out of the raggedy blouse; her breasts, still beautiful, were the only good part left from the old days. *I got this way working like a mule in that goddamn sun!* She muttered in disgust, so that others turned to gawk at her.

Ximena had hours to think of herself, all the while trying to get to her center, to who she really was. As she swayed along with the train's movement, Ximena tried to understand why she had taken such steps. She remembered how she had detached from *El Indio* Medina although she had felt passion for him. In a way, Ximena was confounded by the way she had been. She realized too late that she had loved Tacho intensely, unconditionally, but something inside her knew all along that sooner or later it would all end. *That's me. When it ends, it ends!*

These thoughts led Ximena to think of her future, and how she had thrown herself into an unknown world. Ximena had left behind her daughter as well as a life that, although miserable, was familiar. She had walked away without knowing how she would make a living, or how she would take care of herself. Yet she was taking that chance, although she admitted that just thinking of it made her afraid. On the other hand, she wondered if she really had a choice, or did powerful forces drag her onto the path she was following? *Did I choose this life, or did it choose me?* Frightened by that tangle of thoughts and unanswerable questions, she shook her head and decided to stop thinking, to accept it all because it was done.

Chapter Twenty-Six

Ciudad Juárez, 1923

XIMENA GODOY felt lost as she stumbled off the train. She slung the *mochila* over her shoulder and followed the mob toward the exit of the terminal. Right away, she was caught up in a sea of confused people who shoved trying to get out of the place, but she held her ground and pushed back just as hard, cursing with even stronger language others were using to get their way. It worked like a charm. A path opened up and she made it to the street.

Once outside, she was confronted with a blur of cars coming and going in different directions, others at a standstill, their drivers cursing and shaking their fists out the open windows. The noise, a jumble of honking, shouting vendors and babbling people, was deafening, and she felt intimidated. The thing that really frightened her was the mob of people who looked so strange in clothing so different from hers.

There were some *Indias* who looked like her, but most of city women were decked out in short, revealing dresses, the like Ximena had never before seen. Their haircuts were short and waved, with spit curls pasted onto their cheeks and their lips were smeared bright red. Ximena couldn't help gawking: it was as if she had stepped into a foreign world, one in which she felt threatened. As Ximena walked past a handful of those women they glared at her and then laughed out loud, obviously mocking her. One of them lit a cigarette and blew smoke in her direction.

Ximena caught on that they were making fun of her, but she ignored them and strutted past to take a look up and down the street. What she saw nearly overwhelmed her: so many buildings! Some were single-story, others had two or even three floors; some rickety but others new. All were packed together in a clutter of bail bond houses, eateries, swanky nightclubs mixed in with dance halls, honky-tonks and brothels. There were hawkers roaming the street shouting out their goods, as well as vendors manning stands, and kids peddling Chiclets and trinkets.

Ximena had walked into the heart of Juárez of the middle 1920s, and now realized that she stood right in the middle of *Avenida Mariscal*, the city's hotspot. She shut her eyes to keep her head from spinning. Ximena remembered that she was hungry, thirsty and tired, with nowhere to go. She stood as if in a trance, until she opened her eyes and spotted a man selling fruit. Taking a chance, she went to him.

"*Señor*, do you know a woman by the name of Concha Urrutia?"

Ximena was remembering that name from her camp days; it was the fat girl who talked of making her way to Juárez, and although years had passed, who knew? Maybe Concha had made it after all.

"Does she walk the streets?" The man stared at her, slowly taking in Ximena's tattered *campesina* look. There were so many streetwalkers in that town, she thought, maybe one name wasn't enough. Maybe he could help if he knew a little more. Ximena hesitated as she grasped that maybe Concha had gone the way of the streets to make a living in this scary city.

"I don't know. I haven't seen her in years."

The man was friendly, but he didn't know how to help without more information. "Women come and go in this town, and dozens are called *Concha*. But look, why don't you go over there to that store, the one called *el Humo*. Do you see the sign? Maybe someone there can help you. They sell tobacco and other things that attract customers."

With a quick *gracias* Ximena headed to the store. Inside it took a minute or so for her eyes to adjust to the dimness, but when she did, she saw shelves loaded with boxes and other smoking gadgets: pipes, cigarette holders; some simple, others elegant. She made out a man behind the counter.

"How can I help you?" His voice was mellow and friendly.

"I'm looking for my friend. Her name is Concha Urrutia."

"Hmm. Concha Urrutia."

Like the fruit vendor, this merchant gazed at Ximena and knew right away that she was an newcomer, probably running away from something—maybe a blighted crop, or a man who wanted to get his hands on her. Looking up at the ceiling, he scratched his chin while squinting his eyes, as if searching his memory.

"Well, the only *Concha* I know is my sister, and her last name is Huerta. No, I'm sorry. I can't help you."

"Do you know someone who can help get me information?"

"Why don't you go across the street to *el Manglar*? People meet there all the time, and maybe they can help you."

The man flashed what Ximena thought was a lewd grin, so she backed away and left the place, frustrated and hesitant to go on with the search for the girl from so long ago. *I'm tired. I'm hungry, and I have to do something to help myself.*

Eventually she crossed the street and went into the dark smoke-filled place. It was cluttered with tables and chairs, packed with loud, carousing men and women. The smoky air stank of tequila and beer. In the background a Pianola clanked out rowdy music that was nearly drowned out by shrieks of laughter, and cursing. Intimidated, Ximena slunk into a corner, afraid of being assaulted, and there she stayed until one of the barkeeps noticed her. With a sharp nod of the head, he sent one of his waitresses to check out this raggedly girl who had sneaked in.

"What do you want?" The girl, even younger than Ximena, got so close to her that she felt the heat rolling off the girl's face.

"Nothing." Ximena's voice was weak, not so much out of fear, but because of dizziness.

"Nothing? Then get out!"

The girl abruptly turned her back on Ximena, took a few steps, but then stopped to take a second look over her shoulder. When she saw that Ximena was not moving, she returned.

"*¡Epa, muchacha!* Do you want a taco?"

"Yes!" Ximena was feeling so faint, she was about to slide down onto the floor.

"Follow me."

Ximena, grateful that the girl's voice had lost its edge and that her expression had softened, trailed behind her. They slid past the long packed bar into the back part of the place, where the loud music and deafening chatter faded.

"Sit here and wait for me."

Ximena plopped onto a chair, and right away drifted off. She didn't know how much time passed when she felt someone shaking her shoulder, saying, "Here. Eat."

When Ximena's eyes snapped open, she saw that the girl was smiling, and again she felt grateful. She snatched the plate, and without even wondering what was on it, wolfed it down. The kind girl watched her with a telling expression on her face, but she did not speak; she just stayed on, as if to keep Ximena company.

After a while Ximena mumbled, "*Gracias, amiga.* I think I was close to dying, but you saved me."

"*¡Ay, amiga!* We die when our time comes, and that happens when we're finished with what we're supposed to do. So don't thank me. I think you still have lots more to do, and that's why you're here. Am I right?"

"Yes."

"What's your name?"

"Ximena Godoy. And you?"

"I'm Enriqueta Ramírez, but everybody calls me Queta." She paused for a moment, and then went on. "Well?"

"Well, what?"

"Why are you here?"

"I'm looking for my friend, Concha Urrutia. Do you know her?"

"*¡Uy, uy!* First of all, only God knows how many *Conchas* live in Juárez. After that, let me tell you that many women change their names as fast as they can when they land here, so you can bet that your *amiga* isn't known as Concha Urrutia here. You'll have to dig up something else about her to help."

Ximena heard what Queta was saying, and realized that she

had planned on finding Concha right away, and had not made plans beyond that.

"I don't have anything else to tell about Concha, except that she's fat and she laughs when she feels like it."

"¡Dios Santo! That's nothing! Most women around here are fat, and about the laughing part? Stick up your ears and hear what's going on out there. Most of those women are laughing like howling monkeys."

When Ximena sank back in obvious disappointment, Queta pushed her shoulder. It was a friendly, encouraging nudge.

"Look, Godoy, perk up. It's not the end of the world. You'll think of something—you look like that kind of woman. Where have you come from?"

"A village outside Guadalajara."

"¡Chispas! That's a long way from here! You see? That tells me you have what it takes down there between your legs to make it on your own. Don't be afraid! Later on you'll find this Concha Urrutia."

"Can you help me find work? I have to feed myself and get a place to sleep."

Queta took a step back the better to look at Ximena. "Well, you're not going to get a job here; at least, not in the main business of *el Manglar.* You're too skinny and worn out."

Stung by Queta's snub, Ximena took a hard look at her with the intention of getting even. The girl was about eighteen, maybe a little more. She was lanky, round-shouldered, and knock-kneed. Her skin was sallow, her hair oily and thin. But before lashing out, Ximena paused to admit to herself that Queta had beautiful eyes, and there was something about her that made her likeable. Ximena pushed aside her bruised self-esteem.

"Why can't I work here? It's a *cantina,* isn't it? What does it matter what I look like?"

Queta broke up laughing. Squeaky cackles from deep in her skinny belly made her shake all over. When she got over the attack she said, "I suppose you could call it that since people drink a lot of tequila here." Then she stopped and stared at Ximena. "Are you serious? You don't know what this place is all about?" Then she clammed up, but after a while went on.

"Godoy, men pay money here, and women fuck them in return. Does that tell you what *el Manglar* is all about?"

Ximena glared at Queta. This time she was really incensed. What got her goat was the girl's way of speaking to her, as if she were a child without imagination, or experience, but about to return the insult, Ximena decided to hold her tongue.

"Now I understand, but I'm still asking you to help me get something to do so I can make a living."

Queta caught Ximena's expression and regretted that she had mocked her, so she changed her tune.

"I'm sorry Ximena. Not everyone here is a *puta*, as you can tell by looking at me. We do need girls for clean-ups. I work in the bar clearing tables and washing glasses, but up there," she pointed her chin toward the ceiling, "the rooms need to be taken care of. It's hard, even filthy work, cleaning beds, sheets and other stuff. You know the mess people make when they fuck."

Ximena stared at Queta, but then nodded, letting her know that she wanted the work. Queta wiped her hands on her apron and said, "I'll talk to the boss. Wait here. I'll come back to let you know."

Chapter Twenty-Seven

DON PEPO, the owner of *el Manglar*, was a short, fat, good-humored man; sometimes he was affectionately called *el Gordo*. He enjoyed being called the fat man just as much as he liked a good joke, especially if the joke had a naughty twist to it. Don Pepo was always quick to flash a big, toothy smile whenever anyone approached him. No one would have guessed, by taking a quick glance at his five-by-five build, that he loved to dance. Not only did he enjoy it, but Don Pepo was really good on the dance floor because he was surprisingly light on his feet. His favorite was the tango which he performed with incredible flair at least once a night, always with one of his most beautiful ladies. When that happened, all the flurry of activity in the jam-packed house stopped just so the customers could follow his gyrations with their own rhythmic clapping, wild hooting and whistling.

But Don Pepo was more than a jovial roly-poly entertainer; above all, he was a shrewd businessman who had built up his profitable enterprise from a tiny fast-food stand into one of the city's thriving brothels. He took pride that his customers came from the upper crust. And not only were the customers locals, but also rich *Gringos* regularly crowded into *el Manglar*, knowing that Don Pepo provided the most beautiful ladies in Juárez come nighttime. Not only that, he was also sought out because of his classy and attentive style—his motto was

"The customer is always right!" and his customers loved it. What people didn't know, however, was that beneath that jovial veneer lurked a steely streak; if the occasion warranted, Don Pepo did not hold back from firing anyone who sidestepped his requirements. Once he said "Out!" that person was on the street almost before he or she knew what had happened.

He was a hands-on boss regarding every aspect of his business, especially when hiring *el Manglar* girls. The process began with an interview that included a leg-bust-and-butt check to make sure that everything was just right about the girl. He also demanded that his doctor examine his women at month's end for anything catching, so when those moneyed men came around, they could be sure not to take anything contagious back to the wife.

No one could tell how he did it, but *el Gordo* also had his hands on the everyday details of his upstairs business, which took time. He kept an accounting of every bed, mattress, sheet, pillow, towel and chamber pot. In a word, he was in charge of everything necessary to make his establishment's rooms welcoming. Unbeknownst to those gentlemen customers, each room was equipped with a ceramic bowl, a packet of alum and sulfate of zinc, along with a plunger. Don Pepo required each of his ladies to combine those ingredients with water and flush herself after each intimate encounter.

His girls knew that if there was anything that saddened Don Pepo, it was when one of them got pregnant. "*Damas*, I hope you never fall into that misfortune. Do your best to avoid such a setback." He closed his interviews with those words, but if it happened—and it did—he did not hesitate to fire that lady when the truth came out.

As if doing all of this was not exhausting enough, Don Pepo was also in charge of supplies. He knew exactly how many bottles of tequila, mescal, beer and even soft drinks were ordered, how many were sold, and the money to show for all the sales. And he did the accounting every night at closing time. Even after all that work, he still had the stamina to dance at least one polka or tango before the night ended.

It was to this Don Pepo that Queta ran, hoping to get Ximena a job, and she found him behind the, bar sipping a Coca-Cola.

"*Jefe*, we need a girl to help clean the rooms."

"Why? We had enough help yesterday. What's changed?"

"One of the girls went away."

"Which girl, and where did she go?"

"I don't remember her name. You know, the short, fat one? And I have no idea where she went. She disappeared this morning."

Don Pepo gave her a suspicious look. "Queta, why am I plagued by so many ungrateful people?"

Queta shrugged her shoulders. "There's someone in the back room looking for work. I think she's the one for us."

"Is she dependable?"

"I don't know, *Jefe*."

"A hard worker?"

"I don't know that either, *Jefe*."

"How did she get here?"

Queta shrugged, but showed that she was ready to bring in the new girl.

"Take her to the empty table over there. I'll take a look at her from here. Maybe I'll talk to her."

Queta disappeared. In a minute she re-emerged almost dragging Ximena by the hand to the corner table. "Wait here for *el Jefe*. I think he'll give you the job." Then she hesitated, "Well, maybe, if you're lucky."

Ximena sat down, nervously looking around the crowded *cantina*. She didn't know who she was looking for; no one she saw had the looks of a boss. But it was not long before she was startled by a smooth voice that came from behind her.

"*Chica*, I hear you want to work for our Manglar family."

Ximena jerked around to locate the voice and almost crashed her nose into the belly of a rotund, round-faced man, whose rosy cheeks and pencil-thin moustache reminded her of an overgrown boy. She was confused; the man did not look like someone in charge.

"Yes."

Don Pepo took a chair and then calmly stared at Ximena for a long time until he said, again in the same satin voice, "Please stand up so I can look at you." When she stood, he took more time to run his eyes up and down, first looking at her legs hidden by her long, dirty skirt; then up to her chest; and finally, his narrowed eyes lingered on her face. All the time Ximena self-consciously switched her weight from one leg to the other.

"¡Ay! You're all skin and bones aren't you? Are you sure you can do a day's work?"

"Yes!"

"What if you can't?"

"Try me."

Don Pepo leaned back with his arms folded over his large belly, obviously studying Ximena all over again, because he detected something deeper than her skin, something buried inside her, hidden somewhere under the raggedy clothes hanging on her bony shoulders. But that something eluded him at the moment, so he gave up probing. His eyes could not penetrate what he sensed was this woman's protective shield. The real woman was hidden from him. *Maybe later on,* he thought, intrigued by Ximena's mask.

"What's your name?"

"Ximena Godoy."

"Hmm. That's a good name. I like it."

Still trying to make her out, Don Pepo burned up time with small talk. "I'm called Don Pepo. Please call me by that name. Right now, I'm not going to ask you where you're from, or why you're here. It's nobody's business. But I will ask you if you know what we do here at *el Manglar.*"

"It's a brothel."

"*¡Chispas!* You're frank." He sat up, looking just a little surprised. "Good! I like it. On the other hand, you already know that if I hire you, it won't be as one of our *damas.* You're a bit over the *sierra* in age, although I think time will bring out what I think I see inside you. But that will take a while."

Ximena held her ground, looking hard into Don Pepo's eyes and thinking *When I lay with a man, I do it out of desire, not money.* Out loud she said, "Give me work and you'll see what I'm made of."

Chapter Twenty-Eight

XIMENA STAYED with Don Pepo until 1932, and in those six years she proved her mettle. The first months were hard for her: she hated the flow of rough men who crowded in every night to go into a dingy room and have their way with a hired girl. This disgusted Ximena so much that every night after dark, when the parade began, she seriously planned on leaving *el Manglar*; but when daylight came around again, she always reconsidered. As she began to cut through that veil of crudeness, she began to have second thoughts: she saw there was something better that might be fashioned out of such a bawdy place. The business could be changed, Ximena thought, so she forced herself to put aside her personal feelings and instead, focused on what could be done to transform the place into an elegant, moneymaking enterprise.

Ximena knew that others thought of her as a simple-minded village girl, good only for cleaning soiled beds and scrubbing toilets. She alone knew she had the instincts that pulled her to bigger, better things. So each time she overheard people gossiping about her, she steeled herself to prove them wrong. In time, Ximena found it amusing that no one imagined that she wanted so much more out of life than to be just one of them, just another drab girl out of nowhere, and going nowhere fast. She focused on the finer things that money brings, beyond material possessions: she yearned to be the one to decide her own life's path, and once on that path, she knew that money would come to her. Ximena listened to the powerful sound of ambition that filled her more every day.

She was dreaming big, but for those dreams to take shape, *el Manglar* had to be cleaned up; it had to be transformed, which meant it could not go on as a brothel. When this idea hit her, she stopped dreaming and began the real planning, and that had to begin with Don Pepo. Ximena's aspirations had taken her this far, and she was lucky because the turning point was approaching. It happened as soon as she regained her looks, prompting Don Pepo to move her from cleaning rooms to working tables in the *cantina*.

When Don Pepo made this move he did it cautiously, keeping a watchful eye on how Ximena handled herself. When he felt confident about her work, he put her in charge of the bar. She stepped up to that position and *el Manglar* soon doubled in traffic, and then nearly tripled its customers. *Maybe it's a coincidence, but maybe not,* the fat man told himself. The important thing was that business was booming. But it happened so fast that Don Pepo was taken off guard, with hardly any time to deal with the increase in customers. When Ximena suggested that he expand into the space next door, he hesitated. *It's too much, too soon.* But then, one look from her filled him with courage, and shortly *el Manglar* was on its way to becoming one of the biggest draws in all of Ciudad Juárez.

From the beginning Ximena showed that she was happy to be up front with customers. She was relaxed and casual but poised, friendly and not overbearing. She soon adopted the latest fashion in glamorous short dresses, heavy make-up, as well as a bobbed modern hairstyle. Movies were big in Juárez, so it was not surprising that women mimicked Hollywood's leading ladies, and no one was more stylish than Ximena Godoy, who showed off in feathers and costume jewelry.

Don Pepo was happy knowing that his customers delighted in Ximena Godoy's company; they returned to *el Manglar* over and over again, just for a drink, if it meant being close to her. This was especially true with all those thirsty *Gringos* and their flapper girlfriends who flocked to Juárez, drawn by its wide-open ways: horse racing, bullfights, gambling and lots of booze made Don Pepo's *cantina* a big hit. He snorted through his nose every time he thought of Prohibition. *That crazy Gringo law is making me a rich man.*

Everything was going well for him, but Ximena still intrigued him. He watched her as she moved from table to table, greeting customers, assuring their satisfaction, prodding waitresses to be more attentive.As he did this, he smiled, but he still could not crack that outer shell that kept him from really knowing her. Eventually he decided: *enough is enough!*

It happened one night after the last customers had left, when he and Ximena sat, as they often did, having a cup of coffee just to wrap up the day. After a lull in their conversation, he coughed a little, cleared his voice a couple of times, and then took the leap. "Ximena, I'm going against what I said in the beginning about prying into what isn't my business: Where are you from? What about your family? Why is it that a woman with your looks doesn't have a man?"

Upon realizing that he had sputtered out more questions than he had intended, Don Pepo shut his mouth. Ximena looked at him so intensely that he regretted crossing that line, but it was too late, so he sat gazing at his cup, waiting for whatever answer might come. A few minutes dragged by before she opened up.

"I'm ordinary, Don Pepo. My family was from Guadalajara. We had a home and nice things, but the revolution came and swept it all away. I have sisters and a brother, but I don't know where they are. Maybe up in *el norte* along with so many others who were chased out. When I found myself alone, I had to go out on my own. I'm like many others who had the same thing happen to them."

As Ximena heard herself telling her story, she knew that she had left out the most important parts of her life. She had not told him that she ran away with Tacho Medina, that she fornicated with him, and then betrayed him with another man. She left out the part that she caroused, got drunk on tequila and high on marijuana, and that she took up arms against her own class. She didn't admit that she disgraced her father and in doing so, shattered her family. She simply could not force herself to say those things.

When she stopped talking, he patted her hand and, feeling a strong impulse to reveal his own secret life, he talked.

"I didn't suffer what you did, Ximena. Somehow the revolution passed me by. What I did lose was my wife and little son." Don Pepo felt his face get hot, but he went on. "She—my wife—got involved with another man, and one day she disappeared along with my boy. As you can imagine, I moved heaven and earth to find them, but nothing came of it. I searched for years until I finally gave up. After that I became the man you and everyone else knows."

Don Pepo abruptly stopped, shocked that he let slip what he had kept private for so long. He fidgeted with the cup.

"I have a daughter, Don Pepo. Her name is Ximenita Medina."

Surprised by that revelation, it took a while before he answered. "Where is she?"

"She lives with her *abuela*, her father's mother. He was a revolutionary, probably dead by now. The old woman heads an Indian family; some are mule drivers, others work the land, but all of them are poor."

"Is that why you left?"

"Being poor? No, I can live with very little. What I can't tolerate is being hated."

"You were hated? Why?"

"I'm a *mestiza*, and they couldn't accept me."

Again, Ximena heard herself covering up her past. She lied about the real reason for that family's hatred. She did not tell how her father had tried to murder Tacho, and how her affair with another man had driven Tacho away, probably to a certain death. She did not explain how deeply all of this wounded his mother and family, but she left it out anyway, although it would have explained more honestly why they hated her.

"But that's crazy! Your daughter is a *mestiza*! What about that, Ximena? No one can forget that part of you is in her."

"I never forget anything about Ximenita, but some things are too big to fight. What I mean is that most of her is made up of them, the family. I'm just a tiny part of her."

Don Pepo made a loud noise that squeezed out through his noise, and he squirmed in the chair. "Have you lost your mind?

Your daughter is mostly you, and you must not forget it."

He suddenly stopped talking, again afraid he had gone too far. Ximena, too, was silent. Only the sound of cups clinking against saucers filled the *cantina's* empty space.

He murmured, "Have you returned to the village since you left?"

"No."

Don Pepo wanted to ask *Why not? The train to Guadalajara runs every day. Why don't you bring Ximenita back with you, put her in school here, keep her by your side?*

Those words were on his tongue, but he kept them to himself because by now he knew that Ximena's innermost thoughts were still seriously guarded. *If she wants to tell me, she'll do it when she wants.*

"I want to return for her, and I tried it, but at the last minute I changed my mind. I have to admit that I'm afraid."

"What scares you, Ximena?"

"I don't know."

After that they kept quiet until Ximena got to her feet.

"*Buenas noches*, Don Pepo. Thanks for listening." She moved toward her room, but before leaving him she turned to look at him. "I had already heard about your wife and little boy. I heard it rumored, but I didn't believe it because I thought it was just that—a rumor. Now I know, and I'm sorry that she left you."

That conversation changed Ximena and Don Pepo's relationship. Their words that night tightened their connection in a way neither would have imagined, and from that time onward they understood one another.

After that night, Ximena thought even more of Ximenita. She thought of how her child was growing up uneducated, without knowing people beyond the village, and this weighed heavily on her mind. On the other hand, she was aware of what was happening in her own life since coming under Don Pepo's wing. She saw how men responded when she walked into a room, and she liked it. She knew that Don Pepo was satisfied with her work, so she worked harder. She was content that Queta and others among the ladies of *el Manglar* were friendly, and she was easygoing with them, but this was Ximena Godoy's public face, this was what everyone else saw. It was a different story when she was alone, when she drifted to a hidden place, where thinking of Ximenita anguished her more each day.

In private, and especially in the quiet of the night, images returned to Ximena to perform a weird dance: Memories of her beloved daughter seemed to float in the dark. *You're growing up, my darling muchacha.* Then there was old Señora Epifania, who looked at Ximena with the same narrow, suspicious eyes. And far away, in the innermost recesses of those dark memories, *el Indio* Tacho Medina lingered, waiting for her just as he used to do outside her window when she was just a girl.

Tacho, I couldn't love you as you wanted, I was too young. My heart had not finished growing.

Ximena did try to get to Guadalajara. She had even bought a train ticket on two different occasions. Each time she had packed a bag and made her way to the station, but each time, as she waited, she lost her resolve and hurried back to *el Manglar*. Ximena could not force herself to return to that village of sadness, to the place of so many bitter memories. She just could not do it, not even for Ximenita, although she yearned to be with her. Instead, she promised nearly every day, *I'll come for you soon, and we'll live a wonderful life together. I promise you that much, Ximenita. Soon! Soon!*

As time passed, however, that promise went unfulfilled but she was able to bury her growing guilt and shame somewhere deep in her heart.

Ximena fought off her demons by plunging into the work of transforming *el Manglar* into a fine, classy nightclub. She had the ideas, and Don Pepo was there to give her the backing to put it all together. But he was not a pushover: he demanded details, costs, justification for whatever proposal she had, whether an expansion of the bar, remodeling this, that, or the other, putting ads in newspapers, even upgrading the outfits worn by the help.

Don Pepo and Ximena often disagreed, back and forth, and squabbled, too. They even seriously argued, until a deal was cut. In the end, Don Pepo would say, "¡Ay, Ximena! You're going to ruin me!"

It was hard work but Ximena was up to it, always directing whatever expansion or renovation was in the works. She put in as much time as Don Pepo, with the difference that she always looked more beautiful. Her ideas seemed endless. Getting rid of the little rooms upstairs, along with the ladies, came from her, although Don Pepo was shocked when she proposed it.

"Ximena, have you lost your mind? What's a brothel without ladies?"

"No, Don Pepo! Let *los muchachos* go elsewhere to get it. There are too many brothels in Juárez; one more or less won't make a difference."

As usual he repeated, "Ximena, you're going to ruin me!"

"Just think, Don Pepo: we can turn el *Manglar* into a club for people to come to sip high-end tequila, cognac, whiskey, champagne, and dance to modern smart music. It can be a place for our dressed-up customers to come to feel good about themselves."

"A monkey dressed in silk is still a monkey!" He mumbled.

"I heard what you said, but you know that I'm right."

"Let me think about it."

Eventually no longer a brothel, el *Manglar* morphed into the most elegant club in town, and people flocked to it. It did not happen overnight; it took most of the years of Ximena's association with Don Pepo, who took his time adapting, but once he finally convinced himself that he had stumbled onto his "right-hand man", as he called Ximena, the makeover took off. Yet, in the middle of all that change and action, he still danced the tango every night. Now Ximena was his partner of choice. When that happened everything stopped: the sight of Mr. Five-By-Five guiding the beautiful Ximena Godoy across the polished dance floor dazzled people, even though she towered over him.

Ximena was a success, and admiration for her grew. She blossomed, appeared confident, yet was inwardly still in turmoil and unsettled. That is, until the night an elegant man walked into the club, ordered a private table along with a Cuban cigar and a bottle of champagne. His name was Amador Mendoza.

Chapter Twenty-Nine

XIMENA MET Amador Mendoza the night she danced *La Comparsita* with Don Pepo. Well-dressed, self-assured and handsome, Amador sat at a table close by the dance floor, and on that first night he was spellbound as he watched Ximena taking the intricate tango steps. He appeared so captivated by her that he became tense, his back stiffened and straightened, and his eyes, riveted on her, were filled with the same hunger with which Tacho Medina had looked at her.

El Manglar was at its best that night. Its musicians were inspired, and the club was filled with laughter and chatter. Elegantly dressed patrons matched the glamorous setting of white tablecloths, sparkling crystal and dressed-up waiters. When Don Pepo and Ximena finished dancing, a wave of applause broke out, followed by cries for more. *"¡Otra vez! ¡Otra vez!"*

Don Pepo bowed low in every direction, smiling his toothy grin, all along holding Ximena's hand and hoping that she would agree to do just one more tango. When she whispered in his ear, however, he looked out to his guests and shrugged, letting everyone know that the crowning moment was over, and it was their turn to come onto the floor to dance.

As Ximena began making her way from table to table, greeting friends, the maitre d' approached her, said something, and gestured toward Amador's table. She looked, evidently trying to place the man seated alone, and for a moment she hesitated, but then she made her way in his direction. By the time she got to his table he was already on his feet straightening his tie, smoothing down his double-breasted jacket, and when she stood in front of him he bowed, introducing himself as he took her extended hand.

"Amador Mendoza at your service."

"I'm Ximena Godoy. How may I help you?"

"Please join me, if only for a glass of champagne." When he saw that she was about to turn him down, he quickly cut her off. "There's something of importance that I'd like to discuss with you. Won't you take a chair? I know you have to attend to people, but if you'd join me for a few minutes I'd be grateful."

Ximena looked at Amador with the intense expression she reserved for only a few other people. It was a short moment, but in that brief second she decided that she liked what she saw, so she took a chair and watched as he signaled a waiter to pour the champagne. Meanwhile her eyes were taking in Amador's looks: olive complexion, straight nose, gray-green eyes, slicked-back brown hair, and a sensual mouth. She glanced at his hands, strong but evidently not used to manual labor, and she admired the signet ring on his little finger. She gauged his height and the cut of his suit, taking in everything, all the way down to his polished wing-tip shoes.

"I like this club. I understand that you're part owner?" Amador smiled, exposing straight white teeth, but Ximena did not answer his smile or his words; instead, she sipped champagne with her eyes calmly focused on him. Smoothly ignoring her icy demeanor, he reached into his breast pocket, pulled out a cigarette case and lighter. "Cigarette?" She took one, put it up to her lips and waited for a light, all without uttering a single word.

Amador, however, still did not lose his poise; he just went on with the small talk. "I rarely come to this city, but now that I'm here I'm glad for the opportunity to meet you. I'm sure I'll be returning..."

Ximena cut him off before he finished. "Señor Mendoza, you said you had a matter of importance. Please come to the point. I've things yet to do."

Now Amador did begin to lose some composure; his hand shook just a bit, and the ash fell from his cigar. Nonetheless, he put on a thin smile and tried again. "I understand that you've transformed this place from a shabby business into what it is now."

Ximena abruptly snuffed out her cigarette and got to her feet. "Senor Mendoza, I don't consider what you're saying to be a matter of importance. So please excuse me." She turned to leave, but he jumped up and took hold of her wrist. He did it gently, courteously, yet she made it plain by her reaction that she disliked the familiarity. He let go immediately.

"You're wasting my time," she said, turned and left him. But no sooner had Ximena walked away from Amador than she began to wonder why she had been rude to him: she was ordinarily friendly, especially with new patrons. It meant nothing to her to smile, say silly things and to joke. It was all part of her manner and the reason she was so well liked by everyone who came in contact with her. Yet she had been different with this stranger, and she could not explain why.

Although she had not looked back, Amador Mendoza stuck in Ximena's mind all evening up to closing time, and even after she returned to her room for the night. As she undressed, bathed and got ready for bed, he was in her thoughts. She could not stop thinking of the way he looked at her that first time, and especially vivid was his touch when he took her wrist. *Why did I make him think that I hated his touch?*

Ximena didn't believe in love at first glance, although Tacho claimed that he had loved her from the moment he first saw her. *Well, that was Tacho.* She thought that falling for someone like that was not her way. Nonetheless, the truth was that the more she tried to shake Amador from her mind, the more she thought of him.

When Ximena turned off the light she did not fall asleep. Instead, she thought even more of Amador. After a while she flopped over on her side hoping to doze off, but there was too much going on inside her. Amador's image swirled in her mind and she forced herself to think of other things, and it was only then that she slipped into a haze that was neither waking nor sleeping. It was a place where she was adrift, twisting and turning aimlessly, all the while pulled by a powerful current that dragged her deeper into that tricky in-between place where her thoughts morphed into images of uninhibited passion, of sex and sensations of pleasure. She was again a girl copulating with Tacho in the desert. Or was it Amador? Ximena could not tell; her lover's face was blurred by sand, or perhaps it was intense desire. Then, still in that dream world, the face clearly became Amador's, and without resistance or reservation, she unconditionally surrendered to him.

"Enough!" Ximena's groan suddenly jogged her wide-awake, but the dream left her restless and edgy; she could not explain what was happening to her so suddenly. She had encountered Amador just briefly, and yet he had penetrated her innermost being; he had breached the wall she had built up years ago.

Exasperated and confused, Ximena sat up, turned on the lamp, and went to a cabinet where she kept a bottle of tequila. She poured a shooter, gulped down its sharp liquid and returned to bed. When she turned off the light she finally fell into a deep sleep filled with dreams that she found impossible to remember when she woke up the next morning.

Chapter Thirty

TRYING TO understand why his encounter with the beautiful Ximena Godoy had gone so wrong, Amador stood watching her as she walked away. It took some moments before he returned to the table where he slumped into a gloomy mood. When the waiter approached, Amador motioned him away: he did not want more champagne, or even the cigar in the ashtray still streaming a limp string of smoke. All he wanted was to know why he had been treated so indifferently.

He stared at the cigarette snuffed out by Ximena just minutes before, and he felt resentment, not at her but against the cigarette, as if it had been responsible. Amador wished that he could push back the clock just a few minutes. Maybe he could have reached out to block her hand in mid-air as she was about to mash the butt into the ashtray, then maybe she would not have walked away. Maybe. Maybe not. But it had happened and nothing could change that now. Yet, he could not help telling himself that the encounter might have had a different ending if, in that split second when she was about to put out the cigarette, he had shown that he *did* have something serious on his mind.

If! If! If! ¡Carajo! *She was right. I don't blame her. I was babbling stupid things!*

Amador motioned to the waiter that he was ready to pay the bill, when he felt a heavy hand on his shoulder. When he looked up he saw a short, fat man with a round face highlighted by a pencil-thin moustache. It was the same man who had danced with Ximena Godoy.

"*¡Hola, Amigo!* Don't tell me you're leaving."

"Yes."

"The night is still young. Please, may I join you?"

On the verge of a bad mood, Amador looked at Don Pepo's cheery face and, although he did not really feel like it, he decided to be polite. He mumbled, "I was here when you danced."

"You liked my style?" Don Pepo lifted his chubby arms as if embracing an invisible partner.

"Yes."

"But you liked my partner even more?"

Amador avoided answering, shifted in the chair, and made it clear that he was ready to leave. Don Pepo reached out and put a hand on his shoulder. It was a gentle and friendly gesture.

"Wait! I haven't introduced myself. My friends call me Pepo, so please call me that! I feel that you and I can be friends. Join me in a drink, won't you?"

Without waiting for Amador's answer, Don Pepo waved for a waiter and ordered him, "Take a bottle of tequila, ice and lemons to my office." Then he turned to Amador, "It's quiet and private there, and we'll enjoy our drinks even more."

Again, without waiting for a response, Don Pepo got to his feet and motioned Amador to follow him. Secluded in the small office, Amador relaxed, relieved that something had come along to snap him out of the dejection that filled him after Ximena walked away. Don Pepo, feeling good about the stranger said, "I don't know your name."

Obviously embarrassed, Amador flushed. "Forgive me," he said, and showing a better-than-ordinary upbringing, got to his feet and extended his right hand. "Amador Mendoza Rivera at your service." Then he sat down.

Don Pepo, a little amused but at the same time impressed, studied Amador's movements; he was not used to such etiquette from his everyday customers. When his order arrived, he poured two large tequilas and lifted his glass. "*¡Salud!*" They each downed the drink, and Don Pepo went on. "You're not from Juárez." It was a statement, not a question, but this time he waited for Amador to speak.

"No."

"What brings you to our town?"

"I represent my father's business affairs."

Without knowing exactly why, Don Pepo was again impressed, and he sighed a barely audible *Ah!* He didn't say more. He poured refills and they exchanged small talk about nothing entertaining banter which both enjoyed. The hours passed while they sipped tequila and chatted until they both were a little drunk; Amador's bad mood had melted away, and Don Pepo was ready to trot out another tango.

"Amador, I feel I can be frank with you. Am I right?" Don Pepo took the lead to open a new subject.

"Yes. Let's both be frank."

"I have eyes, and I saw what happened between you and Ximena Godoy a while ago."

Amador's tie was now hanging loose on his rumpled white shirt, his jaw showed the beginnings of five-o'clock shadow and his hair stuck out unevenly, all of which gave him a disheveled look. The alcohol had relaxed his body so he was slouching in the chair, but when he understood the direction of the conversation proposed by the older man, he stiffened and thought, *what's it to you, old man? Don't stick your nose in my business.* But Don Pepo was ahead of Amador. He knew that he was treading on private ground; that the intrusion might kick back and blow up in his face. Yet Pepo needed to talk about what he had seen. "Amador, I know what you're thinking."

"Tell me what I'm thinking," Amador's voice had tensed.

"Amigo, you're thinking that what happened between you and Ximena is not my business."

"You're right! It's not your business." The voice was growing edgier, even a little threatening.

"Well, maybe you're right. But listen to me very carefully."

"Say what's on your mind, Pepo. Get it over with."

"Only that I know that I don't know Ximena."

"What?"

Amador waved his hand back and forth under the fat man's nose. *"You know that you don't know?* What's that mean? You're drunk and not making sense. It's the tequila talking."

"Ha! The day hasn't dawned when half a bottle gets me

drunk! ¡No, Señor! Listen to me because, if you've fallen for her, you need to hear what I have to say."

"I haven't fallen in love with her!"

"I think you have—up to your eyeballs."

"Don Pepo, I don't want to hear anything about her."

"You see? You *have* fallen for her."

Amador, suddenly clear-headed, shut his mouth to listen, weighing what Pepo was saying because he sensed danger. Maybe he would hear something about Ximena he did not like. Or would the old man tarnish her beauty by revealing ugly secrets? But after a few moments, unable to resist hearing anything the fat man had to say about Ximena, he finally said. "I'm listening."

"Calm down! I've already said what you need to hear, and it's this: I *don't* know Ximena. *No one* really knows her."

Amador gawked as Don Pepo went on, "Does this sound like I'm talking Chinese? Or maybe you think I'm playing a game of riddles?"

"No. I'm listening, and what I hear tells me that you *do* know her."

Don Pepo drained what was left of the bottle into their glasses, and swigged the silvery liquid all at once, as did Amador. He knew now that he would pursue Ximena, that nothing would stand in his way, and furthermore she would love him; maybe not right away, but in time. So he listened and watched as the fat man smacked his lips after sucking on a lemon and went on, his words a little slurred. "*Amigo*, Ximena is a mysterious woman, a secret inside a secret."

After that he plopped his round head onto his folded arms and fell asleep right there on the office table.

Dawn was breaking when Amador stepped out of the club, his rumpled jacket thrown over one shoulder. He took a few minutes to look around while he sucked in a deep breath, enjoying the quiet hour. While he waited for a taxi he tried to decipher Don Pepo's words about Ximena: *a secret inside a secret*. Though intrigued by those words, he vowed he would discover their meaning. *Maybe later,* he told himself.

By the time the taxi left him at his hotel, he had assembled a plan on how to win over Ximena's love. By the time he slipped into bed he knew that one day she was going to be his wife.

Chapter Thirty-One

IT WAS still early morning when Ximena left her room in search of coffee. In a while, glum and in a bad mood, she sat in the deserted bar absentmindedly stirring the brew, but just as she had poured a second cup, Don Pepo appeared and sat with her.

"Morning." Don Pepo, just a little bit hung over, made the first move to begin a conversation but Ximena sat in stony silence. She neither responded nor gave a sign that she was aware of his presence. He said, "You're up early, aren't you?"

When she finally turned to look at him, he saw that her eyes were red-rimmed and bloodshot as if she had been crying. "I couldn't sleep." Then she went back to staring at the cup.

"You don't want to talk?"

"No."

Don Pepo was in a cheerful mood despite the poor sleep he'd gotten on the office table, so shrugging his shoulders, he got to his feet, went to the bar, poured his own cupful and returned to sit by Ximena. After savoring a mouthful of coffee he said, "I spent a few hours last night with Amador Mendoza."

Curiosity jogged her to look at Don Pepo. "What's that to me?" Her voice was raspy and irritated.

"¡Calma! Take it easy. I just want to say that we talked for a while after you walked out on him last night."

Don Pepo held up his hand when Ximena made a move to interrupt him so she shut her mouth. "He's a cautious man and hardly said anything about himself."

He took more sips from the steaming cup and sat back, eyes closed, waiting for the caffeine to kick in. Don Pepo took his time knowing that he had Ximena's full attention. "Amador Mendoza is a good man, but it's against all odds. I know it's a curious thing to say about him, but the truth is that he comes from a rich family, a clan so wealthy that anyone would expect him to be spoiled, or even corrupt. Well, he isn't, and this much is in his favor."

"How do you know? He just walked in for the first time, and you know all this about him?"

"Well, Ximena, it's not from him, that's for sure. I know because I'm old, and because I've lived in Juárez all my life. The Mendoza family is known all over Chihuahua. That's how I know what I'm talking about. Amador didn't say anything about that last night; he didn't have to, that's for sure."

"Why are you saying this to me?"

Perhaps because Ximena had slept badly, or she sensed that she was not going to like what he was about to say, the truth was she felt her stomach tying up in knots.

"I don't want you to get hurt. That's why." Don Pepo's voice was gentle because he had more to say on the matter, and he knew perfectly well she would not like it. "Ximena, consider this. Amador is the privileged son of a family of wealth that goes back generations, and they make sure that only those of their own kind are allowed into their circle."

Ximena caught what Don Pepo was getting at. *"¡Dios Santo!* Don Pepo, I just met the man for a few minutes, and you have me marrying him!"

"And you're not thinking that way?"

"No! I'm not thinking that way."

Don Pepo got to his feet, served himself more coffee, and returned to Ximena. "His mother is more than just a mother. She's a *doña*, a matriarch. Amador is one of four sons; the oldest and youngest are already married to wives hand-picked by Doña Marcela Mendoza. That leaves Amador and the other brother waiting for mamá to choose a wife for them."

"Are you saying she wouldn't approve of me, that I'm not good enough?"

"I'm saying the contrary. You're too good for him."

Ximena looked at him and murmured, "Thanks." Yet, she sensed that the worst was still to come. She was thinking so hard that she missed part of what he was saying. She finally turned back in to what Don Pepo was saying, asking, "What's that?"

"I'm saying that Doña Marcela's idea of the good wife is striking, and I'll tell you how I know. Back in the days when my place was what it used to be, when men came to visit the ladies, there was a lot of talk besides the other business. The story about Doña Marcela went that, among other things, her sons' wives had to belong to the best families, and they had to come to the altar pure as transparent glass." Don Pepo took a deep breath. "Ximena, I'll bet everything I've got that Amador has those same crazy ideas built into him. You can be sure that his chosen bride will have to be as pure as the driven snow, just to make mamá happy. At least in his own mind." The fat man stopped suddenly, an expression of warning stamped on his face. "Take care, Ximena. Otherwise, you will be hurt."

Ximena sat, her back rigid against the chair, knowing what Amador Mendoza would think if he ever found out about her past life. She said, "I am grateful, don't think that I'm not. I've listened to you, and I promise that I won't be hurt."

Chapter Thirty-Two

AMADOR MENDOZA was a romantic. He was polished and gentlemanly, the sort of man who gets to his feet when a woman enters the room, always tips his hat to greet her, never uses bad words in her presence and believes in the language of flowers and poetry to express love. Amador was born late, someone who belonged to a bygone era of manners and graciousness, not to the runaway Juárez of the twenties.

That afternoon, Ximena was headed to Don Pepo's office when a worker handed her an envelope. Baffled because the letter had not come in the usual mail delivery, she stood looking at it, attracted by its pale color and dark gray edging. She put the envelope to her nose, sniffed it, and realized that it was perfumed with a faint but alluring fragrance. After a few moments she tore open the envelope and pulled out the single sheet.

I send this brief note to you, beautiful Ximena Godoy, with the simple message that you're on my mind and in my heart. Your eyes haunt me as does your voice. Please allow me to see you. I'll be at the same table tonight.

Your servant, Amador Mendoza

Forgetting her business with Don Pepo, Ximena reversed her steps to find a quiet place to think. Once alone she read

Amador's message over and over again, each time capturing a different meaning, as if his words were layered, and with each reading she felt vibrations on her skin, in her mouth, on her breasts. These feelings were not new to her. She had felt them before, when she was a girl with Tacho Medina, and again when she worked in the fields and felt men's eyes riveted on her. Holding the note, Ximena remembered the days when she worked alongside *peons* who would have given anything to lay with her in the shadows of the tall *milpa*; she remembered, too, the times that she had surrendered.

Yet Ximena's mind moved with caution because now she was a changed woman, a woman who knew where desire leads, and knew the mistakes that can follow. She was a different woman from the girl who had walked away from the rebel camp pregnant and hungry. Since then she had battled a powerful old lady who wanted nothing else but to be rid of her, and again, she walked away. But that time she walked away with a broken heart because she had left Ximenita behind. That time, she had vowed never again to give in to the feelings now assailing her, but she could not help responding to the powerful attraction Amador Mendoza held over her.

That afternoon and into the evening, Ximena struggled with memories and feelings, and especially with questions prompted by what Don Pepo had said about the Mendoza family. Could it be possible that Amador was socially so far above her and was just toying with her? After all, what did she have to offer him?

Will he think that I'm cheap if I go to him? On the other hand, why shouldn't I? Isn't he just another customer? I talk with the others, don't I?

It wasn't like her to be nervous as she dressed for the evening, and even more so later on as she danced with Don Pepo. She was so unsure of what to do about Amador that she did not allow herself to look toward where Amador sat with a bottle of champagne, his cigar smoke curling above his head.

She followed Don Pepo's lead, bending and draping her leg around him, just like the tango should be done; all along thinking *I'll be honest. I'll tell him about my days in the revolution, about my relations with Tacho, Sosa, and the others. I'll tell about Ximenita, Señora Epifania, and the hut, and the mud, and the endless hours in the fields. I'll tell everything, even what I sometimes did in the dark corn furrows. I'll feel better if I'm honest. ¡Carajo! He can walk away if my life scares him. I don't care! After all, it's not as if I want to marry him.*

The last chords of the accordion ended, and as usual there was wild applause and whooping, but Ximena hardly heard the racket— she had made up her mind. She would go to Amador's table and let happen whatever was to happen.

"¡Hola!"

When she reached the table, Ximena's voice was husky, not because she was trying to be seductive but because she was nervous. Amador stood up, took her hand, bowed and kissed it.

"I'm happy that you've come, Ximena. Please join me, won't you? This champagne is good. Will you have a glass?"

"Yes."

When he filled her glass he offered, "Cigarette?"

"Yes."

Ximena knew that she could not go on as tongue-tied as she was, but nothing came to her. When she looked at him, she saw that he was relaxed and smiling, and he did not seem to be uncomfortable with her silence. After a while he broke the ice, "I meant what I wrote in my note."

"Señor Mendoza..."

"Please call me Amador."

"Amador, I don't know what you expect."

"Expect? I want to be close and special to you." He paused, but then came to the point. "Ximena, I want to be the only one in your life."

His voice was soft, and he uttered his words with an assurance that made Ximena's nervousness melt away. But it also put her on the defensive. "What do you mean?"

"I mean that you would belong to me, and to no one else."

Amador's bluntness nearly took Ximena's breath away. She knew right away that the conversation had gotten off on the wrong track. But she would not pretend that she did not hate what he was saying, so when she spoke up, she matched his bluntness.

"I don't *belong* to anyone, Señor Mendoza."

Anyone would think that Ximena had slapped him, because

Amador jerked back against the chair, responding like a man who had never been denied anything. He behaved like someone so used to having his way that denial was beyond his imagination. He stared at her, but now with her confidence recovered, she glared back at him defiantly.

"I don't belong to *anyone*! I never will!" Ximena repeated what she said to make sure that he heard her.

But Amador stood his ground. "You *will* belong to me, Ximena, when you marry me."

"What?"

"Yes! You will be my wife!"

Ximena got to her feet, not even trying to hide her outrage. "Señor Mendoza, you and I haven't been together for an hour, and you're saying that I'll be your *wife*? You're crazy!" She turned to leave but he jumped to block her way. "Move aside, señor. I've got matters to attend to," she spat.

Amador didn't move, obviously making time to put his thoughts together, trying to think of how to patch up his blunder, but when she tried to edge around him, he was forced to speak up. "Ximena, please don't leave! I'm a fool! I'm whatever you want to call me, but please, don't leave! I take back those stupid things I said."

He held her arm and looked into her eyes, pleading for her to change her mind. They stood that way for a time, he holding her arm and she showing that she intended to leave.

Ximena knew that she should walk away, but something urged her to stop, to love again, to surrender. She returned Amador's gaze, and though she knew it was a mistake, she gave in to him. She slipped back into the chair, pleased because he wanted only to sit by her side. It crossed her mind that maybe he still intended to seduce her. But now he would be subtle and unhurried. Anyway, it didn't matter, and it didn't scare her; on the contrary, it enticed her even more.

She stayed. They sipped champagne, talked and smoked, they even danced, and all along he treated her with the courtesy owed a lady. Hours passed and they enjoyed themselves like ordinary young people interested only in chatting and dancing They kept company until the club emptied, and during those hours Ximena fell in love with Amador.

"Amador, who do you think I am?"

Not surprised by her question, he answered, "I think you're the divine Ximena Godoy."

"No, I'm not divine. I'm a woman, and I want to know what you think of me."

"All I know is what I see: a beautiful, graceful and intelligent woman. What else is there to know?"

"There's more. While still a girl I joined the revolution, I lived among revolutionaries, and I even took part in the conflict. I witnessed bloodshed and suffering."

At first, Amador took a long look at her through the corner of his eye, and then shook his head as if trying to focus on what she was saying. "How did that happen?"

"What do you mean?"

"When I look at you, I see a well-bred, well-educated woman, not someone who would join the lowest of our society who caused so much suffering and disruption for the rest of us." Amador's pretentious way of speaking irritated Ximena, and now she was the one who looked at him through narrowed eyelids, thinking *the lowest of our society? Why don't you say scum, outcasts, trash, because that's what you really think.* But Ximena kept quiet, prompting him to ask, "Why did you do it?"

"What?"

"What made you join that ragged mob?"

Ximena knew that this was the moment to be honest with Amador, to reveal that she really had not given a damn about the revolution; she had tagged along with Tacho and the revolutionaries because she hungered for her own freedom, to be able to achieve greatness in what she saw as a different world from the one she was used to. She knew that now she had to admit how, along the way, she behaved just as debauched as those misfits. Now was the time to tell him how, even at that young age, she had already lusted—not just for one man, but for many, and she had given herself to all of them.

Ximena understood that she had to reveal this part of her story so the rest would make sense, but she threw away her chance to be honest. Instead of telling Amador the truth, she covered up her past because now she was afraid of losing him. From now on, everything that came out of her mouth would have to be a lie, and she knew it.

Ximena said, "I joined because I believed in the cause. I didn't see the revolutionaries as you do."

Amador bowed his head and thoughtfully leaned his elbows on the table. She waited for his next words. "Well, Ximena, no one can blame you for being deceived by what those liars preached. You were young, and others more experienced than you also followed like sheep." Amador cut off what he was saying because he seemed to have something else on his mind. He looked up and asked, "What about your family?"

"They immigrated north, but I don't know where they settled. I'm still trying to find them."

"That happened to many people. I'll help you find them, if you wish." He stopped, but there was yet more on his mind. "Tell me, what brought you to this place?"

"After the revolution, I lived with friends for some time in Jalisco but eventually I couldn't impose any longer. I knew that I had to make my own way, so I came here to Juárez. And here I met Don Pepo. He hired me as his assistant."

"I've heard that this place wasn't always what it is now."

"What do you mean?"

"Well, I've heard that it was once a place that housed women of bad reputation."

"That's why Don Pepo hired me, to help him in transforming his old business into this popular club. It's taken a few years, but together we did it."

Amador looked into Ximena's eyes and she thought she saw doubt there, but his next words did not reveal distrust. "Ximena Godoy, you're a mysterious woman, but I love that mystery." He ran his hands through his hair and rubbed his eyes. "It's late, so I'll go now. Can we meet tomorrow?"

"Yes."

Amador took her hand, brushed it lightly with a kiss, and walked into the dark night. Ximena returned to her room. She felt weighed down, her movements were sluggish. She took off her clothing piece by piece, pausing, thinking. There was lethargy in the way she smeared cold cream on her face as she gazed into her mirror.

Chapter Thirty-Three

LETTERS AND flowers arrived for Ximena, sometimes even twice a day. There were other gifts; a bracelet, and then a pearl ring, and once a gold chain with a dainty pendant attached to it. Yet, because she was still not convinced that Amador was serious, she kept a certain detachment. A part of her suspected that, in his mind, she was just a plaything, although he went on behaving like a gentleman. At first Ximena found excuses to turn him down, but she discovered that Amador did not get discouraged easily, and instead came up with more invitations. Finally, Ximena took time off from her work with Don Pepo's blessing.

"Go! Take as long as you want! Have a good time! Enjoy yourself, Ximena. You work too hard. It's about time someone special stepped into your life. But remember what I said to you in the beginning."

Ximena discovered that, once she accepted Amador's invitations, she liked his style and his company. She enjoyed taking in the sights that included meals at fine restaurants, betting and shouting at the horse races, gaming at casinos, and even picnicking along the river. And they joked and talked about favorite things, about funny experiences, but most of all he spoke of his family, their names, their personalities, and he especially talked of his mother. Behind all the talk Ximena detected, or thought she did anyway, that he wanted her to like his family and feel a part of them.

Just once did Amador ask, "Ximena, what about your family?" But because she did not want to talk about that part of her life, she put on a smile and said playfully, "Oh, that's a long story that I'll tell you one day."

After their first few outings, Amador rented a car to take them across the river into El Paso, and this thrilled Ximena more than anything so far, just knowing that she was in the United States. But once was not enough, so they went several times just to see sights that were new to Ximena. She especially liked the elegant Hotel Camino Real, where they gambled at roulette tables under the Tiffany Dome. After gambling, they danced to soft music on the hotel's rooftop, and later on gazed at the faraway lights of Juárez. This was a new world for her, dazzling and unforgettable, and she did not forget that it was Amador who introduced her to it.

The long days of summer grew short. Time passed and the season slipped into fall. Amador and Ximena enjoyed each other's company so much that they became inseparable. She went on being reserved about her past life but he didn't seem to mind. Instead, he talked more and more about himself and his own family. Ximena got to know much about him—what he liked and didn't like, and about his role in the family's business. When it came to explaining how he managed to stay away from work so long, he chuckled, saying that he attended to business right there in Juárez. Although Ximena didn't swallow it, she told herself that the very wealthy were different when it came to work.

Amador showed that he enjoyed Ximena's company, but he didn't return to serious talk about himself and Ximena, not as he had done on the first night. He seemed to be playing a boyish flowers-and-holding-hands game that she began to find tiring. A little bored each time they met, she now longed to be intimately involved. It was time, she thought.

One night, on their drive back from El Paso, Ximena decided to make the first move: even if he didn't feel love, she did.

"Amador, invite me to have a drink at your place."

After a stiff silence, he said, "It's what I planned, but you got ahead of me." Annoyed that she beat him to what should have been his move, he went on, "My hotel has a good cabaret. It's not as fine as *el Manglar*, but you'll like it."

The cabaret was not what Ximena had in mind, but she smiled and tried to look pleased. When they arrived, the maitre d' showed them to a table laid out with a lacy tablecloth, crystal and candles, and she knew right away that something special was going on. When she took her place, a waiter handed her a long-stemmed white rose intertwined with ribbon; the champagne came up right away. All along Ximena smiled, but inside she was thinking *this whole thing was already planned.*

She tried to feel romantic to match the setting, but she disliked the ritual too much; it was artificial, and not spontaneous. Nonetheless, she sipped the champagne and accepted cigarettes Amador offered from his silver case. The music was good so she agreed when he asked her to dance; she even yielded to his tight embrace and endless whisperings of trivialities. Finally, he led her back to the table where he produced a tiny box that held a large diamond ring.

"Soon, you'll be my wife."

Ximena was not surprised. She was thinking that the whole set-up was so obvious that the ring hardly caught her unaware, and what she was really feeling was a sense of entrapment. Ximena was in love with Amador, and she wanted him intimately, but without conditions or rules.

After searching for words to express her thoughts, she mumbled, "You hardly know me." When Ximena heard herself, she knew that it was an empty and stupid thing to say because it was not what was weighing heavily on her mind. But it was too late to take it back; it's what had come out of her mouth.

His shoulders slumped, he even appeared to be shocked. After a long pause, Amador came up with a shaky, "I thought that you would be happy."

Ximena could not respond because her mouth had gone dry. Actually, there was not much she could say anyway, but after a minute she spoke up. "Let's go up to your room."

This turned out to be a serious mistake because Amador caught her meaning, and his face darkened. "Aren't you afraid of what people will think?"

At first Ximena seemed startled by the question, and then she suddenly broke out into loud jeering laughter, and she loudly mocked his words. *"What people will think?* ¡Dios Santo, Amador! What people?"

She slid to the edge of the chair, turned to the right, to the left, and then twisted around to look behind her. "I don't know anyone here. Maybe you do, but I don't, and even if I did, I wouldn't care what they said."

By now Ximena's voice was so loud and shrill that it rose above the din of music, clinking glasses and chatting couples; people turned to stare at them, curious to know why the couple was squabbling. Some of them seemed amused, others whispered, still others pretended not to notice.

Stung by Ximena's mockery and sarcasm, Amador tried to silence her. *"Shhh!* For God's sake, Ximena, lower your voice! You're making a scene and people are staring. Why are you acting this way?"

"I don't give a *carajo* that people are looking! I just don't give a shit!"

"Shut up, Ximena!" Amador hissed at her, mortified to be the target of all that gaping. As Ximena quieted down, he mumbled, "Don't make fun of me! If you don't care what people say, then try to understand that I do."

She stared at him thinking *are we going to have a real fight? Right here in front of everyone?* She then sat back calmly in her chair, picked up the glass and sipped her champagne, but continued to return his cold stare. *Well, why not? I think it would do us good. We're stale and boring.*

After a few moments, Ximena cooled off, and decided that perhaps she had gone too far. She backed down: "It's just that I'd prefer to be alone with you, but if you think it's not the right thing to do, let's not do it."

Amador and Ximena sat glaring at each other in gloomy silence, neither one willing to break through the wall of ice that had erected itself between them. She stared at him but she could not get inside him to make out what he was thinking or feeling; he was so different from the men she knew. Crazy thoughts crossed her mind, leading her to think that maybe Amador was not a lover of women.

Had Ximena been able to get inside Amador's head, she would have seen how mistaken she was. Despite what she was thinking, he was a worldly man, experienced with women, who could easily read the signals given off by a woman on the hunt for intimacy. Amador knew right away that Ximena was trying to maneuver him into seduction, and more than anything else, he resented her immodest behavior.

But Ximena didn't understand his disenchantment. She didn't see that she had shattered the perfect image he cradled in his mind. She didn't grasp that he really had wanted to make her his wife; that in his mind, that woman was someone he would not take up to his room. Perhaps this was Ximena's biggest blunder and at that moment, it altered the nature of their relationship.

On his feet and about to leave the table, he mumbled, "I *wanted* you to be my wife." He snatched the ring off the table, but stopped when she spoke up.

"Then why not be alone with me? What are you afraid of?"

"This is too much!" Insulted, Amador felt the sting of Ximena's words just as if she had slapped him, and his anger only escalated. "I'm not afraid of anything. I was only trying to give you the respect I thought you deserved. Do you think that I'm less a man because of that?"

Without waiting for an answer, he grabbed Ximena's arm, yanked her out of the chair, and pulled her past the gawking, curious guests. He coerced her past the elevator and up the stairs to his suite where he threw open the door, switched on the lights, and pushed her in. Amador's romanticism evaporated right then and there. Enraged, he pulled off his jacket, undid his tie, and muttered, "Take off your clothes! Get on the bed!"

For a moment, this side of Amador startled Ximena, it even scared her a little. But she liked him better, too. She stared at him, unsure whether he was making fun of her. When Ximena saw lust in his eyes, she knew he was serious and she liked him even more. She did as he asked. She took off her clothes and got on the bed thinking that, at last, he was acting like a lover.

Amador came to Ximena in a rage. There were no caresses, no words of endearment or tenderness, and his body penetrated hers with quick, painful thrusts. He went on plunging himself into her with a ferocity that none of her partners had ever shown when making love to her. Soon she cried out for him to stop, that he was hurting her, but he went on and on, groaning, pushing, tugging, until he climaxed. Only then did he stop to roll off her.

Whatever love Ximena thought she had for Amador disappeared. Instead, she hated him because she knew that it had not been love that drove him to that sexual frenzy; it had been a desire to hurt and insult her. In that instant, she also understood that the other Amador, the love-letters-and-flowers Amador, was a fake, an imposter. She realized that this man who had just assaulted her was the real Amador, and she hated him even more for being a liar. She jumped from the bed and lunged for her clothes.

"I wasn't the first, was I?"

"What?"

Ximena was half-dressed when Amador spat out the question. "You heard me. I wasn't the first."

Disbelieving, she stopped what she was doing to glare at him. "¡*Carajo!* Amador, how can you be so stupid? I told you that I lived among revolutionaries who did battle, killed, got drunk, and smoked marijuana. How much imagination does anyone need to know that we also fucked every time we could?"

"Is that when you learned that dirty language, too?"

"You can be sure that it wasn't by sleeping with angels." She finished dressing and stood by the bed, staring down at Amador. He had not moved, and instead lay sprawled on the bed, naked, almost tempting her to grab the lamp to bash in his skull.

"Listen to me! I'm almost thirty years old, and I've lived in a brothel for years. How could you think that I was a virgin?"

"Because you said so."

Ximena's voice shrilled. "I never said such a thing! You dreamed it!"

"You pretended to be pure."

"I've never pretended to be what I'm not." Ximena was enraged. She wanted to hurt Amador even more than he had injured her, and so she did it with words. "And there's something else. I have a daughter. Her name is Ximenita."

"Get out, *cabrona!*" He shouted, not caring if everyone in the hotel heard him. "I don't want to see you again!'

Ximena left Amador in that dark room where he lingered

for hours. He thought of the night when he first saw Ximena Godoy dance the sensuous tango; when he had known that the woman he nurtured in his mind had become flesh. Now that she had offered herself, shamelessly inviting coarse sex, that image shattered. Worse yet was that she didn't even try to hide that she was tainted. The moment Ximena admitted that she was the leavings of other men, his dream collapsed in a heartbeat.

Mortified by what had happened, Amador wondered how he would go on without Ximena. What would take her place? Emptiness? When he finally left the bed, he threw on a robe, packed his luggage, and then contacted the concierge with instructions to book a passage on the early train south to Ciudad Guerrero. He planned to return to his family, and no one would ever know of his mad love for the woman called Ximena Godoy, whose image would haunt him for the rest of his life.

Chapter Thirty-Four

XIMENA STREAKED out of the room, ran down the stairs and through the lounge to the street where she hailed a taxi. She did not look back because she felt only disgust for Amador, but even more so for herself, knowing that she was the bigger liar because she had not been truthful when she had the chance. She jumped into the taxi, told the driver where to go, and then crouched down in the seat. *Would it have made a difference if I had told him everything? Would he love me despite it all?* Then her mind moved in another direction. *I've done bad things, I don't deny it, but who in this world is blameless? Is he so pure? I was honest when I told him that I didn't want to belong to anyone. Why didn't he listen?*

Ximena was mumbling and the driver glanced back to look at her, but she impatiently waved him off. He turned back to driving, and she to her thoughts. She had allowed herself to dream of a life with Amador and Ximenita, a life without rules or ties to harness either of them. Now, that dream was gone, evaporated: it had been a fantasy from the very beginning. She knew that now.

Ximena had forgotten what Don Pepo told her, that Amador was neither spoiled nor corrupt, but that he did have an image in his mind of what his wife should be: that image was an ideal as fixed as if it had been carved in stone. The fat man was right—

despite Amador having known and slept with many women, in the deep recesses of his mind the figure of a chaste, untouched woman waited for him.

When Ximena returned to the club that night, Don Pepo took one look at her and he knew; yet he said nothing, and neither did she speak. But Ximena was a scorned woman, and the days and nights that followed did not make matters better. Instead, time only brought her more pain. The breakup hit her hard, and she struggled to shake off loving Amador so intensely, more passionately and more stubbornly than any of her other loves. It hurt even more when she realized that, this time, she was not the one who walked away: it had been Amador who spurned her.

Ximena's resilience forced her to begin a reinvention, a restoration of herself without Amador, and she slowly became different in ways difficult for others to detect because it was deep inside her. There was something different in the way she spoke and went about her business, in the way she walked and moved, that gave those around her cause to wonder and gossip. Outwardly, she was just as glamorous, and her personality the same, always as open to the club's patrons as she had always been; yet she had become remote, even aloof, and people knew that something was going on. Only Don Pepo sensed the inner turmoil in Ximena, and he was not surprised when she revealed to him what she needed to do to regain her peace of mind.

"I need to do two things in particular."

It was a morning when she and Don Pepo met in his office to talk over the upcoming day's work. Ximena was dressed casually, and she was not wearing makeup, which was unusual for her.

"I'm listening." He, too, was in work clothes and had just poured coffee for each of them.

"I've thought it over carefully."

"I said I'm listening."

Evidently searching for words, Ximena took her time, squirming just a little in the chair, and then taking more time fussing with a loose coil of her hair. Don Pepo gazed at her with a curious expression.

"I intend to return to the village."

Her words came out in a rush, as if they were burning her

tongue and she had to let go of them fast. Don Pepo sat up stiffly in the chair.

"To stay for good?"

"No! I didn't mean to say it the way it came out. What I meant was, I'm returning to bring back Ximenita."

"*¡Chispas!* For a minute I thought you meant that you'd stay there. What a relief! Fine! You know that I've thought all along that you should bring her here to live with you. When do you plan to go?"

"I want to do it right away: tomorrow, or maybe the next day. The problem is that I don't know how long it will take; maybe a few days, but maybe more."

"Ximena, take all the time you need. You know that we can take care of business here, so don't worry. I'll lend you money if you need it."

"Thanks! I have my savings but I'll turn to you if I have to."

The two fell into that kind of silence that only happens with friends who know each other so well that talk isn't necessary. Don Pepo knew that this decision was a consequence of Ximena's split with Mendoza. He was glad that at least some good would come out of the failed affair. He, like everyone around her, saw how withdrawn she had been since the breakup. Maybe her child would revive her spirit.

"I'm glad, Ximena. It's the right thing to do."

"It's not going to be easy."

"You're thinking of the *abuela*, the old lady who keeps the girl?"

"Yes. I know her ways. She won't let go right away, and this time it's going to be different." After a few moments she said, "There's more, Don Pepo. I know that Ximenita loves Señora Epifania. After all, the old woman is the only one she's known all these years."

Ximena stopped what she was saying as she worked something out in her head; she was counting.

"She was seven when I left six years ago, and that many years in the life of a girl who is now thirteen is most of her life."

"Forget it! Kids have short memories and they adapt faster than we do; much faster than an old fart like me."

Don Pepo got to his feet, waving his arms as if making an

announcement to his patrons, and then he poured himself another coffee.

"Ximena, do what you have to do, and don't come back without that girl."

He headed for the desk but then, as if on second thought, he turned back to look at Ximena.

"You said there were two things. What's the other one?"

"I want to find my friend, Concha Urrutia. If she lives here in Juárez—and I think she does—I want to get in touch with her."

"Who in the *carajo* is Concha Urrutia?"

Ximena, who had been glum all along, finally broke into a smile, and that made Don Pepo flash an even bigger grin back at her.

"She's a girl I ran into once when I was in the rebel encampment."

"Once? And you call her a friend? Ximena, you have the craziest ideas!"

"No, Don Pepo, it's not crazy. Haven't you ever met someone that you knew right away would be your friend forever?"

The fat man looked intensely at Ximena and nodded. It was a slow gesture filled with meaning. "Yes, Ximena, I met someone like that a few years ago right here in our club, and you're right, it's not crazy. It's a blessing. Now get out of here. I've got work to do."

Two days later, Ximena got onto the train and headed for Guadalajara. It was a cold November morning just after dawn, and she was bundled up in a full-length coat, gloves and hat. When she settled down on the reserved seat, she remembered the time she made the same trip in the opposite direction, when she was clinging like a monkey to the rooftop of the train.

The day was ending when Ximena finally got off the train at her destination. She made her way down the road toward the village. By that hour the winter sky was filled with a golden-lavender light that made a sharp backdrop for the bare branches of the trees. The cool air was filled with the aroma of *maguey* cactus and the sweet scent of prickly *tunas*. Ximena had forgotten the beauty of that land, but also forgotten was the rough trek from the station to the village.

"This won't take long," Ximena said hopefully to herself,

"just enough time to put together Ximenita's things and then get back to the train."

Once she got off the main road and onto the path to the village, the ground became uneven; her heels caught and slipped; several times she came close to twisting an ankle. When Ximena finally reached the village, she stopped to look at that dismal sight, taking in the dingy huts and the rundown paths that led nowhere. The silence that wrapped around the place made her think that it was a village of the dead. She wondered how she had survived there all those years.

Slowly, heads furtively stuck out from around corners, and over there she caught prying eyes trying to observe the elegant lady striding through the center of their village. They seemed afraid to show themselves until one woman, then another, appeared from around corners and shelters. They were garbed in black, reminding Ximena of crows crowding in for pecking and scrounging. But no one recognized her, and they kept their distance—until one of those *comadres* came forward. "What are you doing here?"

"I'm looking for Señora Epifania. That's her hut over there, isn't it?"

The woman looked around, but then turned her wrinkled face back to curiously gawk at Ximena. "Yes. Who are you? What do you want?"

"You don't remember me?"

"No."

"I'm Ximena Godoy, Ximenita's mother."

"*¡Ay! ¡Dios Santo!*" The woman clasped her hands over her mouth but words slipped out of her mouth anyway. "You have changed so much! Señora Epifania won't recognize you!"

"She has a good memory. I know that she will remember me."

"But she has suffered so much."

Ximena shook her head. She did not want to hear more about the old woman. But she asked, "Where are her sons?"

"Gone. One day they disappeared, and the rumor is that they went to fight for *los Cristeros*, you know, the ones killing each other over priests and churches, and only God knows what else. They're heartless fools, those sons of Epifania. God will punish them for abandoning their old mother."

Ximena made a move toward Epifania's hut, but *la comadre* grabbed her arm. "Wait!"

"Let go, old woman!"

"Very well, but don't say I didn't try to stop you."

Ximena looked at the woman with curiosity, on the verge of asking her what she meant, but instead decided to head for Epifania's hut. She followed the craggy path all the way into the hut, and without calling out, entered the dark hovel. It was lit only by light that seeped in through the low entrance. It took a few moments for her eyes to adjust. Then over in the corner, she made out what at first looked like a bundle of rags—until she saw that the mound moved.

"Señora Epifania?"

Unsure, Ximena's voice was shaky. She moved closer, expecting the tough, wiry woman she remembered to step out of the gloom, but then she realized the Epifania was under the layers of ragged covers. All that Ximena could see of her was the long nose that poked out from the folds of a threadbare *rebozo*. Then Ximena saw those familiar tiny eyes, filled with the same old fire, and she caught how those eyes now glared at her.

Ximena stood struggling to believe her eyes, until she overcame her fright enough to blurt out, "Old woman, you know why I'm here." But Epifania did not answer. Instead, she retreated back into her ragged shroud.

"Where is she?"

The old woman stubbornly refused to answer, so Ximena scrambled to her side, took hold of the *rebozo* and yanked it away from her head, exposing the wrinkled face.

"Tell me! You know that I'll find her wherever she is, so don't put me off."

The old woman still did not speak, but when Ximena shook her back and forth, this time by the shoulders, she finally opened up.

"Ximenita is where even you can't reach her."

"Don't play games with me! Tell me! Where's my daughter?"

"Dead."

That dreadful word took a moment to break through the fog that had wrapped itself around Ximena. When it did reach her, she was so devastated that she fell onto her knees where she remained, stunned and confused. But almost immediately, she lunged toward Epifania, tearing away her coverings as if there, under that rancid pile of rags, she would find Ximenita hiding, playing a childish trick on her mother.

Ragged pieces flew, tumbling and scattering onto the hovel's dirt floor, until Ximena left the emaciated old woman shivering in her soiled underskirt. Ximena glared at Epifania, and then again shook her by the shoulders, this time more furiously.

"Tell me! Where is Ximenita?"

Then she pushed the old woman aside to make sure that the girl was not crouching behind, maybe under, maybe somewhere else, and all the time tears of rage and frustration streamed down her face.

Ximena was losing control of herself, although her instincts told her to stop. *Enough! Your daughter isn't here. Stop this torture! You're making yourself sick!* But Ximena could not stop herself—she was gripped in a vise of unspeakable anguish.

Breathless and gasping, she teetered backward and fell hard on her butt; her eyes remained pasted on Epifania who now would not shut up.

"You heard me and I'll repeat it! Ximenita is dead!"

It was clear that the old woman relished the pain she was inflicting on Ximena. She had somehow willed herself to live long enough to thrust that knife into the woman she hated, even before coming face to face with her; the woman she detested since Tacho told of his love for her.

"She's dead and you killed her! You're an evil mother!"

A voice inside Ximena shouted *This is intolerable! Run! Get out of this hovel!* The voice screamed but she did not listen to it, and instead fell into a trance, and a mysterious power compelled her to stay and hear more of what came out of the old woman's hateful mouth.

"You're a cursed woman! I curse you! *¡Maldita!* Go! Nothing you ever do will be good!"

Finally, Ximena scrambled away from that dark place, but it was too late. Epifania's words were already burned into her heart. Still, she bolted headlong without looking back, knowing that she would never again see that hated old woman or hear her evil words. She ran, but was stopped by the same black-shrouded *comadre* who had tried to stop her from encountering Epifania.

"I warned you! Don't say I didn't."

Barely able to whisper, Ximena asked, "What killed her?"

"Nobody knows. Epifania didn't tell."

"Did a doctor come?"

"No. The healer came but it was too late."

"Did she suffer?"

"Nobody knows."

"Where is she buried?"

"The cathedral has its holy ground. That's where you will find the girl."

Ximena turned away from that evil place, but she did not go to the cemetery. Instead she fled until she reached the desolate station to wait for the train back to Juárez. There she wept for the loss of her child, and for herself.

Chapter Thirty-Five

AFTER HER daughter's death, Ximena Godoy yearned to become a recluse. To all outward appearances she was the same friendly, glamorous woman, famous for her presence at *el Manglar*; the same woman who managed, organized, greeted patrons, and danced with Don Pepo. However, Ximenita's death had opened a wound in Ximena's soul, a hurt much deeper than a lost lover, or the humiliation of being turned away by Amador Mendoza. In truth, Ximena's soul was thrashed by guilt: she was convinced that she had caused her daughter's death by not having returned to her as promised.

Señora Epifania's curse took root in Ximena's soul, and she tried but couldn't stop thinking of her last encounter with the old woman. *You're a cursed woman!* Epifania's words plagued her, and remorse became her daily companion. No one knew that at the end of each day, when Ximena returned to her room, she retreated into a cold and solitary world. There, in the still of darkness, she passed sleepless nights smoking cigarettes and drinking *Cuervo*, trying to summon the strength to fight off the demons of grief and recrimination haunting her. But no matter how much tequila she drank, there was no letup to her ordeal until dawn finally broke, when daylight crept into her hiding place.

No one imagined this about Ximena, nor did they know that

time stopped when she secluded herself in that retreat. No one knew that she looked inside herself, as if peering into a mirror, and she encountered the reflection of a woman with accusing eyes. Maybe it was a trick of her tired eyes, or even the effects of the tequila, but Ximena saw a face whose eyes compelled her to make a daily confession that went like this:

"Bless me," Ximena always implored of the woman in the mirror, "for I have sinned." Then she fervently recited the opening prayer as she opened her soul to allow her sins to creep out. Each time, the uninvited woman answered, "How many times have you sinned?" And to this question, Ximena whispered, "I've lost count."

"Are they mortal sins?"

"Oh, yes!"

"Name them!"

When pressed to name her sins, Ximena resisted. No one should know that much, not even her other self.

"They are many, yet they are all one."

"Don't fool around with me, Ximena! Many can't be one!"

"I'm not fooling around! My sins are many yet they are one."

"If that's so, then name the capital sin, the mother of all the others."

"I can't."

"You're evading. Remember that I've been with you all along, and I know each of those sins."

"Then why do you ask?"

"Because this is a confession, and your lips must name the sin. That's what a true confession of guilt means."

"I can't!"

"That means you're not sorry."

"I *am* sorry!"

"Then name that sin!"

"It's a sin with no name."

"This is no time to joke!"

"I'm not joking. I truly mean that my sin is the unforgivable sin, the one without a name."

"Name that sin, I tell you!"

"I killed my daughter."

At this point, the woman in the mirror always paused as if

shocked, although she heard Ximena's confession every dawn.

"How?"

"How what?"

"How did you kill your daughter?"

"If you were there, as you say, then you would know the answer!"

"Again I ask you: How did you kill your daughter?"

"I abandoned her."

"Abandonment doesn't kill."

"No, but sadness does."

"I can't absolve you."

"I know. I've already told you that mine is the unforgivable sin."

"No, that's not the reason."

"Then why can't you absolve me?"

"Your confession is incomplete, that's why. Something is missing. You're leaving out something that comes before your daughter's sadness and death. A secret that you're hiding."

"I deny that!"

"Yes! You're hiding something!"

"I've confessed that I killed my daughter. What more could there be?"

"Oh, there's something else. Think! Only when you admit that previous sin will you be absolved."

"I'm a cursed woman."

"Yes, but I also know that you're evading again, so stop playing your little games!"

As if on cue, Ximena then falls into morose silence. *How can I admit what I don't remember?* Then she returns to the inner woman's carping.

"If I tell you that I can't remember what the mother of my sins is, will you believe me?"

"No! And now I'm tired, and I'm leaving."

"Wait! Will you absolve me?"

"No."

"How can I make up for what I've done?"

"That's for you to answer."

"How can I make amends if I don't know how?"

"I've told you that I don't know. That's why I can't absolve you."

"What can I do?"

"Wait until the end of your life, maybe you'll find the answer then."

"Will you absolve me when that happens?"

"Maybe."

Who are you?"

"I am you."

Then, like clockwork, the confession ended. When the inner woman disappeared into the mirror of Ximena's soul to wait for tomorrow's dawn, Ximena was left sleepless, exhausted and shaky. She dozed off after that, but always, when she rose from her bed to face the day, Ximena felt burdened by an unimaginable weight.

Chapter Thirty-Six

IN TIME, Ximena did snap out of that self-punishing ordeal to return to her old self. It happened when she finally discovered where her friend Concha Urrutia was living, tucked away on a Juárez backstreet. Finding her friend helped Ximena break out of her downward spiral of sadness and guilt. But the impact of Epifania's curse had not disappeared, and Ximena's sleepless nights continued their relentless punishment. Nonetheless, finding Concha helped Ximena begin to pick up the pieces of her life.

Concha Urrutia was not easy to find, and it had taken a long time for the search even to begin: the effect of the Amador Mendoza affair had to play out and then crash, and no sooner had Ximena started looking for Concha after that fiasco, when she was struck with her daughter's death, leaving her inconsolable and indifferent to everything, including the whereabouts of her lost friend.

Months passed and Ximena gradually regained some inner serenity, and she decided that it was finally time to find the woman who inspired her to come to Juárez in the first place. But tracing a lost person was not easy. Although Juárez was still small in those days, it was not a village, so Ximena had difficulty and hired a detective. Eventually the snoop reported her friend's whereabouts, and Ximena didn't waste any time; she made her way to look up the long-lost Concha Urrutia right away.

During the years since she and Ximena had first known each other, Concha had done well for herself. She was now the owner of a small gambling joint she called *La Conchita,* located in the midst of the seediest part of town. It was so rickety and low-class that only the riffraff of neighboring *barrios* hung around. Still, they were steady customers, eager to lose wages barely scraped together. These men didn't think twice about wasting even more money trying to make up for their gambling losses. *La Conchita* was popular, and even if the place was lowbrow and shady, it was all hers, and Concha Urrutia was proud of it.

The spot was a dim, smoky place with a tiny bar on one side and a couple of dilapidated gambling tables that hugged the opposite wall; one was for craps, the other for poker. On the day Ximena walked into the *cantina* it was still early, but there were already a few shabby customers trying their luck. Tending bar was a man who blended in with the dismal surroundings; his face reminded her of a famished, long-nosed, watery-eyed dog. He sported a straw hat that might have been stylish years before, but now it was sweat-stained and frayed, and his faded vest emphasized his skinny body. The outfit was finished off by oversized, baggy trousers.

From where she stood, Ximena could not see the man's shoes, but she imagined that they, too, must have been clownish. When she got close enough for him to make her out he smiled big, losing the lost-dog snout, and looking more like a toothy *caiman.*

"*Dama*, how can I help you?"

"I'd like to speak to Concha Urrutia."

His slanted eyes narrowed even more as he checked out Ximena up and down, evidently liking what he saw.

"Who is looking for *la Señora*?"

"I'm Ximena Godoy, a friend of many years ago."

"The same lady of *el Manglar* and...?"

Anxious to see Concha, Ximena cut the man off at mid-sentence. "If you please, I don't have much time. I'd be grateful if you'd call her right away."

The man turned and disappeared through a beaded curtain behind the bar. While she waited, Ximena looked around.

What a dump! Right away she imagined what she would do with that small space, and how to convert it into an attractive little casino. With her back to the bar, she was thinking of tables, chairs, paint and lamps, when a heavy hand landed on her shoulder.

"*¡Caramba!* Is it really you? Are you *la loca* who gave me beans, tortillas and a lot of questions way back when we were a pair of *chingonas*?"

Startled, Ximena spun around to face Concha.

"Yes! You're the one with the big belly, the one who beat the shit out of *la Malvada!* Ximena Godoy! That's your name, and I remember you like it was just yesterday that we sat by that *pinche* little fire. You saved my ass from freezing off." And with that Concha let out the loud carefree cackle that Ximena remembered so fondly.

Ximena stared at Concha; she wanted to take in every detail. Concha was a little heavier than Ximena remembered, but still very attractive. She wore a short flapper dress that emphasized her ample bust and hips, and her hair was bobbed in a way that flattered her round, friendly face. Dainty spit curls gave her the perfect final touch.

"And you're Concha Urrutia, the one who was alone but not afraid. You laughed and didn't care what others thought, but you could be serious too. That's why I remember you."

Ximena got that much out, then threw her arms around her friend and held her close for a long time, thinking that it was hard to believe that so many years had passed.

"*Amiga*, I've been looking for you for a long time, and here you are, just a few streets away."

Concha was quick to answer. "It's another story for me because I knew where you were when you got famous."

"Then why didn't you come to see me?

"You're too famous."

"*¡Mierda!*"

Concha let out a cackle that made the broken-down drunks swivel around to gawk in their direction, but she glared back and told them to mind their business. Then she took Ximena's arm and led her to a little table on the side, out of the way. There the two women sat, feeling like it was 1916 all over again, like they were still young girls, like the revolution would go on forever.

"Bernardino, bring us double tequilas; make it your good stuff! This is my friend, and she deserves the best." Hardly taking a breath, Concha kept on babbling, "Bernardino nearly had a heart attack when he found out you're the famous Godoy, the one who owns *el Manglar*. And ¡carajo! I nearly choked myself!"

"Concha, I'm not the owner."

"No? Then what the hell are you?"

"I'm the manager, that's all."

"Shit! People think you're the owner, so that makes you the owner. Don't mess with it!"

Bernardino brought the tequilas, lemon and salt, as Concha jabbered on. *"¡Dios santo!* Godoy, you're beautiful! When did it happen?"

Ximena disregarded the question, picked up the shooter, held it high and waited for Concha to do the same.

"Here's to us, *amiga*. I hope our paths never separate again. We've got things to do."

The women clinked glasses, drained them in one gulp, let out a yelp, and then a howl that made the barkeep look over his shoulder and break out with his hungry-dog grin.

"Bernardino, bring two more, right away! Oh, hell! Forget the little chickenfeed shooters! Bring the whole *pinche* bottle and leave it here!"

Then the women went on to get tipsy, smoking cigarette after cigarette, while they brought each other up to date on how they had come so far from the little campfire that had brought them together.

Ximena's voice was raspy with the effect of the tequila. "I woke up that morning and you were gone. Where did you go?"

"I jumped on the train headed up here. *¡Ay, amiga!* There were hundreds of us from all over Mexico; men, women and even kids, all of us fighting over a little space just to hang on to the sides and roof of the train. The lucky ones hung out of windows, and it didn't make a difference what side of the Revolution anyone was on.

"In the middle of that craziness there were *carrancistas, villistas, zapatistas, obregonistas*. There was even a bunch of *pelones,* deserting the *federales.* It didn't make any difference because all we wanted was to escape all that killing that didn't make sense to any of us."

Concha stopped to catch her breath, poured two more tequilas, hoisted her glass and then went on with her story.

"I landed here in Juárez, but right away I hated it. So I crossed the border into El Paso where I lived for a couple of years."

"Doing what, Concha?"

"I worked in *cantinas,* what else? I know you're going to ask what kind of work I did, so I'll tell you right away. I did everything from tending bar, to making and sprawling out on beds." She stopped abruptly to look hard at Ximena's wondering expression. "Well, what's a girl to do when she's hungry? She lies down and opens her legs, that's what she does. Sometimes, Ximena, that's all a woman has left to do, and you know that better than anyone."

Ximena did not answer, but asked, "You stayed in El Paso?"

"No. I hated the *pinche gringos* and their stingy ways, so I made my way over to Los Angeles."

Mention of the city so far away captured Ximena's imagination instantly; she had never met anyone who had traveled so far.

"But isn't it just filled with *gringos,* like El Paso?"

"Maybe. It's just that there are more of us there. You know, *Raza,* and it's easy to feel at home."

"What did you do there? Did you like it? Do you know anyone there? Why did you come back?"

"¡Orale! I can't answer all those questions right away, not without another tequilita. C'mon, *amiga, ¡Salud!"*

"¡Mierda! I'm getting drunk." Ximena's words were slurring.

"I was a good girl in Los Angeles. I think it's because this time I found work at a factory, and I had the chance to hang around with a bunch of good girls. I even got a little room in a boarding house, and for once I was decent. Can you imagine? Me, decent? Me working at a factory that made stuff that we eat all the time! Ha! Those *gringos* love *tamales!* What a bunch of *pendejos!* They go to stands that sell them and pay good money because they say it cures hangovers!" With that, Concha let out a huge bellow, now crackling with hiccups.

"What made you come back to Juárez? I would have stayed in Los Angeles."

"La *migra* caught me. Well, not just me. It happened when they raided the factory; all of us were caught like fish in a net. ¡Zass! Just like that!" Concha snapped her fingers. "We were loaded onto trucks and dumped on the Mexican side of the border at a little chickenshit town called Tijuana. Well, I thought that since I was on the move again, I'd just keep going until I made it back here again, and here I stayed. *¡Salud!*"

While Ximena listened, memories of her own years crowded in. Images of Señora Epifania, the hut, begging the old woman to take her in, Ximenita's birth, the cornfields, the deadly epidemic. All of those pictures and so many others swirled in her memory. She tried to remember when it all happened, in what order, and what Concha could have been doing at the same time, at the same moment. Ximena felt that she and Concha, as if tied onto separate ends of the same thread, had been moving toward one another, step by step, all the time fighting to stay alive, each in her own way.

"*¡Chihuahua!* I've been babbling like a fool! Let me hear what you've been doing, and how you got to be so famous."

"It's a long story, Concha."

Ximena knew that she was not up to reliving the steps that had brought her to this moment because she still found revealing herself too painful; the memories were buried too deep. Instead, she stalled and tried to think of at least some memory, not too important, more on the surface. "*Amiga*, pass over one of those cigarettes." When Concha handed her the pack, Ximena lighted up, taking time to wipe a speck of tobacco from her lips. She looked toward the bar and then, contrary to what she had intended, blurted out, "I had a daughter."

"*¡Caramba!* That's wonderful!"

Concha shimmied her butt on the chair. At the same time, she clasped her hands together as if ready to applaud.

"Yes! I remember the belly you were carrying. Well? Tell me more about her. What's her name? I want to meet her. She's in school, for sure."

Before the rat-a-tat-tat of Concha's slurred jabbering could go on, Ximena stopped it.

"She's dead. I lost her."

Concha stiffened, her brow furrowed and she seemed to go breathless. This time, there were no wisecracks, much less laughter; neither did she unleash the foul language that came to her so naturally. Instead, Ximena sensed a Concha she had not imagined buried deep inside that fat body; what she said expressed unexpected compassion, a deep feeling for Ximena.

"*Amiga*, I'm sorry! Please stop! No more!"

"I want to tell you. I need to tell someone because if I don't, my heart will explode." Finally Ximena opened up, letting a torrent of grief spill out; the words burned her tongue as they scrambled to reach daylight. "I killed her."

Concha reached across the table, took Ximena's face in her cupped hands, and whispered, "Don't say such a terrible thing! I know you didn't kill your daughter. I know it, so don't say it."

Maybe it was the tequila, or maybe just being with someone she trusted, but the inhibitions and control that guarded Ximena's heart melted away and she opened up. Her voice was choked. "I abandoned her. I promised to return but I didn't keep that promise."

"Some promises can't be kept. Don't punish yourself. If you only knew how many promises I've broken."

"Concha, my girl died, and I never saw her again. I'm cursed."

"*¡Dios Santo!* What put that ugly idea in your head? No one is cursed. I don't believe in that kind of thing."

"No? What do you believe?"

"We take wrong steps, do bad things, make mistakes, but we're not cursed. That's what I believe."

"Then why do I feel so miserable?"

"Ximena, we lose precious, beautiful things in life, and because it hurts so much we feel heartbroken. That's what life is all about, but we keep on living. We don't say we're cursed."

"How do you know that?"

"Don't you think that I've ever lost something blessed and wonderful?"

Ximena stared at Concha thinking, *You, too have lost something irreplaceable.*

"Ximena, I'm not religious, much less educated, but I know

one thing: we're not cursed. What we've done, and even what we're yet to do, will be forgiven, just as we must forgive others. We have to think this way, or go crazy."

"What about the unhappiness we cause?"

Concha's hands fell away from Ximena's face but her gaze was steady and filled with understanding. "I don't know the answer to your question because I don't know what you're thinking of. All I can say is that we must forgive ourselves, even when we cause unhappiness."

After that the two women fell into a deep silence that did not need words to be understood.

Chapter Thirty-Seven

CONCHA URRUTIA was more than just the girl that Ximena liked because she laughed, stuck her tongue out at conformity, and attracted so many people. She had her story, an interesting one. She was born in a village outside of Uruapan, not far from Jalisco. She was the middle child in a string of sisters with only one brother, who happened to be the oldest of the brood of kids orphaned when their mother died giving birth to the last girl.

Concha's father was a woodworker by trade, a good man whose only weakness was that he really believed Mexico would provide its people with a better life, and that revolution was the way. Although most of his fellow villagers agreed with his way of thinking, it just was not practical, so unlike him, they did nothing.

When Concha was about sixteen years old, the revolutionaries finally made their way through her village, and her father was among the few to pawn his tools, buy a mule, a saddle and a Remington repeater to join up. After he rode away, he was never seen again, and that meant that his children were now truly orphaned.

The Urrutia children were hardworking and had learned to fend for themselves, and that was true of Concha who, although not pretty, had something that made her more than likeable. She was born chubby, and that roundness stuck to her so that her face and cheeks resembled a brown apple. Even her body was shaped like a pear. Concha's eyes were small, but because they sparkled they were her most striking feature along with her mouth, even though it was too large for her face.

On their own, her features were not attractive, but together they were enchanting, especially when she let out that loud, cackling laughter. When Concha laughed, everyone laughed, and that alone endeared her to everyone.

But she had her inner darkness, mostly because she suffered from loneliness no matter how many people surrounded her. It was a constant, nagging feeling that afflicted her since her earliest memories. She longed for one person to love, that special one to occupy her world and rescue her from that hurtful feeling of isolation. She could not really say who that person might be; perhaps it would be a man, or maybe a woman. In the end, it did not matter to her. The important thing was to be loved and thought of as a friend, as someone special.

Since her early years, Concha had floundered about in confusion when these thoughts came to her because they were still blurred, undefined and formless; all she knew was that she longed to be cherished.

When the rugged-looking revolutionary wearing the oversized *sombrero* galloped into her village mounted on a beautiful pinto, and when he reined in the horse and stretched down his arm to her and murmured, *"Orale, Chula!* Come with me to fight the revolution!" she did not even think it over. Concha latched on to that extended hand, leaped up onto the rump of the animal, wrapped her arms around the revolutionary's slim waist, and rode away to join in the battles of Jalisco and Sonora. As with their father, her family never saw Concha again.

But she was disappointed, even deeply hurt, not only by the man's almost instant indifference toward her, but more so by the aimless revolution itself. It was not long before Concha saw that her father's aspirations were betrayed, and the revolution had turned into a string of one pompous general after the other, each toppling the other in deadly power grabs. Those who started out as revolutionaries were soon transformed into hordes of displaced, hungry people, while bands of turncoats infected entire armies. No one knew where to place their loyalty;

no one could even guess who was right and who was wrong.

On the night that Concha had crept over to the young woman, the one with the swollen belly, to ask if she could sit with her by the little campfire, Concha already knew that she was on a new road leading away from all the futile fighting and meaningless death. That was the night she met Ximena Godoy, but she had no way of knowing that, although the strands of their lives were destined to separate for a long time, they would meet again.

Chapter Thirty-Eight

THE 1930 New Year's Eve Fiesta at *el Manglar* was a dim version of the usually over-crowded, spirited year-end celebration: in fact, the place was barely half-filled. There were the usual party hats and whistles, confetti, balloons and plenty of champagne, but the magic and loud celebration of other years just was gone. Whatever was happening north of the border was hitting Mexico hard, and the towns that depended on *gringo* dollars were sinking fast.

That night, most of Don Pepo's workers joined in an effort to drum up the craziness of past years, but there was nothing there. He and Ximena tried hard to enliven the evening, but the customers who had shown up were glum, and not even their usually magical tango cast its spell; everywhere there were long faces.

Outside, the feeling was the same. *Avenida Mariscal*, usually the heart of the city's nightlife, was subdued and nearly deserted. Missing were the animated, laughing, carousing crowds that usually packed the street. Some of the club and casino lights had gone dark, dance halls were nearly empty, and musicians along with cooks and waiters hung out in front of their businesses smoking, looking dejected, and obviously trying to figure out what was happening.

Someone turning the corner heading for the raunchy part

of town would arrive at Concha's place. At first glance, her little spot did not seem to have been hit like other businesses; it was packed with the same old *compadres*, and maybe that was because the place had never depended on *gringo* dollars to begin with. *It's better to be poor, so when hard times hit, nothing changes. You don't even notice.* At least, this is what those old drunks murmured.

On that New Year's Eve night, in her element, Concha moved from one rickety table to the next, greeting one and then another of her customers, and her words to each little group made the old geezers laugh and hoot with wide-open mouths. Above that racket, her uninhibited, boisterous cackle broke out each time.

In that year of 1930, the Great Depression hit Juárez hard, particularly Don Pepo, who was forced to make plenty of cutbacks just to survive. First to go was the big band that featured famous singers and soloists, leaving him to wonder *what's a nightclub without music?* He hired a more affordable *marimba* combo that provided wonderful dance tunes, but when money dried up even more, he had to let them go as well. Then he brought in a trio, but even that little group had to be dropped, so finally there was no more music at *el Manglar*. Food and drinks alone were offered to bring in patrons.

Worse still, along with having to do away with his beloved music, the fat man was forced to cut his staff to a fraction of what it used to be. It was heartbreaking to see how he cried when the time came to say *adiós* to his waiters, barkeeps and cooks; some of them had been with him from the beginning. A few chose to stick around, although there wasn't any money to pay them, but the others, for reasons of their own, had to leave, and they too left crying.

Don Pepo and Ximena tried to stay optimistic, but it was hard. Still, despite heavy hearts, they spent hours thinking of different ways to attract customers. They put together a simpler menu, one that stuck to basic local food; no more fancy stuff or imported delicacies. They decided to cut down on tables, and the few they kept were set up with less decoration and frills.

Ximena made up flyers to stick on telephone poles, and hired a *muchacho* to hand them out at the bus and train stations. She thought of giving out flyers to other casinos, as well as the horse and dog racetracks, but those places were in worse condition than *el Manglar*, so she gave up on the idea.

Ximena and Don Pepo talked for hours devising cuts here and there, but no matter how many changes they thought of, the problem grew worse every day. "What happened to all those dollars?" But no matter how many times they asked this question, they could never explain the disaster.

The biggest blow came in 1932: Prohibition was repealed in *el norte*. Now, legal access to liquor in the States eliminated the last reason for the *gringos* to cross the bridge into Juárez. So after this catastrophe, in a panic, the fat man proposed returning to the roots of his business. "Let's bring back our *muchachas*! Who can resist a pretty girl along with a nice private room?"

When Ximena got wind of this latest proposal, she hated the idea and fought it. Don Pepo, however, did not buy into her way of thinking: he just could not understand it. "What's the matter with you, Ximena? Work is work! Who gives a *carajo* if it's flopping on a bed or washing dishes?"

And when Ximena pushed back hard, they had their first really serious fight. "Don Pepo, how can you even think of returning to such a thing?"

"Why not?"

"Because it's shameful!"

"What? It's work, and all work is good, never shameful! Besides, look around you! We owe everything to those women. Don't fool yourself!"

"Don't you feel rotten about taking advantage of human beings that way?"

"Ximena! Women who work with men in rooms are grownups, and they do it because it's work! It's that simple! No one is taking advantage of anyone. What a crazy idea. What are you thinking?"

"First of all, Don Pepo, most of those you call women are just little girls, some of them just past their first bleeding. Don't you find that disgusting?"

By now their voices had gotten louder and they were shouting at each other. Sometimes the fat man's yelling drowned out Ximena's, but not always: she had good lungs, and even though they were in the back office room, people out front could hear every word of the screaming.

"*¡Carajo!* Why should I be ashamed? It's a living! It's been going on since the beginning of the world. Don't forget that it's what gave you the opportunity to be where you are now, so don't pretend to be so pure!"

The fat man's words implied something that hit Ximena hard, leaving her nearly speechless, but only for a moment: she shot back in self-defense. "How dare you say that? I never opened my legs for money. Never! You know that better than anyone!" Her voice caught in her throat, then quieted, letting him know that he had stumbled into a forbidden part of her soul.

He, too, backed down, while long minutes passed in silence until he broke down. "Ximena, I'm sorry! *¡Chingo!* I'm going crazy, and I don't know what I'm saying. I'm not thinking straight! I'm sorry! Let's forget the ugly words we've said, and let's begin again. Let's try! Together we can find a way out of this trap we're in. After all, it's only money. Somehow we can find the way to get it to come back again."

Ximena felt just as sickened, not so much by the words they exchanged, as by the bitter feelings of frustration and anxiety buried deep in those words. She knew that both of them were floundering, that they had lost their footing, and they were just plain scared. She moved close to the fat man and took his hand, letting him know that she, too, was anguished.

"I'm not pure. I haven't been that way for a long time, and I know that I'm a hypocrite, but I can't make *putas* out of little girls. I hate that business!" She stopped speaking for a short time, trying to stop her voice from trembling. "Look, Don Pepo, I owe everything to you. I can't forget it, not for a minute, and I'd do anything for you. I'd even trade myself for money, if I thought it would change the mess we're in."

"No, *Hija*, don't say such a thing! I told you I was talking crazy. We'll find a way, I know it." That he called her daughter startled them both just a little. He had never used that word with her, and although they did not say more, still they felt the powerful meaning of the word.

During the months that followed, Don Pepo and Ximena worked hard trying different ways to attract customers to *el Manglar,* without success. And the day came when they had to admit that the business had failed; they were bankrupt. The only thing that eased their anguish was that ruin was everywhere. They found small consolation hearing that others had it even worse; some owners were facing severe penalties, and even being jailed for failure to pay debts.

Through it all Don Pepo anguished, hardly slept or ate, and he lost weight. Everyday kilos melted off his once portly body, and people noticed how his round cheeks and fully packed double chin, once so firm and glistening, flattened out like a *tortilla*, leaving flabby skin dangling over his frayed shirt collar. And what about his trousers? This was a serious matter because he did not have the money to buy new ones even though the old ones sagged off his deflated butt so much that he had to shorten his old suspenders.

However, his spirit was intact, and he swaggered around as if he was still the best-dressed man in the club. But despite his put-on strut, no one called him the Fat Man anymore, and just looking at the shadow that had replaced the jovial roly-poly man of the old days was enough to make anyone choke up.

By this time even Concha Urrutia was forced to accept that her enterprise could not go on either; even the old codgers had disappeared. Not that Don Pepo was happy that her place had gone under, but it did tell him that the money disaster was not because of any mismanagement or blunders on his part, but because it was widespread. The day Concha came to him with the bad news he began to feel sorry for her, but only for a minute because right away her indestructible spirit flashed, reassuring him that she might have been knocked down, but it would not be for long.

"Things happen for a reason, Don Pepo. Maybe we needed this kick in the *fundillo* to remind us that the good times go away as easy as they come. It means that we have to look around for another way to make a life for ourselves. True or not true?"

"True, Conchita, true."

The inevitable happened when Don Pepo and Ximena had to accept that it was the last day for their club; that it was closing time. Just thinking of it was painful for them, and also for the few workers and friends who had clung to what was left of the business even though they had not been paid in months.

That night they clustered together determined to close down the place with nothing less than a *fiesta* and happy faces. They were all there: Concha and her faithful barkeep Bernardino, two guitar players who had stuck around for old times' sake, and even Queta Ramírez, who had stayed by Ximena's side since the beginning at Don Pepo's. Naturally, Don Pepo and Ximena were the heart of that *fiesta*.

In the supply room someone discovered a few bottles of tequila, along with a pile of lemons. Just the sight of the Cuervo and little yellow fruits filled the friends with the spirit to say *adiós* to their club, and to each other. Shot glasses were filled, lifted and clinked. Shouts filled the room. *Salud! ¡Buena Suerte!* The revelers did it once, twice, over and over, until they lost count. When the tequila kicked in, the musicians scrambled for their stashed-away instruments and in no time the sensuous notes of *la Comparsita* filled the back room, and when that magical tango broke out the shouting got louder. *¡Oralé! ¡Don Pepo! ¡Ximena! ¡Tango! ¡La última vez!*

And just like in the old days, the beautiful Ximena Godoy and the fat old man danced, this time as they had never danced before, with so much rhythm and grace that the others were inspired, and they all joined in. Concha Urrutia grabbed gawky Bernardino, Queta danced with a shadow partner, and even the musicians swayed as they plucked the strings of their *guitarra* and *guitarrón*.

When *la Comparsita* was over the little crew, sweaty, tipsy and nostalgic, made their way to the deserted front hall of what had been Club *el Manglar*. Together they fastened down shutters, windows and entrance doors, switched off the inside lights, and last of all, the outdoor neon sign identifying *el Manglar,* was shut off telling the whole street that the club was gone.

Chapter Thirty-Nine

"MAKE IT your new world, Ximena. Don't look back. Don't come back. Remember that wherever you plant your feet, there you will belong."

These were Don Pepo's words of farewell as they stood together, looking across the bridge. Ximena suspected that Don Pepo's legs were shaking, and that his heart was sad. But she also knew that he wanted her to go. Her legs were shaking too; she found it scary to face that unknown space where she didn't even know the language spoken by its people. Her consolation was knowing that she would not have to brave it alone, for standing beside her was Concha Urrutia who would come with her. If they were together, she would have confidence.

"¡Vamos, amiga! Why the long face?" Concha put her hand on Ximena's shoulder to reassure her. "It's not like we're going to fall off the earth. Anyway, everything here is falling apart, so do we have a choice? Think of it that way. So c'mon! Pick up that bag, and ¡vámonos!"

Although not as sure as Concha, Ximena knew that her friend was right. Besides, she had given this move much thought, but when everything was said and considered, it was Don Pepo who made her see that el norte was the place to go. And his opinion counted. He was the one who assured her that there was nothing in Juárez to hold her back, not even him.

"Don't worry about me, Ximena. I'll be fine. Remember, I've looked after myself since I was a *mocoso*."

Ximena looked north toward the edge of El Paso where she could make out the outline of buildings and people moving around. She still remembered some places from her days with Amador Mendoza, but very vaguely. More vivid were thoughts that took her in the opposite direction, down to Guadalajara, to the villages that she knew from her childhood, and to when she lived under Señora Epifania's sharp eye. Ximena's thoughts made their way into the hut that had witnessed so much of her unhappiness, but also the joy of giving birth to Ximenita. She thought of her baby's umbilical cord, now buried deep inside that hut, waiting for its owner to return to claim it.

She knew hard times were ahead of her, but that did not scare her; it had been worse when she ventured into Juárez alone. What *did* scare her was that mysterious unknown world across the bridge. She knew that she and Concha were going against the tide of people that was flowing back into Mexico— some because they chose to, others because they were rounded up and deported by the trainload. Whatever the reasons, *mexicanos* were coming this way every day by the hundreds, and her stomach tightened up as she thought how she and her friend were going against that current.

She turned to Don Pepo. "I don't want you to worry about me either. You know that I, too, can take care of myself. I'll never forget what you've done for me and taught me, and neither will I forget how good it was working with you."

They fell silent as they gazed north, the three dark silhouettes with their backs to the world they knew and loved, but all three now facing the unknown. Time crept by until Ximena shattered the reverie: she embraced the old man, and then Concha did the same. Of the three, it was Don Pepo who was crying when the women slipped away from him to make their way across the bridge. The parting was on a windy afternoon in November of the year 1932.

PART TWO

Chapter Forty

WHEN SHE crossed over from Mexico, Ximena Godoy left behind a string of memories, hopes and withered loves. She also left behind a beloved daughter buried in a remote cathedral cemetery. But unlike so many of those other left-behind joys and sorrows, Ximenita would never be forgotten. As Ximena Godoy and Concha Urrutia made their way to Los Angeles, their pathway was not smooth or straight, and certainly not easy. The two women struggled and nearly fell to pieces when they reached that city which was trapped in the worst of times; but they held on and moved forward. They remained intact, knowing that they were just two women out of thousands of other migrants in search of a better life. They accepted from the beginning that living in a strange, new world was going to be a hardship.

When Ximena made it across to the American side of the border, she arrived empty-handed, but not purposeless—she was filled with an ambition, a dream to make something of herself, and a drive to achieve something big. It was grounded in what she had learned about herself in Juárez. There, Ximena had discovered that she had the gift of making a business work, a knack for conceiving an idea and making it come together. Knowing this made her different from the others; it filled her with self-confidence and vision of her new goals. Her conviction outweighed any shakiness she might have felt when she first breathed American air.

In the years that followed she never wavered, nor did she doubt that one day she would reach her intended aims, the goals she set for herself. From the beginning, Ximena burned with ambition and hatched big ideas; but it took years and hard work for her to fully execute those plans.

Alongside Concha, Ximena's first job was in Boyle Heights at a poultry market. They worked processing chickens for market, and the stink of boiling feathers and slimy guts repulsed most people, even those desperate for work. Yet Ximena and Concha toiled there for a couple of years, holding on to that backbreaking job only because of their determination to make it in that new world. Hardly a day passed that Concha would not complain, *"¡Ayi ¡Qué peste!* This stink is driving me crazy!"

Like clockwork, Ximena's answer sounded out over the boiling mess: "Just think of the poor chickens, and feel lucky you're not one of *them!*"

Concha's responding cackle pealed out, making the other workers stop to wipe their brow and chuckle, even though they didn't know why. This is how the two women coped with their misery, and their friendship deepened and grew stronger, perhaps because they endured those hardships together.

After years of working with dead chickens, they followed a tip from a fellow worker about openings at an industrial laundry at the corner of San Pedro and Central. There they landed jobs that were a step up from the poultry market. Grateful to be rid of the chicken stink that every day had soaked into their skin and hair, Ximena and Concha worked folding hotel sheets and pressing pillowcases.

This will happen for just a few more years. Wait just a little bit more. These were Ximena's thoughts at the end of each exhausting day, but it wasn't long before she hit a point where she couldn't fold linens any longer. One day she turned to her friend and blurted, "Concha, we're going to take over a food stand. It's a good little spot over on Third and Soto where lots of hungry people hang around, and it's for rent. We'll call it *El Encanto.*"

Concha looked at her with startled eyes. "I've saved enough

money to start, and what's important is that we'll be in business again. You'll be my right hand. How about it?" After catching her breath, Concha's reply was an unconditional *"¡Seguro!"*

Once Ximena started up the food stand, word got around that the food was really good and *El Encanto* eventually got very popular. However, it had taken many long hours of work for the two women, beginning at sunrise and sometimes not ending until midnight. Some days business was good, some disappointing, but the two women did not give up until profits began to exceed the debts Ximena had taken on.

After a couple of years, she stopped renting and bought the stand, and soon afterward she took over the empty lot next to it. The best times for Ximena came when World War II kicked out the dreary Depression, when there were suddenly plenty of jobs and money to be spent. It was then that her business got strong enough to move ahead, and she had a real restaurant built, a big place: the kitchen put out hundreds of meals a day.

El Encanto became so well known that people flocked to it as much from the east side as from the west side of town. By the time the late forties rolled around Ximena Godoy had expanded her business to three more locations, and her name had spread beyond the restaurant owners on Olvera Street. During that time her business reputation grew, and her network now included some very influential people.

While Ximena focused on the business during those years, Concha was having plenty of fun. So it did not surprise Ximena one bit when, early in the war, Concha fell head over heels in love with a soldier, and on a whim, married him the day before he was shipped out to Guadalcanal. Ximena, happy for her friend, hosted a big party in the couple's honor with music, champagne and a banquet, although she warned Concha not once, but many times: "Concha, this could be a mistake. Horrible things happen in war. Remember the revolution? Remember all the dead people?" But Concha went ahead and married her soldier who, as Ximena had warned, returned in a coffin. A sad and more subdued Concha returned to work full-time.

Ximena, too, attracted her fair share of men. Although now in her forties, she was one of those women who grow more beautiful with age, and there was not a shortage of interested suitors in her life, most of them younger men. Usually amused, Ximena gently waved those would-be lovers aside. She did not want to get distracted from the business she was building. Ironically, it was her energy and ambition that attracted those men, although some admitted they were just a little bit intimidated by her ways. Still, they pursued her.

Ximena had accumulated countless friends and contacts, but they saw only one side of her personality: her public face, the one she chose to let them see, was the steady, centered and in-control businesswoman who earned more admiration with each deal she cut. But there was another side to her: the solitary life she led at home, after her dealings were done.

Although recollections of her checkered past occasionally came to nag her when she was alone, Ximena nonetheless enjoyed her solitude. No longer did the shadows and reflections that tortured her after her daughter's death return to haunt her, and Ximena found a freedom, a serenity, that she liked. She enjoyed those quiet hours when she was alone to think of how far she had come from her past life in Ciudad Juárez. Fifteen years had passed since she and Concha Urrutia had crossed the border, and in that time she had transformed herself.

But during one of those long nights, her thoughts were interrupted by a phone call which was destined to change the course of her life. Although she had heard the name of the caller, she had not met him and yet, what he said caught her attention right away.

"Miss Godoy, my name is Camilo Ibarra. I'm the owner of a restaurant in downtown Los Angeles. It's called *El Tenanpa*. Have you heard of it?"

She paused for a moment, recognizing this was a business call, and that maybe it could lead to something.

"Yes, I've heard of the place. It's got a good reputation."

"Thanks! I can say the same for your place. In fact, I've visited it a couple of times, and I can't say enough about the good food, and even more about the way you run it."

"Thank you! What can I do for you, Mr. Ibarra?"

"I'll come to the point. I'd like to set up an appointment to meet with you so I can lay out a plan for us to discuss."

"What kind of a plan?"

"A business venture that I think might interest you. I don't want to waste your time, so I'll tell you right away that I'm looking for a partner to invest in the project."

Ximena took a few moments to consider what Ibarra had said, thinking she liked that he was frank and to the point. "When would such a meeting happen?"

"As soon as you can give me the time."

"If I meet with you, Mr. Ibarra, it would be just to discuss your idea. It wouldn't mean a commitment on my part. Do you know what I mean?"

"Sure! I wouldn't expect more. Does this mean that you will meet with me? I'll come to your restaurant whenever you say."

"Alright."

"How about tomorrow? It's short notice, but the sooner I speak with you the better."

"I'm not available tomorrow, but I can meet with you the next day, at three. Is that good for you?"

"Perfect! Three o'clock it is. I'll see you then."

Ximena returned the phone to its cradle, went to the liquor cabinet and poured herself a drink. Then she went over to a chair, lit a cigarette, and stayed there for a long time watching the smoke curl toward the ceiling; all the while she was thinking. Ximena was paying attention to a feeling coming over her; she had a strong sense that something good would come of the meeting with Camilo Ibarra.

Chapter Forty-One

PEOPLE CALLED him the Cesear Romero of Downtown Los Angles, not because Camilo Ibarra had Romero's Hollywood matinee idol looks, but because he had a similar toothy smile and curly salt-and-pepper hair. Aside from that, Camilo was ordinary looking—not tall, but not short either. While he was considered by many to be average, there was more to him than just that exterior. Down deep, Camilo was a good and honest man who would do just about anything for a friend, or even a stranger, when he saw real need. He was a loving man, too, who especially respected women to the point of putting them up there in the clouds, although at his age—he was pushing fifty—he had never married. He had had flings with women he really loved, but for some reason or another, marriage never developed from those affairs. *I'm waiting for the right one,* he would say before anyone asked him, flashing that winning smile filled with long white teeth. No one doubted that he was waiting and looking for that right woman who would fill the gap in his life. It was just a matter of time, and everyone knew it.

His close friends knew that Camilo had a weak spot, which was that he trusted too often and too much. But though he had plenty of scars to prove that he had been burned many times, nothing could make him change; it was his nature to be trusting. Maybe he got it from his family of nine sisters and brothers, plus mamá and papá. Camilo was the middle child of that brood; he was a sort of bridge, the one who learned early how to smooth things between the other children. It must have been this in-between role that convinced him trust had to come into play if things were to work out.

Camilo was hard-working, too. It was something he learned back on the dusty streets of Canoga Park where he grew up. He usually told people that he could not remember how old he was when he started working, but there had been all sorts of jobs: picking fruit in the summer, shining shoes at bus and streetcar stops, selling newspapers on street corners, and even washing dishes in the little café down the street from where he lived.

I was a hard-working little cabrón. He laughed when telling this part of his story. *Mamá loved the few bucks I brought home. But it was in that little café that I felt the best, so that's where I stayed to learn the ropes.*

But that was Camilo Ibarra on the outside—his mask, if you will. Anyone who could get inside of him to tear away that disguise, past that easygoing, people-loving smooth guy, would find a lonely man who longed for a special someone, but who, for some unlucky reason, had missed crossing paths with her.

Maybe it began in his childhood when he often felt alone, despite being surrounded by his rowdy brothers and sisters. Or perhaps it was his destiny to be alone, a destiny he did not wish for but had no control over. Who knows? On the other hand, whatever the explanation, his lone-wolf veneer seemed to fuel, not dampen, the image of the happy, successful man.

By the time Camilo met Ximena Godoy, he was the owner of the popular Mexican eatery called *El Tenanpa*, located at the corner of Ninth and Broadway, right in the heart of old Los Angeles. That location was a hot spot where things really jumped, especially on weekends when people dropped in to eat before going off on a night of drinking and dancing.

But there was more to his success than just the restaurant. It was 1947 and Los Angeles was still crazy with postwar excitement. This town was overflowing with gangsters—some of them petty, others big-time—along with their glamour girls, and plenty of con artists who latched onto the winners. But not only lowlifes filled up the city —Los Angeles was also a place of hardworking people who now could own a little house in one of the tracts recently springing up in El Segundo, Hawthorne, Compton and other spots just beyond downtown. The building frenzy was mirrored in the way couples were having babies as if caught up in a contest; it was as if each couple wanted to be the family to have the next baby on the block.

Not only ordinary working people jammed Camilo Ibarra's place. There were still plenty of sailors, marines and soldiers waiting for their discharge papers who swarmed into *El Tenanpa* on weekends, always looking for a good time. After a big meal, they would leave the restaurant and head to the corner of Seventh and Broadway to catch the latest movie at the Orpheum, the Paramount, or the Million Dollar, all of them first-rate movie houses. In the city blocks between were bars and more eateries, all of them packed with laughing guys and flirting women. The world had turned young after the Depression and the War; everyone felt that it was a good time to be alive. And it was in this world, at this special time, that Camilo Ibarra had become a very successful businessman.

Chapter Forty-Two

IN HER restaurant's back office, Ximena Godoy first met with Camilo Ibarra. It was a coming-together of equals, of two cautious businesspeople eyeing one another with scrutiny, and just a little bit of distrust. After the necessary amenities, Camilo opened a manila file folder and got to the point.

"Here's what I'm planning to do, Miss Godoy. Hopefully you'll like the project enough to partner with me. I want to set up a nightclub on Sunset Boulevard, and I already have a spot in mind, a location right off Alvarado Street. The place is empty and run-down right now, so we can pick it up for a song."

He stopped what he was saying and looked at Ximena; his gaze was intense, and he expected a reaction from her, but when she did not speak up, and her face was expressionless, he went on.

"Do you think it's crazy?"

"I don't know. It's too soon to say. I'm just listening. Go on!"

"Well, I see it as a swanky place where people will come to dance and have drinks, maybe a little supper. The place is big enough for a great dance floor and space enough for a band or combo. I have contacts with musicians like Tito Puente, Eddie Cano and Cal Tjader—those guys can pull in people who appreciate good music. We'll put cozy little tables around that dance floor, you know, intimate settings, each with a little lamp.

Couples will love it! I can see a cocktail lounge with a long, beautiful bar worked by bartenders dressed in sharp vests and slacks. Nothing but the best booze will be served."

Camilo stopped talking a moment to catch his breath—he was excited— and went on,

"Well, what do you think of the idea so far, Miss Godoy?"

"I'm thinking that it'll take money. Lots of it." Ximena was also thinking of her own ideas, the ones she had when she had persuaded Don Pepo to transform *el Manglar*.

Without blinking, Camilo said, "That's right! It'll take lots of money."

Ximena returned his gaze, and then spoke up. "I have a few questions."

"Shoot!"

"First, I'm wondering about location. Since the place is on Sunset Boulevard, won't it be just another club to add to the many already on that strip and on Hollywood Boulevard? I'm thinking of Ciro's, the Brown Derby, the Palladium, and all the others."

"No. Those clubs are all in Hollywood and Beverly Hills— our place will be closer to downtown Los Angeles. People will find it easier to reach since most folks start a night out closer to downtown." Already Camilo was saying *our* instead of *my*.

Letting it pass, Ximena asked, "What kind of people would come to your club?"

"Our customers would be a classy crowd, Miss Godoy. Sharp dressers, glamorous people with good jobs and plenty of money to spend, those would be the ones to flock to such a club. Oh! And another thing. Our clients would be people who have had enough of the big-band sound and are now craving those *timbales* and conga drums that get people dancing."

Ximena sat still as she gazed at the wall behind Camilo. "Aside from conga drums and timbales, what else would make the club unique?" She paused and looked into his eyes. "Why would I be attracted to that club in particular, instead of, say, Ciro's? Also, have you checked out the area to make sure there aren't other similar clubs that would compete?"

Momentarily stumped by her barrage of questions, Camilo sagged a little in the chair. However, in a few moments he recuperated enough to come up with a few answers.

"Look, Miss Godoy, our club will be unique because it's going be a place that's meant for our people, you know, not only for *Gringos*. It'll have that *Caribeño* flavor, that Mexican feeling— you'll get it the minute you walk in. People would come running from all over East Los Angeles, even the Hollenbeck district and Boyle Heights. My God! What a mob! I can see them now." He waved his arms excitedly, but then stopped talking.

Ximena, too, kept quiet. She was thinking hard, and as always when she concentrated, she looked into space, her right eyebrow slightly raised in an arc. She was again remembering Don Pepo and *El Manglar* at its peak, with its wonderful music and fancy settings. She sat back in the chair.

"Well, Miss Godoy, what do you think? Would you consider partnering in this venture?"

"What would be my investment?"

"Fifty percent."

"What would I have to put up front by way of cash?"

Camilo spread out a couple of sheets he pulled from his folder and, pointing to a column of figures, he explained: "My calculations show that we can put the whole project together for forty grand; that includes remodeling, permits, hiring and other incidentals. I know that's a lot of dough, but if you and I each put up ten thousand, I feel confident that a bank will match our twenty, and that way we can secure the forty."

Ximena's eyes were riveted on Camilo. "Ten grand upfront! That's a lot of money, Mr. Ibarra. What about collateral?"

"Only my gut feeling that it's a winner from the start."

When Ximena's eyebrow shot up showing her skepticism, he spoke up right away. "Yes, Miss Godoy, it's a risk, but I know that our club will be a big success mainly because it'll be one of a kind. People are hungry for this sort of place. It's time someone put it together, and I know it'll be you and me." When she kept looking at him, waiting for more, Camilo smiled and chirped, "I've even come up with a name for the place. Want to hear it?"

"Yes."

"We can call it *Los Timbales*. How about it? What do you think?"

"It sounds ordinary." When she saw that her blunt opinion

took the wind out of his enthusiasm, she added, "But then, maybe you can come up with a more glamorous name later on."

Camilo managed to overcome the letdown. He smiled, realizing right away that she was not easy to please, but he liked that. Undaunted, he asked, "Well? What do you think? Will you be my partner?"

"I'll consider it, but I need some time."

"Sure! Sure! How long?"

Ximena laughed at his impetuousness, and did not try to hide her amusement. "Give me a week. I don't think the place will run away in the meantime."

"No, but it could be snapped up by someone just as smart as you and me."

"It won't be snapped up. Give me a week to think it over. Also, let me have the address. I'd like to look at the location."

"I'll be happy to drive you there. Right now, if you can make it."

"Thank you, but I prefer to do it on my own."

Camilo scribbled the address on a piece of paper, handed it to Ximena, and then knowing that the meeting was over, got to his feet, picked up his folder, and asked, "When can I call you?"

"Call next Friday at the same time you called me the other night. At that number."

When he was at the door, Ximena asked, "Mr. Ibarra, why me? Why are you asking me to be your associate? I'm sure you have many other contacts. Or am I the last of a line of people who have turned you down?"

Ximena's skepticism was a little surprising to Camilo, but he grasped that it was part of her good business sense. It was one of the reasons she was successful.

"You're right, I do have other contacts, but you aren't the last. In fact, you're my number one choice, and that's because no one runs a business like you do. Believe me, you're my first choice."

When she didn't say more, he opened the door, and then paused when he heard her next question.

"Do you speak Spanish, Mr. Ibarra?"

His face showed surprise; nonetheless, after a few seconds he answered. "No. I guess you could call me a real *Pocho*. I know that sometime, back in the old days, my family's folks came here from Mexico, but their way of talking had faded out by the time me and the kids came along. Why do you ask? Does it make a difference?"

"No. I was just curious." This time Ximena was looking straight into Camilo's eyes and he caught what he thought was a little joke playing around in that look, and he found it intriguing. He opened the door and was about to leave when Concha Urrutia suddenly appeared, blocking the way out. Nearly bumping into him, she blurted out, "¡Chispas! I almost knocked you down." She said this, smiling big, because she liked him right away.

"It's all right. Come in, I'm just about to leave."

Ximena got to her feet and approached Camilo and Concha. "Mr. Ibarra, meet my friend and best support, Concha Urrutia. We've worked together for years, and she's really the one who runs my business."

Camilo flashed his big smile at Concha and took her hand. "A pleasure, Miss Urrutia."

When Concha smiled back at him, she felt emotion streaking through her. As she watched him walk away, Ximena's friend was feeling that maybe this man was the one she had been waiting for.

The meeting ended with a good feeling for Ximena Godoy. Experience told her that she and Camilo Ibarra were on solid ground to do business. Their personalities, too, meshed in a good way, she thought, and although it took a few days before she reached her final decision, she didn't doubt her judgment once she made up her mind.

Chapter Forty-Three

XIMENA GODOY was living the best years of her life. Her star was still on the ascent as she neared her fiftieth year. Clearly, she was in her prime and her determination to succeed was at a higher pitch than ever before. She had good reason for thinking that she was living her best years: the new club was a success and she was admired as never before. But the icing on the cake was that she and Camilo had fallen for one another.

But their love affair didn't happen suddenly. It developed gradually while they got the club on its feet, and they bonded while supervising the remodeling, hiring workers, advertising and taking charge of all the small details like designing glassware for the bar and choosing colors for the table settings. Through it all, they struck a balance. Of the two, Camilo was the ideas guy, and Ximena had the nose for running the business. After that, falling for one another was not a surprise.

Along with the new club, Ximena and Camilo still owned their other restaurants, and those were thriving, too. But Ximena knew that Concha deserved the credit for that side of the business. She recognized that, without Concha, who was now manager-in-chief, those enterprises more than likely would have suffered. So with Concha in charge, Ximena could relax. She hardly visited *El Encanto* or the other sites anymore; she left that up to Camilo, who worked out the everyday details with Concha.

One day, in the flurry of that crazy activity, Camilo, certain of the answer he'd receive, asked Ximena, "Will you marry me?"

She looked at him for a few seconds, and answered, "No."

Taken off balance he asked, "You're kidding! Why not?"

"I've never wanted to get married." Her cool way rattled Camilo: he was sure she loved him and wanted to live with him for whatever years were left to their lives. But when he took a hard look into her eyes, he saw that she meant what she had said.

She went on: "Camilo, I love you, but I've never wanted to be married. Please understand me."

"I thought you wanted us to live together."

"I *do* want us to live together, but that doesn't mean we have to get married, does it?"

He gawked at her, hardly believing what he was hearing, but she seemed so calm, so at ease with the whole conversation that he, too, calmed down. "I guess I'm just an old-fashioned son-of-a-bitch."

She impatiently waved an arm. "Let's buy a house, Camilo, and let's just live there without all the strings that come with being married. We would still be partners, wouldn't we? We would still run our business as we've done from the beginning, and we can love each other because we want to, not because a piece of paper says we should. The only condition that I would expect from you is for you to love only me. I'm a jealous woman, Camilo. I can't stand competition. I want you to know that from the beginning."

It took Camilo a while to adjust to Ximena's point of view, but in the end, he really didn't see why they should not just live together. They bought a house in the Silver Lake District where, at the end of each day they talked business and tied up loose ends. Afterwards they made love. Every night they did it, and every night their lovemaking was followed by intimate conversation. He told her about himself, his family, his childhood, and how frustrated he had been not to be able to fight during the War; he had been too old.

Ximena, too, shared her memories, and finally, she didn't hold anything back. She told about Tacho and her days with old

Epifania, about Ximenita and even about her fiasco with Amador Mendoza. And for the first time, Ximena even told about her mother who left her family for another man. "This part about my mother is something I've never told anyone. Don't you find that strange?"

Camilo answered, "Nope. Some memories stay buried, waiting for the right moment, or the right person to hear them."

Ximena loved Camilo as she had never loved before. What she felt for him was unselfish and deep, and for the first time in her life she trusted unconditionally. The truth was that she had never been as happy as she was during those months when she lived with Camilo.

Camilo adored her, and he made sure to let Ximena know that she was the center of his life. He spent hours thinking of how next to please her just to show how much he loved her. Although he was not the type who gave flowers and trinkets, his love showed in what he did for her. One of those times was when he bought a life insurance policy naming her as beneficiary.

"You never know, Ximena. I can walk out of the club and get run over by a car. Accidents happen. I wouldn't want you to face money problems if that ever happened. With this policy you'll be set for life."

"Why do that? It might be bad luck." Ximena was superstitious enough to believe what she was saying, but secretly she took it as just another sign of how much he loved her. For that gesture, she loved him even more.

Chapter Forty-Four

CAMILO IBARRA was a nice guy who could not have been thinking straight when he blundered. This, too, could be said about the loyal, steadfast Concha Urrutia. However, the truth was that their lives unraveled, leaving them empty-handed to face the consequences of their irreversible mistake.

It might have started the morning Chucho Arana walked into Ximena's office and found the lady boss focused on a ledger book. When she did not move or show that she was aware of his presence, he cleared his throat. Only then did she look up, removed her wire-rimmed reading glasses, blinked, and stared at him.

"I didn't hear you knock," she said after a few moments.

"I didn't knock. Sorry." His voice was deep and full, like that of a crooner. "The door was open."

Obviously nervous, he shifted his weight from one leg to the other, and at the same time he put on what he thought was a relaxed smile. But he didn't fool Ximena one bit. His posture made him look even stiffer and more ill at ease. Ximena didn't help him out of his obvious discomfort, as she looked him up and down, her right eyebrow arched.

"What can I do for you?"

"I'd like to work here. I'm looking for a job."

Ximena leaned back in the creaking swivel chair as she

narrowed her eyes to look closely at him. He was a tall man with broad shoulders and a wide forehead, a straight nose and large, deep-set eyes highlighting his face. She focused on his dark skin, curly hair and the way he was dressed: razor-edged pleated slacks, a sharp sports jacket and matching tie. Ximena liked everything about him.

"How old are you?" She queried, forgetting to ask his name.

"I'm twenty-five."

He's half my age. The thought flashed in Ximena's mind, wishing to be closer to him, if only in age. All along, she stared at him calmly, impressing and even intimidating him until she finally asked, "What's your name?"

"Chucho Arana."

"What brought you here to look for a job?"

"A buddy told me that there was an opening for a bartender. That's what I do."

"Do you have experience?"

"Yes, I've tended bar at the Latin Quarter and part-time at the Zenda."

"Do you have any references?"

"Yes!"

Ximena took in more of Chucho's looks while he fumbled in his jacket for the envelope that he finally found, and then spread out its pages in front of her. All along, the more Ximena looked, the more she liked him; there was something she saw that reminded her of someone.

Those hungry eyes have looked at me before, but I can't remember who it was, or when.

Now it was Ximena's turn to feel uneasy, for thinking of the young man that way. She put the thought aside, picked up the papers, and read through Chucho's references. She would tell Camilo about her odd feelings over a drink that night.

Chucho went on shifting nervously from one foot to the other, but at the same time he examined her closely as she focused on his references. First of all, he wondered if she was really the tough businesswoman people said she was. *No. She's too beautiful.* His eyes lingered on her breasts and the cleavage peeking out from the neckline of her blouse, and from there he treated himself to look at her hair, her neck and her hands with their long, delicate fingers.

When she suddenly looked up, he flinched with the idea that maybe she had read his mind, so he smiled sheepishly, exposing uneven teeth and adding a rich sensuality to his lips. That thought crossed Ximena's mind as she fought off another sensation that had made its way down to her groin.

"These references look good." She got to her feet and pointed toward the empty cocktail lounge. "Come with me so you can meet Mr. Ibarra."

The three met at the bar and talked in low, friendly voices. The lounge felt good at that time of day, bathed as it was in a soft light that slid through arched windows, casting long shadows on the polished floor. Camilo liked Chucho Arana right away because he saw in him just the kind of bartender he wanted for the club. Chucho was young, but not a kid. He was smooth in his manner, good at conversation, and he showed a sense of humor.

"Okay, Chucho, the job's yours, but we want you to come on board right away so you can catch on. We have a classy crowd, and I think you'll fit right in." Camilo turned to Ximena, asking, "What do you think?"

She gazed into Chucho's eyes for a second, and then quickly backed up Camilo's opinion. "I agree. Welcome to *la familia*, Mr. Arana."

During Chucho's first months on the job, Ximena, aware that she and Chucho were attracted to one another, kept her distance, mostly by being businesslike whenever the occasion came up that required interaction between them. But even though she tried, Ximena could not help being conscious of his presence; she felt the heat of his eyes riveted on her, even when the lounge was crowded. Whenever she glanced in his direction it was to discover that he was looking at her, and it felt good.

Sometimes his allure made her slip and she smiled at him, maybe just a little too intimately; other times she teased him and even flirted. When that happened, he responded eagerly so it worked as a warning for Ximena, and she forced herself to back off for days, and sometimes weeks. Hardly a day passed that she did not remind herself of how much she loved Camilo Ibarra, and that nothing could interfere with that love.

Chucho's just a kid. I'm old enough to be his mother. What a laugh!

But even when days passed without an encounter between them, Chucho's image stuck in Ximena's mind, and no matter how many times she resolved to stop thinking of him, her resolution worked for just a few days. Afterward, thoughts of him stubbornly popped right back. Yet despite the teasing and flirting, nothing actually happened between them, and reminding herself that she had done nothing to betray Camilo helped Ximena push away the guilt feelings that nagged her.

During that time business went on as usual, which meant that Camilo and Concha met every Tuesday to discuss day-to-day work in the clubs. It was that simple, with nothing special or particular about their encounters.

This Tuesday seemed like any other Tuesday. Camilo and Concha sat at the desk facing one another. The room was the same office where Camilo and Ximena had first met.

Their discussion was about numbers, dollars and cents, workers and supplies, all of it cut-and-dried, routine and mostly boring. On that day, however, Camilo looked up, then Concha did the same, and their eyes connected. There was nothing new or different about that small gesture, except that something moved inside each of them, a sudden, powerful sensation.

What Camilo felt was so deep that he became instantly aroused, and he became hard. He broke away from looking at Concha, shocked by what he was feeling. He had never thought of her that way—sexually, that is. He had always found Concha intelligent, pleasant, and more than that, he liked her ways, especially her laughter. But never before had he felt the unmistakable impulse now overcoming him.

For her part, Concha, in love with Camilo from the beginning, felt her breasts and vagina tighten, even though the image of Ximena's face flashed through her mind. In that split second, Concha thought of her friend and of their close bond, of their years, of shared tears and laughter, of frustrations and successes. All of that crowded into her head; and yet it evaporated just as quickly, leaving only the powerful desire to be intimate with Camilo.

What followed happened in silence. Neither wanted to talk;

and it was fast, as if they had been waiting a lifetime to surrender to that powerful urge. Camilo threw down the pen he held and took Concha's hand, thinking that it felt like a soft, plump dove. He kissed it, and then her wrist, her arm, and finally he sealed her mouth with a long, hard kiss.

Concha did not resist. She yielded, and in seconds she was on top of the desk on her back struggling and wiggling to kick off her panties. It took Camilo less time to tear away his jacket, open the fly of his slacks, and before either realized it, they were plunging and heaving, one against the other, belly against belly, thighs against thighs, and their ecstasy was so intense, their sighs so thick and heavy, that they did not hear the door open.

It was not until they each climaxed and let out final, rapturous groans that Concha turned her head to look in the direction of the door. As if in a daze, she saw a woman standing there, gawking like a fool, her face pale and twisted. What was she looking at? But it took only an instant for the answer to that senseless question to cut through Concha's afterglow, and she realized that it was Ximena standing at the doorway.

Chapter Forty-Five

XIMENA GODOY spiraled headlong into a nightmare of disbelief and depression that made it impossible for her to think straight, and she was assailed by emotions she had never experienced. She locked herself in the house for days, depriving herself of food, sleep, or anything else that might have helped her. Instead, she paced from room to room, rarely staying in one spot for more than just a few minutes. Throughout the turmoil, Ximena surrendered to a mental undertow that battered and pulled her apart.

At first, confusion and self-pity wrestled with her desire to forgive Camilo and Concha, but she found it impossible to accept their betrayal. Days passed, but no matter how many times she turned it over in her mind, the truth was undeniable and in the end, hatred—along with an indescribable desire for revenge—overpowered her.

Ximena's mind continued to flounder, dragging her in different directions, probing and searching in dark corners for the fragments of her shattered life. What had caused its breakdown? Why had she gone to the office that day? She had never done it before, preferring to leave Concha and Camilo to work alone. What then had moved her to make that decision?

In that blur of questions to herself, Ximena remembered it was a spur of the moment impulse that made her drive to the office with the intention of inviting them to all go out to cocktails and dinner. They worked too hard, she thought, and it was time for a little relaxation. That had been the stupid urge that inspired her to take the step that now utterly had transformed her life. Ximena would never forget that she did it to herself: it had been she who ruined her life by making that goddamn decision.

During her many hours of seclusion she became convinced that her face, her nose, her forehead, her entire body was in pieces, held together only by an invisible string. But when Ximena stared into a mirror she saw that she was intact. She could see that it was, instead, her soul that was damaged and falling apart, mangled by jealousy and loathing. Time passed and she descended far down into a hell of rage; she wept dry, bitter tears that flowed from her veins to her chest, heaving with painful sobs.

Eventually she lost track of all time, and only when daylight filtered into night did she understand that many hours had passed. It was then that she tried to talk herself into forgiving the lovers, thinking that perhaps absolution would bring her peace. However, every time her mind moved in that direction, the image returned of Concha on her back with Camilo plunging in and out between her jiggling legs. This image filled Ximena with so much disgust that it erased any possibility of forgiveness. On the contrary, the shocking scene forced her to retch into the toilet as she remembered *they were fucking like two crazy rabbits!* The vulgarity of that thought made her vomit again and again.

Still trying to find a way to forgive, Ximena reminded herself that there was nothing new about what Concha and Camilo had done. *Hadn't people fornicated in secret since the beginning of time? Didn't it happen every day? Didn't I betray Tacho Medina the same way when I slept with that soldier whose name I can't even remember?*

Those nagging questions took her back to other fearful places in her past, forcing her to wonder why Tacho had not killed her when he had the chance. *When he put the revolver to my head, why didn't he pull the trigger?*

Still thinking of Tacho Medina, Ximena surrendered to hours of pondering, trying to decipher the difference between wanting to do something, and actually doing it.

Maybe wanting to do something is enough, she thought. *Maybe desiring to kill someone, if it's desperately desired, is the same as actually doing it. If that is so, Tacho may as well have pulled the trigger, because in his heart, he had already murdered me.*

She clearly remembered that long-ago day, wanting to believe that the wish to murder, and the act of committing murder, really is the same. *If it happens in the heart, then it really happens. There isn't a difference!*

Ximena muttered these words countless times, trying to admit that in her heart she had already committed murder. Yet for her, it was not enough. She was not ready to resolve her anger and grief with wishes. She still needed to act.

Ximena abandoned herself to these dangerous thoughts while another black night turned into morning, and she finally fell into a fitful sleep that sucked her into a deep hole. She was more unconscious than asleep when a racket, from a distance growing louder as it got closer, shook her out of that trance. It was Camilo at the front door knocking, banging and rattling the knob.

"Ximena, open up! I'm sorry! Forgive me!"

She shook her head trying to clear it, and when she realized what was happening, she slouched back in the chair unmoved. His muffled pleas meant nothing; she watched when he flattened his tear-stained, blotchy face against the window.

"I don't love her! I don't know what got into me! It was that one time! I swear it! Please believe me! I love only you!"

Ximena felt her jaw tighten with rage, and she did not answer, while he continued the banging and begging.

"Talk to me!"

Ximena sat in the gloomy living room listening, disbelieving what she thought were hollow words, all the time letting disgust grow inside her with each of his sobs.

"At least, let me talk to you. Haven't you ever done something that you've regretted? Haven't you ever been ashamed? You've been forgiven, haven't you?"

She thought of those nights when Camilo turned to her in their bed to embrace her and whispered, "I love you so much!"

She remembered, too, that each time she murmured, "I love you too." Only then did he fall off into deep sleep. But now, jealousy had turned Ximena's heart cold; the unconditional love for Camilo that filled her with so much joy had soured into hatred. She sat stiff and icy, listening to his whimpering but not allowing it to make a difference.

Instead she murmured, "It's too late, Camilo. I can't forgive you. I don't have a choice." Although she knew that her words were beyond his hearing, their meaning evoked in her something close to relief. She sat very still, enjoying the relief. Finally Camilo went away, and it was night.

When deeply betrayed by two loved ones, a woman such as Ximena Godoy can bear just so much outrage and grief before being forced to move in one of two directions: self-destruction or vengeance. She had looked for another way out, for another less drastic option, but the unconditional love she had nurtured for Camilo had evaporated, disappeared, and had left hatred in its place. And because she knew that it was impossible for her to live with that ugliness forever inside her, she made the decision.

Finally, having chosen the direction to take, she knew that the dawn signaled the last day of her ordeal. Ximena went to her bathroom, filled the tub with water so hot that she flinched as she let herself into it. She remained there for a long time. As she sat in the cooling water, she felt her emotions receding. Those emotions had thrashed her with so much violence and now, as they drained away, she thought calmly and her rationality returned. While she rubbed her arms, legs, breasts and shoulders with a soapy sponge she reflected, but no longer were her thoughts scattered or careening, but instead were collected and clear.

Finally the elusive serenity filled Ximena: an idea had sprung into her mind while she soaked. Ironically, it was Camilo's words that planted the seed, something he said to her when he signed off on his life insurance. "You never know, Ximena. I can walk out of the club and get run over by a car. Accidents happen."

Chapter Forty-Six

XIMENA APPEARED radiant at the club that morning. Her hair was swept up in the pompadour style she wore so well, her make-up was perfect, and she looked slim and elegant in a tailored two-piece suit. Surprised by her composure as she walked in, the workers tried to behave normally, but they could not help staring at her, some with sidelong glances, others from behind dishes and glasses. And others gawked, open-mouthed. Word had gotten around; people knew about Concha and Camilo's encounter, and they had all been waiting to see how *la Jefa* was going to deal with it.

When Ximena walked in she paused for a few moments, looked around with a haughty smile and then, with a quick but pleasant *"Hola!"*, she made her way toward the back office. When those waiters, bartenders and cooks saw where she was headed, and because they knew that Camilo was there, they all gasped, wondering who would die first.

She let herself in and found Camilo staring out the window. She saw right away that he had not shaved and his clothes were rumpled and messy. When he turned to see who had come in, he froze. For her part, Ximena appeared calm and so natural that he thought it was his imagination, and that what happened had been a nightmare. Still speechless, he watched as she walked to the desk, put down her purse, reached for a cigarette, lit it and took a long drag.

As she went through those motions she kept her eyes on him. Camilo could not figure out what he saw in that look. All he knew was that he wanted to shout with joy just to see her standing there looking so rested and beautiful again.

Finally she spoke: "Camilo, you and I have to make peace. There's too much at stake, too many people stand to lose, and we have to do everything possible to keep our enterprise from falling apart. This is what I think, and I hope that you agree with me."

Ximena's voice was serene, as if nothing had happened. Her words were direct, at ease, and although Camilo was at first jarred, he forced himself to settle down and try to think straight. He pulled himself together and saw that what she said made sense. He realized she was being sincere, but more importantly, she was being her old self. Thinking this way persuaded him that all was fine, that he and Ximena could go on with their lives as if he had not blundered, as if he had not broken her heart.

"Do you forgive me?" His voice was a whisper.

Without pause she answered, "It was a mistake. Let's just put it behind us."

That was all Ximena said, and at the same time she put the cigarette in the ashtray, moved her purse, sat down, opened a drawer and pulled out her work ledger. She even took off her jacket before she sat at the swivel chair and got to work. All the time Camilo stared at her because her movements were so deliberate and relaxed that he was confused. He had feared the opposite—shouts and accusations—but now she was letting him know that nothing had changed; that it was business as usual.

Yet Camilo was still too unnerved to act as usual. He wanted to speak, to let Ximena know that he regretted the biggest mistake of his life and more than anything, he yearned to tell her how much he loved her, and that no one could ever take her place. Yet, he was afraid of taking the risk of opening up the terrible wound by speaking or asking what was going on, even though he knew their life together could not just pick up where it was before. He knew they would eventually have to thrash out the ugliness that had invaded their lives. So all he said was, "What about us?"

She turned to look at him, but her eyes were sad and empty. "I guess you're asking if we can go on living together. Am I right?"

"Yes."

"The house is yours as much as it is mine, so you're free to return if that's what you want. The only thing I ask is that you give me time to get over this whole thing. What I mean is that I can't sleep with you, not right away."

By now Camilo had edged closer to her; he wanted to reach out and take her in his arms, but he did not dare. Instead he said, "Whatever you say, Ximena. I'll respect what you want, and I deeply hope that soon you'll remember the love you had for me. When that happens, I'll be there, always by your side, always the man who loves you more than anyone or anything."

She nodded, a little impatiently he thought, and went back to her ledger. Camilo gazed at her for a while before turning to get his jacket and hat. When the door closed behind him Ximena looked up. Only then did her eyes betray the storm inside her. She had crossed the first threshold, but it had not been easy.

She held her hands up to her eyes, and saw that they were trembling; each finger quivered as if it wanted to tear away from the palm that held it fast. Then she brought down those hands flat on the desk's surface, hoping to calm the agitation, and she realized that it wasn't just her hands; her whole body was shuddering as well.

It's not easy! These words squeezed out from between clenched teeth, making her wonder if she had the guts to go through with the bigger part of what she planned.

It took time but she finally pulled it together by reminding herself that it was Friday, the beginning of the weekend, and the busiest time for the club. The thought of work gave her focus, so she forced herself to put in a few hours of paperwork, and then more time for the usual rounds to make sure the workers were ready for the heavy load. Only then did she head back home to dress for the long evening ahead. When she got to the house she found Camilo already in the shower, and her stomach turned when she heard him singing, but she pushed the feeling aside.

The night kicked off with a huge crowd of people already in a party mood. It was late November, the beginning of the Holiday Season, open fiesta time for the club's patrons. At first they trickled into the cocktail lounge moving and talking in subdued tones, but when the first notes of the conga drums told everyone that the music was on and that it was dance time, the floor flooded with laughing, noisy, swaying people.

Ximena made sure she and Camilo walked into that scene arm-in-arm, just as always, smiling and backslapping old friends. She needed to let everyone know that all was just fine, that they were still partners and lovers. However, when they separated to greet couples and anyone else who expected the extra attention, she looked toward the bar, and as before, she found Chucho Arana's eyes pasted on her. This time, however, she was glad because more than anyone else, it was Chucho's help that she needed, so she made her way to a spot at the bar where he was serving.

"*Hola, Jefa!* You're looking good."

His greeting was smooth, flirty, and his eyes glimmered as he took her in from top to bottom. Breaking with her usual reserve, Ximena did not hold back, and returned his leer, making sure that it was loaded with invitation.

"You're looking good yourself, Chucho." When he seemed startled by her compliment as well as the look in her eyes, she went on, "Please make me a Seven-Seven, will you?" Thus Ximena's seduction of Chucho Arana began, and luring the young bartender was easy. It even felt good for her.

In the days that followed, Ximena was tireless. She put in endless hours moving from workers to deskwork, then back to the kitchen to order supplies and oversee deliveries, all the time dealing with musicians and merchants as well as floating new ideas, always making sure to ask Camilo what he thought of this, that, or the other idea.

Each night, when the club was in full swing, she danced with favorite partners, injecting a magic that made its way to her patrons, and all through that pretense no one imagined the darkness that had infected her heart, least of all Camilo. He had by now convinced himself that she had forgiven him, and nothing had really happened.

On the last Saturday night of November, when the club's action was at its height, Ximena took a break and retreated into the office to treat herself to a few minutes of quiet. She liked that office, especially after dark when it was lit with soft light, and where she could escape into its privacy and silence.

Once there, Ximena went to the desk, kicked off her platform shoes, and then reached for a cigarette. She had just taken the first drag, leaned back, eyes closed, when she felt a presence that she had not seen. When she opened her eyes she saw Concha Urrutia standing in front of her, just on the other side of the desk.

Although the room's lighting was dim, Ximena saw right away that Concha was not her old self; she looked haggard. It was apparent that she had lost weight and her face was drawn, her cheeks sagging and wrinkled. Despite Ximena's instant reaction of hatred, she felt something close to pity for the devastation that had hit Concha, but she ignored the feeling and forced herself to stay calm, although she could not help the stiffness that gripped her.

"What do you want?"

"I want a chance to explain. Give me just that chance."

"I caught you and Camilo fucking! What's there to explain?"

"Don't say it that way!"

"No? How else can I say it? You tell me if you can."

Intimidated, Concha lowered her face as tears streamed down her flaccid cheeks, but Ximena kept quiet knowing, *she's afraid of me*. When Concha finally spoke up, her voice was trembling so much that she sounded like a little girl.

"Ximena, I've loved him from the beginning, but I kept it a secret."

"You make me sick!" Ximena roughly slid to the edge of the chair, making it squeak. "Love—my ass! You're a *puta*. You've always been one. I knew it from the first day we met. Remember that goddamn little fire? Remember the food I gave you? It was then that you told me what you were. I actually forgot, until you came and stabbed me in the back."

"Yes, I remember everything. I remember too how we worked and dreamed together, how I backed you up all the time. I'm your friend, Ximena, maybe your only friend. Think of what you're doing. Look at me! I'm the only one who knows how you grieved for your daughter."

"Shut up, Concha! Just shut up!"

Incensed even more by the mention of her daughter, Ximena broke in before Concha finished. She sprang to her feet and forced Concha to shrink away, fearing Ximena's assault. But Ximena just went on talking, her voice controlled and low, trying to mask the rage behind her words.

"Friend? You say that you're my friend? You're crazy. Get out of my sight. Go away. You've ruined my life, and I'll never forgive you."

"Ximena, why are you so unforgiving?"

Concha gaped at Ximena for a few moments hoping for some answer, but there was nothing. So she turned, walked out of the room, and disappeared.

Alone, Ximena's control vanished. She was trembling, on the verge of fainting; she slumped into the chair to lean against the desk for a long time; she was nauseated to the point of suffocation. She opened her mouth trying to breathe, but her heart was pounding so hard that she managed to suck in only dry, empty gulps. She clawed frantically at her chest trying relieve the pressure, but it was not until she heard herself cry out that she snapped out of her anxiety attack.

Rigid, cold and sweaty, Ximena sat listening to muffled laughter and chatter that drifted in from the other side of the door. She even felt the vibration of dancing feet, and picked up sounds that made their way along floorboards, vents and cracks. She did not stay that way for long, however, knowing that if she waited, she risked losing her nerve to take the next step. Ximena forced herself to rifle through the desk until she found the phone book and, still shaking, she flipped the pages to the number she needed, reached for the phone and dialed the number.

The voice at the other end of the line sounded groggy. "Immigration. How may I help you?"

Without even trying to disguise her voice, Ximena spoke into the receiver. "I want to report a person who is living in the city illegally."

"Okay. Where's this person from?"

"Mexico."

"Male or female?"

"Female."

"Okay. Give a name and an address where she can be located."

Ximena gave the information, and even volunteered more details. "It's a small duplex on Vignes; you know the little street behind Union Station. The place is white and the person lives in the duplex on the right. If you show up in a while you'll find her, but if she hasn't got there yet, wait. It won't be long before she gets there."

"May I have your name?"

Ximena hung up without answering, but stayed with her hand clamped onto the receiver for a long time, trembling even more than she had just a half hour before. She hung on to the phone as if it were a lifeline. Ximena shuddered knowing that it was she who had now betrayed the person who had been more than a sister. She realized that she had, with that brief phone call, killed Concha just as effectively as if she had put a revolver to her head.

Images flashed in Ximena's mind: Concha squatting with her by a campfire; Concha laughing and joking with customers in her rinky-dink Juárez casino; Concha dancing with the skinny bartender the night el Manglar closed down; Concha walking by her side when they crossed the border; Concha standing by her as they plucked chicken feathers; Concha listening to and encouraging her dreams of becoming something special; Concha feeling with her the pain of having lost Ximenita. The parade of memories shattered, however, when the last image intruded: Concha locked in Camilo's embrace.

Days passed before word reached the club that Concha Urrutia had not shown up for work as usual. Those close to her said that although it was not like her to leave without explanation, they imagined she had been called back to Mexico because of a family emergency. What they secretly believed, however, was that she was afraid of what Ximena Godoy would do to her for messing with Camilo Ibarra. That's what people who worked with Concha really thought, but they didn't have the nerve to come out and say it.

Chapter Forty-Seven

THEY HAD just finished having sex. Ximena reached for a cigarette as she held the sheet against her naked body. When she lit the cigarette, the click of the lighter was the only sound that filled the small dingy bedroom where she and Chucho always met. She leaned back onto the pillow, gazing at his profile and muscular chest, while she inhaled deeply. Chucho returned her look as he reached over, took the cigarette from her lips and put it to his lips. It was a sensuous gesture so she smiled seductively as she took back the cigarette.

All of this happened in silence because, as usual, the lovers hardly spoke during those secret encounters. Their trysts were mostly pawing, kissing and humping, but they were satisfied to be together that way, like mute strangers who fornicated in a dark corner.

Only it was not really a corner. Their love nest was a bungalow that Ximena had searched out and rented, and it was perfect— not too far from the club, yet located at a distance that provided the anonymity and privacy necessary for their get-togethers. The place was one of several rickety cabins, each as dilapidated as the other, crammed side-by-side along a weedy path.

For Ximena, the good part about those shacks was that they housed mostly transient, anonymous strangers passing through Los Angeles on their way somewhere else. These people did not care who walked past their front porch even at all hours, much less did they care about what was going on next door. In other words, those bungalow people minded their own business, which was what Ximena needed.

This day was like Ximena and Chucho's usual encounters, but there was also something special about it: she had something on her mind besides sex, and he sensed it. With his head still cushioned against the pillow he cuddled closer to her, his eyes half closed while his hand caressed her breast.

"What's on your mind, Ximena?"

"What makes you think there's something going on up here?" She tapped her forehead with her index finger and smiled again.

"I just know it."

He took the cigarette from her again, only this time he took a lungful of smoke, and then playfully puffed out tiny rings that danced toward the ceiling. He was quiet, but when he looked at her it was with teasing eyes. Chucho Arana was not an educated man: he had dropped out of school at ninth grade level. But years of living on his own had given him an uncanny sense of what made people tick. Even at half Ximena's age, he was a good match when it came to sensing what others were thinking; it was a skill he had developed while growing up alone.

In fact, Chucho considered himself an orphan—but not the kind that people feel sorry for because a dead mother and father left him behind. He thought of himself as an orphan because he had lost track of his parents sometime during his early years, and the way he told the story was that he did not remember ever having a mother or father. By the time he thought of himself as Chucho Arana, he was alone, a drifter as well as a petty thief who was usually running away from cops or victims, and sometimes both.

As a child, Chucho learned that it was easy to swipe stuff off grocery store shelves, and even easier to turn around and sell those goods. Then as he grew into his teens, he outgrew snatching grocery store junk and took up stealing more profitable things to sell, like bicycles, car radios and hubcaps. So by the time Chucho got to be twenty, he considered himself a pretty slick car thief. Stealing became his only job, one he liked because of the money it gave him to buy the sharp suits and shoes he loved. The only problem was that cops often nabbed him, and he ended up doing stretches in reform school or on some work farm or another.

Chucho's goodtime life took a turn for the worse the time he hotwired a judge's Chrysler and got caught just as he was driving away. This time his luck seriously ran out: he would not get off with an easy stint on a farm because that same judge threw the toughest sentence possible at Chucho: a stretch in prison. But luck didn't exactly abandon him for good because it was late 1944: the war had been going on for years, and the Army was hard-pressed to find new recruits. So when the judge realized that Chucho Arana had so far managed to dodge the draft, he gave him an option: sign up with the Army or go to prison.

"It's your choice! Sign up right here and now, or it's jail time for you. There's a recruiting table just outside this courtroom. It's your choice."

In a matter of hours, Chucho was on a bus leaving Brownsville, his hometown, headed for Fort Ord in northern California, to serve in the Army. He didn't resent it because a soldier's life, he told himself, was better than being a jailbird, although he was scared of dying. And Chucho's luck kicked back in. By the time he finished basic training and was ready to be shipped overseas, the conflict had ended. Chucho was saved at the last minute. He not only beat doing prison time, but he learned a lot from his fellow recruits.

He learned about gambling, especially craps, and at the same time he fell in love with California. When he was discharged he looked around and decided that Los Angeles, with its jumping jazz clubs, gambling, movie stars and mobsters, was the place for him. It was then that he became a bartender and settled in to see what would come up next.

Chucho Arana was a complicated man, mostly because he was contradictory; it was hard to tell who he really was. In his inner recesses, there was a dangerous mix of over-confidence and insecurity that he masked with an outward swagger, a smart-alecky style. His personality also covered up an uncommon self-centeredness that explained his obsessive fixation on his looks and dress, as well as hostility when he sensed a rival. However, there was more to Chucho's complex personality. If anyone dug around looking for a yet more serious character flaw, that person would find greed. Above all, Chucho loved money. He found the allure of cold cash irresistible, so when he met Ximena Godoy he not only sensed her ambition right away, he also sniffed the sweet smell of money that stuck to her like perfume.

"We make a good pair," Ximena said, as she leaned against the headrest and looked at Chucho through half-closed eyes. He rolled over to get closer, and kissed her shoulder.

"What do you mean?"

"We both want more."

Chucho stretched his leg under the sheet and draped it over hers, at the same time his hand wandered up and down her belly until it rested on the soft, furry triangle between her thighs. However, his thoughts weren't about what he was touching; he was thinking, rather, that she was right about the both of them. He was thinking, too, that it was Ximena's lust for more of everything that fascinated him so much.

"Yeah! We make a good pair all right," he agreed but, sensing something more behind her words, went on, "Are you thinking of anything special?"

"¡Ay! You *are* a *cabrón*, aren't you? Can't I come out with something simple without you smelling a rat?"

He flashed his charming smile, knowing it worked each time he wanted something of Ximena. "Why a rat? Can't it be something nice and cute?"

"You think I'm playing a game?"

"I never think that of you."

Chucho felt something moving through Ximena's body, something like a current of energy, so he pulled his hand back and moved away a few inches to prop himself up on his elbow. He wanted to look into her eyes; after a few seconds he reached over, put a finger under her chin and turned her face toward him. Positioned that way, the lovers gazed at each other almost nose to nose.

Ximena saw that Chucho was trying to read her mind, but it was all right because this was the day she had chosen to bring him into her scheme. She had already weighed every word she was about to say, knowing that she risked everything by exposing her private plan. She knew that by putting her cards on the table she was putting herself in his hands. But these misgivings weren't new to her. In her mind she had gone through everything before, step by step, considering consequences, even calculating results that she might not intend, or foresee: at the end of it all she decided to take Chucho in for the simple reason that she needed him. "I need you to help me with a job."

"What kind of job?"

"A special one."

Chucho snuggled up closer to Ximena, his eyes burning with curiosity.

"Shoot! I'm ready."

She knew that he had already caught on to her ways; that she wasn't coy; that when she had something to say, she spoke directly, without playing games.

"I need a holdup to happen."

"What?" He jerked away and stared at her.

"You heard me."

He kept quiet, but not for long. "That means money."

"Yes."

"How much?"

"A bundle."

"And I suppose the crook's gonna be me. Right?"

"You catch on fast."

Now it was his turn to light up, and hers to lift the cigarette from his lips to bring it to her own. As they did this, they followed the sensual ritual, in silence. They were both deep in thought.

"Ximena, let me guess: the guy I'm gonna holdup is Mr. Ibarra. Am I hot or cold?"

"Burning."

"Isn't that like stealing from yourself?"

Her head snapped in his direction, and her face showed frustration. "Chucho, I don't want questions from you. All I want is a *yes* or a *no*!"

Put in his place, he retreated back into his thoughts. But not for long, because he had more questions to ask, even if it ticked her off. "What if something goes wrong? What if someone gets hurt, or even killed?"

"What if I tell you that's exactly what's supposed to happen?"

Chucho's eyes widened as he gawked at Ximena, and she nearly burst out laughing. He never looked confused like this.

But she didn't laugh because she had him just where she wanted him. And Ximena didn't want anything to spook him.

"Jesus Christ, Ximena! What's all this about? You're saying you want me to snuff out Mr. Ibarra?"

"Yes."

"Why?"

"That's my business, Chucho. All I want to hear from you is *yes* or *no*! Make up your mind!"

"I gotta know why!" Chucho showed that he was feeling pushed around, intimidated, and he didn't like it, but Ximena was unmoved: she kept her half-closed eyes pasted on him, hardly blinking.

"Okay, so you want me to rob Mr. Ibarra, but why kill him? Why not just get away with the money?"

"Accidents happen when people mess around with holdups. They get hurt. It's expected because it's part of the picture; it's natural."

"Is it because you caught him and Concha Urrutia fucking?" This provoked a glare from Ximena, but she didn't say anything, so he went on. "If that's the reason, you're crazy! Think of it, Ximena! If people went around killing each other just because of that, half the world would be dead."

"*Yes* or *no*, Chucho." Ximena was unrelenting and losing patience, but she was also thinking that this might be a mistake, that maybe Chucho was just a bag of hot air. What mattered even more to her just then was that she felt something inside her slipping, and she knew doubt was creeping in. Something was telling her that, despite all she had already done, perhaps she could still reverse her direction.

Chucho reached for another smoke, only this time without the sexy pass-the-cigarette routine. He took a deep drag on the fresh cigarette because he desperately needed that lift, that nicotine rush that shoots through the veins up to the brain and gives a guy the dose of heft he needs. Chucho then turned away from Ximena and stared at the opposite wall, taking time to speak. He didn't want to show that he was afraid, yet he needed time to steady his racing heart. "Why me?"

"Because I trust you."

"Ximena, are you joking?"

"Goddamn it, Chucho! You know I'm not joking, so what will it be? Yes or no."

"What if I say no?"

"Then it's no. End of story!"

"What if I blow the whistle on you?"

Ximena stiffened and sat up, on the verge of losing control, but she answered anyway. "Who do you think people would believe? If you want to risk it, go ahead. Be my guest."

Her cockiness brought him down hard, so he retreated into silence, knowing he would be dog meat if he were stupid enough to snitch on her. Beside, no one would believe him anyway, not even Camilo Ibarra. Yet killing someone was something Chucho had never done, and the thought of it terrified him.

I'm a chiseler, not a murderer. Maybe if I'd gone to war and killed a couple of Japs I could do it, but I didn't, so I can't, and that's that!

"Ximena, how would I do it? Where would I do it?"

"Listen to me, Chucho! Every Sunday night, when we close the club, Camilo gets into the safe, pulls out the profits that come in during the week, puts it all in a satchel that he takes out to the car. Then we pack up and leave. By that time it's about three in the morning and no one's around. When we get out on the curb, you can jump him."

"Yeah? Just like that?" Chucho snapped his fingers. "I'll bet he has some kind of bodyguard with him."

"No! He never has anyone else with him. Just me."

"That's what you think! He probably has some guy hide somewhere in the dark just in case he's jumped."

"I'm telling you: he doesn't have anyone!"

"So then how do I do it?" Chucho's stomach was churning. He was scared just listening to what Ximena was saying.

"Do I have to tell you everything? Use your brains for a change! Get a gun! You can do that anywhere on the street! Then make sure you cover your face so he doesn't recognize you right off when you snatch the money. Then you shoot him."

"Jesus Christ! Listen to yourself, Ximena. First you tell me to kill him. Then you tell me to cover my face. What difference does it make if he'll be dead anyway?"

There's gotta be another way around this thing. Why do

I have to kill him? He's never done anything to me. Chucho's mind whirled with anxiety at the thought of killing Camilo Ibarra.

"Look, Ximena, this is big, maybe too big for me. I need time to think it over."

"Yes or no, Chucho!"

"What's in it for me?"

"A week's profit from the club."

"About how much?'

"About ten grand in cash."

His head snapped around to look at her. He could hardly believe his ears, knowing that it would take him years to squirrel away that kind of money, and the risks began to fade compared to the payoff. In moments, new thoughts crept into Chucho's mind.

Maybe if I play my cards right I can do it my way. I could just grab the money and disappear, couldn't I? I mean forever. Gone far from her. She couldn't jump into the middle of the stick-up and force me to kill him. What could she do about it? Nothing, right? She couldn't tell the cops she hired me to kill her partner, that's for sure.

"Yes or no, Chucho."

"Yeah."

Then they had sex again.

PART THREE

Chapter Forty-Eight

Los Angeles — Late 1950

IT WAS noon the day after Camilo Ibarra's killing. The clock on Ximena's mantel ticked, filling the empty room with its metallic sound. As late as it was, Ximena was still in her robe. She was sipping whiskey, smoking and waiting; she had yet to snap out of the trance into which she had fallen now that her plan was completed. Then the phone rang. Its loud bell shattered the silence of the shadowy house, but she did not make a move to pick up until the ringing grew louder, shriller, and she was forced onto her feet.

"Hello!?"

"Miss Godoy?"

"Yes?"

"This is Detective Tieg. We've got some follow-up questions regarding last night's homicide. Can you come to the precinct? Or if it's better for you, we can show up at your place? Whatever suits you."

Ximena did not answer; her breath had caught in her throat. She finally muttered, "I'll wait here. Give me an hour."

"Fine. See you then."

She returned the receiver to its cradle, but she did not move her hand away. It was almost as if it was glued to the phone. She felt numb, incapable of getting her fingers to let go, and the same was happening to her legs which had turned wooden. *Did the cop get wind of Chucho? What kind of questions could he still have?*

When Ximena forced herself to calm down she went to the bathroom, opened up the faucets full blast, and waited until steam filled the room. Then she stood under the shower, its hot water splashing onto her head, face, shoulders, breasts, thighs and legs. She stayed there, feeling wrapped in a protective cocoon. Though she didn't want to leave that shelter, eventually she did move out into the bedroom to dress, all the while trying not to think.

When she finished dressing, Ximena went to the living room where she sat waiting, and it was not long before heavy rapping got her back on her feet. When she opened the door, Detectives Poole and Tieg mechanically raised their fedoras in greeting.

"Good afternoon, Miss Godoy! I rang the bell but it didn't sound." Tieg, obviously trying to be polite, spoke up in his nasal voice, but Ximena didn't bother to answer. Instead, she led them into the living room. Only then did she mutter, "Come in."

"Thanks!"

Making their way toward the sofa and chair, the detectives' eyes darted in every direction, inspecting whatever met their sharp gaze. They glanced up and down, to the sides, and had their eyes been able to see around corners, they would have looked there as well. Once seated, as if performing a ritual, the three lit cigarettes that filled the room with a blue haze.

"How can I help?" Ximena's voice was low and cautious. She was trying hard not to show that her nerves were straining.

"Miss Godoy, I'm sure that you're pretty wiped out and hurting a lot, so I'll get to the point." Tieg took a long drag, gave himself time to exhale, and then returned to what he was saying. "We've talked to some of your crew, but there's more we need to know."

Ximena mirrored the detective and took a drag from her cigarette, giving her time before she said anything. "You found workers at the club this early?"

"No. We hauled them over to the precinct."

Again Ximena stalled before speaking; she wanted to give her heart time to stop racing. *What did these cops find out? What did the workers tell them?*

"Okay. How can I help?"

"Well, we asked about the victim, and even if we did get some good background there's still more we need to know about Mr. Ibarra. We think that you're the best one to give us that information. Uh! By the way, before I forget, we need to know if Mr. Ibarra had insurance."

Ximena's stomach tightened, but she answered calmly. "Yes! Camilo was an astute businessman, and he made sure he had insurances."

The cop asked, "What kind?"

"He pretty much kept that information to himself."

"You were his business partner, weren't you? I'd expect that you'd be in on that sort of information."

"Well, you're right. I know that we had insurance on the buildings as well as coverage for the employees, if that's what you mean."

"Yeah, that helps. What about personal insurance?"

Ximena saw that the detective's eyes were riveted on hers, but she did not evade his look; she stared right back.

"I think he had accident insurance or even a life policy. Maybe both."

"We need that information. Could you give it to me as soon as possible?" But then Tieg paused, and changed his mind. "On second thought, we can get that information on our own. You have enough on your hands."

"Thanks."

Ximena waited for the next probe but was relieved that the detective ended the conversation about the dead man's insurance.

"Okay! Now back to what I was saying. Talking to your workers, we came across another name."

"Which one?

Tieg scowled. "Chucho Arana." He spoke the name without moving his eyes off Ximena's face, evidently looking for a change of expression. "He was one of your workers, is that right?"

"Yes. He was one of the bartenders."

"Some of your workers told us that Arana disappeared a few days ago. In fact, it wasn't long before last night's holdup."

"That could be, but I can't be sure. That was Camilo's department."

Ximena felt that her nerves were taking over, so much so that, despite craving another cigarette, she didn't dare reach for one knowing that her shaking hands might give her away. She kept still, prompting Tieg to go on.

"Miss Godoy, what exactly do you know of this Chucho Arana?"

"Only that he was a good bartender."

"Didn't you check him out before you hired him?"

"He came to us with written references. All of them were good, and that was enough for Mr. Ibarra and me."

"Nothing else?"

Was the floor beneath her shaking? She thought so, or was it the shudder of her unraveling nerves? *Goddamn you, Tieg! Go away! Leave me alone!* Ximena forced herself to say something that would not betray what she was thinking, or the exasperation she was feeling. "Detective Tieg, what are you driving at? Just come out and say it so I can get a clearer picture."

"Okay. This Chucho Arana has a rap sheet as long as my arm that says he's been a thief and con artist since he was a kid. He's been in and out of juvenile halls and reform schools, and only dodged big time prison by signing up for service during the war. I hate to be the one to tell you this, but it looks like he could be the one who held up and killed Mr. Ibarra. The punk's probably deep into Mexico by now, so you might have to kiss your money good-bye."

Ximena felt the air sucked out of her, as if Tieg had punched her in the stomach. Her face drained and her eyes fell shut, but she didn't try to mask any part of this reaction, knowing that it would likely work to her benefit by suggesting her utter surprise and innocence.

"Miss Godoy, can I get you a glass of water? How about something stronger?"

"No, thanks! I'll be okay in a minute. It's just that what you're telling me is so awful. We should've checked him out more carefully. Just give me a little time."

Tieg nodded, then turned to his partner to whisper. Meanwhile, Ximena steadied her nerves. All along she had been afraid that she was suspected, but now she realized she was being regarded as a victim, not a suspect, so she relaxed. She had not known that part of Chucho's past. In fact, she didn't know anything of his life, but now that the cop had laid it out, she felt relieved, not deceived.

From the time she made the deal with Chucho Arana she had fought off nagging doubts about him, and distrust was always with her. There was her worry that he might be tempted to run off with the cash and not link up with her in Mexico as they had planned. She had that lingering suspicion all along, but there was nothing she could do about it. She needed him to pull off the holdup, and there was no way of going back once the plan got going.

But now she was relieved that the cops thought Chucho was the culprit, and she did nothing to change their thinking.

Run, you weasel, and never show up again! The more you run, the guiltier you look. The money you're stealing is chickenfeed compared to what's coming to me.

"What can I do?" Ximena murmured when she saw Tieg and Poole staring at her.

"Leave it to us. We'll catch him, even if it takes a long time." Tieg was quiet for a minute, but then he reached into his breast pocket and pulled out a note pad. "I hate to do this, Miss Godoy, but there's more we need. Are you feeling up to it? We can come back later if it suits you."

Ximena felt that a huge burden had been lifted off her, and she felt lighthearted, optimistic, even cheerful and ready to move on. "No, let's get everything out of the way right now." Even her voice had lightened.

As Tieg flipped pages, Ximena glanced over to look at Poole and saw that he was scribbling in his own notebook. She glared at the paunchy man, and sniggered, "Your partner is a real chatterbox, isn't he?"

Tieg squinted at Ximena with his beady eyes, then twisted over to stare at Poole, grinned wide, exposing his long front teeth, but then disregarded her sarcasm. He returned to his notes, cleared his voice and read out the name.

"Here it is. We need to know about Concha Ur...Urr... Damn! I can never get my tongue around those double letters."

"Urrutia." Ximena helped him.

"That's it! A couple of your guys mentioned her name but

couldn't say much more about her."

"Why do you want to know about her if only a couple of people mentioned her name?"

"Well, we gotta follow up on everything, even scraps, and we hear she took off too, just like the slick Chucho Arana. Are you following me?"

"What are you insinuating?" Ximena returned to being cautious.

"All we can say is, we want to know about her whereabouts. Maybe she quit the job. Maybe she's on vacation. We don't know, but it's gotta be cleared up, because right now it doesn't look good for her. Her taking a powder almost at the same time as Arana has to be explained."

An idea, like a light, went on in Ximena's head: Chucho and Concha, the real culprits! She could not have planned it better, and it was Tieg who came up with the idea.

"I knew her."

"How?"

"I knew her, that's all."

"What happened to her?"

"Nothing happened to her. What gives you the idea that something happened to her?"

"Well, you said that you knew her, making me think she disappeared or something."

"I think she went back to Mexico years ago... I lost track of her."

"Years ago? Your guys sounded as though she took off just a short time ago."

"Well maybe it hasn't been that long. I don't remember! I don't keep track of the comings and goings of our workers."

"That makes sense, but if you can tell me when she took off, just a more or less, it'll be a big help. If it's recently, it'll link her disappearance with Chucho Arana."

Ximena felt worn down by the detective's persistent questions, and she was afraid of saying the wrong thing, so she clammed up. However, because she now felt steady enough, she lit up. Her cigarette held between relaxed fingers, she stared out the window. She knew that this was the moment to clear Concha of any connection to Chucho Arana. It was in her hands to set that matter straight, but she decided to shut up. *Let Tieg think what he wants.*

Looking at her, the detective caught on that Ximena did not want to talk anymore, yet he also sensed that he had tapped into something important. He decided to press for more.

"Well? Why would your guys think she was important enough to remember?"

With her eyes glazed over, Ximena put on a bored look and went on staring out the window, but in a moment she turned to the detective, shrugged her shoulders and said, "Maybe Concha and Chucho were in on the holdup. Who can tell?" She sat back, knowing that she had now sealed Concha's fate in a much worse way than she had originally planned. But she felt nothing, neither satisfaction nor remorse. What went through Ximena's mind were the words, *now we're even.*

Chapter Forty-Nine

XIMENA SHUT her door, relieved to be rid of the detectives, although Tieg's parting words left her feeling uneasy.

"You're free to go back to business, Miss Godoy," he'd said, but added, "for the time being." This last part bothered her. *What did he mean? Is he going to do more snooping?* She gave the thought a few seconds, then shrugged her shoulders and headed back to the living room where she paced for a while longer. Ximena then picked up a cigarette, lit it, and walked over to the front window where she stood staring out at the street.

After a while she moved away to pace around the room as if waiting for somebody or something. Camilo was dead and Concha was gone, but Chucho Arana was out there somewhere, and this weighed heavily on her mind. She let herself linger on that thought, but returned to thinking of what her next step should be.

She would have to deal with business, as the detective said, and the first thing would be the arrangements of Camilo's services. He had a big family who were, no doubt, torn up over his untimely and violent death, and not only were there family members but also friends, workers and associates. Camilo was a well-known and well-loved person and lots of people expected to pay their last respects. There would have to be a rosary and *velorio*, a Mass, a funeral and finally the burial.

A priest was mandatory, naturally. All of this needed phone calls, appointments with florists, catered food for the mourners and contact with the mortuary.

Ximena was expected to take care of that business because she was considered the widow, regardless of the legalities of the relationship. She was struck by the irony of having caused his death, and now having to take charge of those details, all the while pretending to be grief-stricken.

But Ximena Godoy did it all expertly. She went through it all step by step, detail by detail. On the day of condolences she stood, as the grieving partner, shrouded in a black *mantilla* that covered her head and face down to her chest. She accepted expressions of sympathy with a resigned dignity that evoked admiration.

Thank God she's a strong woman! Someone else would have collapsed by now! And to think the terrible crime happened right in front of her! What courage! They say there was blood all over her dress.

Ximena faced the rituals for the dead, knowing that at day's end she would retreat back into the solitude that always gave her strength and kept her going. It was with that same strange calm that she endured the days and weeks that followed. One by one, she ticked off items from a list she had worked out in her head.

The first step was getting through the aftermath that followed Camilo's death. With that behind her, she moved on to the next item: signing the insurance claim documents that stipulated a waiting period of at least four weeks. Fine! She could do that much, especially when she was informed of the dollar amount of Camilo's insurance policy.

Miss Godoy, the amount is two hundred thousand dollars, and you're the only beneficiary. How Mr. Ibarra must have loved you! Although, I know that it's nothing compared to the loss of such a fine person.

Next on the list was the sale of the enterprises that were now totally hers. The restaurants and the nightclub had to be sold, so she set in motion the mechanics of getting a broker and buyers; after that, all she had to do was wait. Ximena went through all of this with a quiet dignity that won over people because they felt sympathy and admiration at the same time.

In the meantime, her days blended into weeks that began to drag, especially at the end of each day when she was alone. It was not as easy as she had thought it would be. She began to feel restless and jittery...

Her anxieties intensified. One day when she returned home, just as she was pouring a drink, Ximena glanced toward Camilo's favorite easy chair, and there he sat, as he always had, with one leg crossed over the other, a cigarette between his fingers, smiling his usual broad, toothy grin. The vision was so real that she dropped her drink. She looked down at the liquid and ice on the floor and muttered in disgust, but when she glanced up again, the apparition had vanished. Ximena realized that she had been mistaken and she shakily told herself it had been just a figment of her overworked imagination.

I'm just too worn out, she whispered. The experience left her shaken. She pulled herself together, poured a new drink, went to the kitchen for a snack and then took a long steamy bath before going to bed. However, the vision of Camilo sitting in the chair stayed with her. He had seemed so real and it stuck in her mind—she could not stop thinking of it for a long while.

Later on, however, when the vision not only returned but continued, and when he seemed to speak, her nerves began to fray again. She knew that something unnatural was happening to her. Terror began to make its home in her thinking, and she went sleepless, fearing that he would creep into the room to watch.

She tried to avoid the frightening nightly visits by inviting friends for dinner and drinks, sometimes a little dancing, and she did this frequently. People understood that she was lonely in that big empty house, so they joined her as many times as possible, but they couldn't stay all night.

Ximena, seeking to deal with the haunting vision that came to her when she was alone, resorted to shutting off the living room. It meant going around the long way to reach the kitchen and other parts of the house, but it worked: the vision of Camilo didn't show up afterward, but Ximena still faced sleepless hours brooding over what she had done.

The memory of her daughter returned, now in Ximena's imagination a grown woman. Had Ximenita lived, perhaps it would have altered the way Ximena behaved, the way she reacted, the decisions she had made. Would she, Ximena, have forgiven Concha and Camilo if Ximenita had been alive?

Childhood stories Ximena heard from her aunties and their old *comadres* about the dead also came back to her. These tales were about poor souls trapped for eternity in purgatory because of unforgiven sins. Everyone knew that the departed returned from the grave for one reason alone: To beg for forgiveness from the living.

Is that why you're haunting me, Camilo? Are you looking for my forgiveness?

When Ximena managed to fall asleep, it was a restless, feverish slumber clogged with jumbled dreams, and in the midst of that confusion Camilo returned to accuse her, not to seek forgiveness. Yet even in that haze, Ximena refused to back down. Instead, she justified what she had done. She even tried to prove that she was the injured and not the guilty one. At one time she even confronted the apparition.

Why did you murder me, Ximena? Was it worth it? Don't you feel guilty?

Why should I feel guilty? You're the one who betrayed me.

Ximena, there's blood on your hands.

Shut up! Go away!

There were nights when Ximena awoke, believing that something slimy was on her hands, and she stumbled to the bathroom to wash, even though she could see that her hands were clean. Her days and nights were filled with this turmoil, and as it became too much even for Ximena, she continued to break down, her spirit unraveling. Even her belief that revenge was its own reward was falling apart. Something was going terribly wrong with her plan.

From the beginning, she had known that revenge was not free, that it had its price. She knew that side effects would come with it, feelings of doubt and guilt. She was tough, and she was prepared for all that, she had thought. Yet she now had to admit that the reality of revenge was more terrible than she had ever imagined. The expected satisfaction refused to kick in, the peace of mind she craved and needed eluded her, and the solitude that had given her balance throughout her life had soured into bitter loneliness.

The weight of guilt was wearing Ximena down. It had not played a role in her careful planning, but now it would not go away. That emotion continued to stubbornly interrupt her thoughts and even the precious few hours when she managed to fall asleep. Her spirit shriveled, making her fear that she was losing her mind.

To make matters worse, Ximena aged visibly during those weeks of waiting for her money. Her hair grew out grayer, thinner. When she looked in the mirror she discovered wrinkles that had not been there the day before. When people she dealt with noticed her decline, they thought it was a result of the trauma and shock of witnessing Camilo's bloody murder, and so they sympathized.

Yet, in the face of what would have broken down anyone else's resolve, Ximena went on living her troubled life, knowing there was no turning back. *It's done, isn't it? I can't undo it.* In the meantime, she went about the business of selling property, signing severance agreements with workers, and depositing money that was already coming in. The only item pending was the insurance settlement which was due in a matter of days. So she bided her time, knowing that while all of this business was going on, her eye was riveted on a future into which she would disappear to begin a new life. Thinking like this steadied her nerves.

Chapter Fifty

CHUCHO ARANA no longer figured in Ximena's calculations. But one Saturday morning, Detectives Tieg and Poole again showed up at her front door.

"Good morning, Miss Godoy."

As usual, they greeted her with fedoras in hand, but their presence did not signal anything good for Ximena. In response, she muttered a faint "Good morning," as she felt her stomach tightening. "What can I do for you?"

"May we come in?"

Tieg was already inside the house when he asked that question; his pushiness made it clear to Ximena that there was a change. Without answering, she trailed the detectives into the living room.

"The room is shut down." Tieg said as he turned to Ximena. "Is there any reason for that?"

"No. Go right through. We can talk there."

The detectives went in and took the same seats as on their first visit, still scanning the room as they had always done.

"May I offer you anything? Coffee? A drink?"

"No, thanks. We'll get right to the point."

Tieg helped himself to a cigarette, taking time to light it. Ximena, in the meantime, began to feel sweat trickle down her spine. The detective finally spoke up as he adjusted the pleats of his slacks.

"Well, the good news is that we've arrested Mr. Chucho Arana." He clammed up waiting for Ximena's reaction, his eyes tiny slits focused on her face. When she did not respond, he went on. "We got a break when the guy actually tried to sneak back from Mexico. One of our snitches spotted him in a dive just outside San Diego where Arana was actually trying to shake down some drunk." Tieg took another drag and muttered, "The jerk's got nerve!"

Again the detective waited for something from Ximena, but still she said nothing. He stared at her, trying to detect some response, at least a tiny clue that would alert him to her feelings about his reporting. Finally he asked her directly, "I want to hear what you think, Miss Godoy."

Now it was her turn to veil her feelings by slowly lighting up and taking a deep drag. After taking time, she shrugged her shoulders.

"What can I say except that I'm glad? But isn't there more to this story than just Arana's arrest?"

"What do you mean?"

"Well, so he's arrested. Does that mean he's the one? Do you have proof that he was actually the hold-up guy who killed Camilo Ibarra? I mean, he'll probably deny having anything to do with the crime."

"Oh, he did that plenty of times until he finally broke down and coughed up the whole mess."

Ximena felt that the floor shift. It first went up, then down, and then sideways. *Chucho confessed! What in the hell did he say? What whole mess?* Out loud she stammered, "How did you get him to confess?"

"We have our ways, Miss Godoy."

The cop is playing with me. Why? What's he getting at?

"You say that he confessed to the whole mess? What do you mean?"

"Well, there was an accomplice."

He is playing with me. It took all of Ximena's power to control the nausea that rushed from her belly up her throat, and lodged in her palate. She wanted to vomit, but she commanded herself to stay steady, to at least look natural. She even took the risk of acting curious, just like any other innocent person might have been, especially one as hurt as she was supposed to be. "Did Arana name that accomplice?"

"He sure did." Tieg stopped speaking, implying that he knew the answer to her question but he was not ready to let her in on that information just yet.

Forced to play this guessing game, Ximena murmured, "Concha Urrutia?"

Still acting coy, Tieg answered, "Nope! She's in the clear, so we can forget about her."

Ximena had not planned what happened next. She sprang to her feet and rushed toward the window to look out, as if someone was coming, as if someone was at the door, as if she was about to leave the room. She moved without thinking, but the detectives also stood up, their bodies tensed and ready for a struggle. But Ximena simply stood motionless.

"Miss Godoy, Arana named you as the mastermind of the robbery and killing. He claims that for him, it was an accident because he didn't really plan to do it. He says that you were the one who ordered it, and even caused it when you yanked at him and made the gun go off."

Seconds dragged by before she gathered enough saliva in her mouth to answer. "And you believed him?"

"We didn't believe the creep at first. It wasn't until he produced a letter from you giving him instructions, details, time and place for the heist. I hate to say it, but it's all there on paper, and in your handwriting."

At the mention of a letter, Ximena jerked around to face the men.

"Letter? I've never written him or any other worker a letter."

"We know otherwise, Miss Godoy. It's the one you wrote to him before he did the job. It's even dated. You're quite the businesswoman, very professional, I must say, except for the ending, which was more than a memo to an employee. At least in my opinion."

"What are you talking about?"

Ximena was now throwing out anything that came to her mind to slow down what Tieg was saying. She wanted to put off hearing what she did not want to hear.

"I mean the ending was pretty lovey-dovey, and not how a business letter usually ends."

"Detective, be careful! Why should I have anything to do with any of my workers, much less write a stupid letter? How do you know it's from me? Is it just because that thief says so? Didn't you tell me that he also has a record of forgery? That he's a liar? How can you prove that I wrote such a thing?"

Ximena's heart was racing, but she controlled her voice enough to bombard Tieg with as many questions as she could think of, hoping to derail him. But it didn't work: he ignored all her questions but the last one.

"How can we prove that it's a letter from you? Well, Miss Godoy, let me explain by first of all refreshing your memory. When you put in a claim with the insurance company, you filled out a bunch of documents, and among those papers you wrote a long paragraph listing the reasons that justified your inheriting the money. Remember that? You know those insurance guys! They're probably bigger crooks than anyone else, and naturally, they don't take just any old reasons. No sir! They have to have it all down on paper.

"So, to make a long story short, we got our handwriting experts to compare the writing on the letter slick Chucho gave us with your handwritten long paragraph, and what do you know? The two samples match just fine, even better than that. In fact, we have a perfect match. Miss Godoy, that's why we're sure that Arana blabbed the truth about you, and that's how we can prove it."

As if coming up for breath after being underwater for too long, Tieg stopped talking to gasp for air. Although quiet, he did not take his beady eyes off Ximena who had again turned her back on him.

"Miss Godoy, you're under arrest. Here's the warrant. Please get your coat and bag. You're coming with us to Central." He rattled off this last part without pausing, obviously nervous and expecting a big reaction from Ximena. Then he added, "Don't resist! It will only be held against you."

Was it possible to calculate the seconds it took for the detective's words to penetrate Ximena's understanding? Perhaps such a calculation was not possible. What difference did it make anyway? She understood she had blundered in a grievous way. *The letter!* She had forgotten that she had written the goddamn letter. She had erased it from her mind, and now it had returned to blindside her.

Ximena closed her eyes trying to control the throbbing in her ears, a drumbeat that grew louder, drowning out what the detective was saying until the pounding ebbed, and she heard his high-pitched nasal voice.

"You see, Miss Godoy, every criminal slips up somewhere, no matter how smart he...excuse me...she is. All we cops have to do is wait and keep our eyes peeled."

Was Tieg mocking her? Was he gloating? Or was he preaching? Whatever it was, Ximena knew that she was trapped, and she had done it to herself. She turned to look at the detective, sensing that he was waiting for something, maybe a denial. But that would be useless. Did he expect her to scream or run? She wanted to, but she didn't because she couldn't.

Nothing happened because Ximena's will to survive was draining out of her. It was seeping out of her, drop by drop, until she was deflated and pinned down by fatigue and inertia. All she felt now was a desire to put a stop to the planning and calculating. Gone was the fire in her guts that had fueled her desire to get even and defy anyone who got in her way. She was tired, more than she had ever been in her life.

Ximena became still and quiet. Perhaps she understood that what was happening was really not captivity but release, freedom from being on the defensive, from dread of nightly shadows and phantoms, and that it was a liberation from the insatiable desire for revenge. Maybe she understood that what was happening was inevitable; that it was her destiny and what she deserved. These were the feelings and thoughts that compelled Ximena Godoy to surrender without a struggle.

Detective Tieg had expected resistance from her, so he was surprised by Ximena's submission, and he was even suspicious that perhaps she had something up her sleeve. He muttered, "You can call anyone from the jail."

Chapter Fifty-One

THE PROCESS after Ximena's arrest was swift, mostly the result of her refusal to defend herself or to speak to anyone except a lawyer who at her instruction cut a deal with the District Attorney. Ximena proposed to plead guilty to the double charge of murder and conspiracy to commit fraud, in exchange for life in prison. Her gain was that she would not face having her story dragged out for strangers to probe and scrutinize, and even more important, she would avoid the death sentence that was certain if she faced trial.

This bargain was all Ximena's making, and she did it because of the grim alternative facing her. When she chose a lifetime in prison, it was not because life was still precious to her. The truth was that her will to live had nothing to do with her bargain with the prosecutor. In fact, life had lost all its value for her. Rather, she chose a lifetime behind bars because she was tortured by a morbid fear of death. Just thinking of the electric chair made her head spin so violently that it brought on fits of nausea and vomiting. Ximena hated living, but she was even more terrified of dying.

But there was more. She made the decision to deal with the prosecutor not only because she was paralyzed by the fear of death, but also because she was nauseated by the thought of facing a judge and jury that would be free to pick through her life and intimate relationships. Surely, Concha Urrutia would be dragged up from Mexico to testify, and the thought of what she would say mortified Ximena. So it was this tangle of fears and punishing thoughts that compelled Ximena to seek a life behind bars instead of certain execution.

When the deal was reached and the process complete, she was committed to the prison for women at Tehachapi, located in a desolate, windswept valley in Central California. It was early 1952 when Ximena Godoy dressed in a drab shift and heavy work shoes, joined countless other women convicted of murder, robbery, extortion and many unspeakable crimes. But this meant little to Ximena: in her mind, those inmates did not exist. Instead, she stepped into a solitary world of her own making, a place where she took refuge within herself, rarely speaking to anyone except to respond to curt orders from guards.

The Ending

Tehachapi, California, 1952.

IT WAS past midnight. Darkness filled the cellblock housing Ximena Godoy, but despite the late hour, her cell was airless and sultry, a leftover from the July heat that usually gripped the valley at that time of year. Up and down the concrete corridor the inmates were silent. They slumbered like caged, wary animals, and only the wind's incessant sighing fractured the stillness as it sifted through bars and wired openings. Sleepless, Ximena stared at the dark ceiling. She did not have a cellmate so she was alone to wrestle with boredom and insomnia.

Months had passed since her arrival at this prison for discarded women. In that half a year, she withdrew so deeply into self-imposed isolation that other inmates hardly recognized her voice when she spoke. She was friendless by choice, although she understood that each day of solitude was a risk. She knew that no one survived in that place without the consolation of at least one friend. But she had her nights that brought her a lifeline, not to the present but to her past. It was during those long, empty nights that images returned to her, images of people who had inhabited her lifetime. And this was enough to give Ximena a strange comfort.

Each night, as soon as the procession of memories began, she sat on the narrow cot and leaned against the brick wall to watch the images drift by. Tacho Medina, Don Pepo, Señora Epifania,

Amador Mendoza—all of them came to pay their nightly visit.
She stared at them as they emerged from one side of the cell and
moved to slide through the barred window until they vanished
into the bleak desert night.

Those phantoms didn't frighten Ximena. She knew they
were only thoughts and memories, and they got her through the
dreary night. In a strange way, they even helped her understand
her life. Somehow they gave Ximena answers to longtime doubts
and questions that took her as far back as her childhood.

Every night like clockwork, the apparitions sauntered
by Ximena, not in the order in which they had lived in her
lifetime, but jumbled and mixed up. The only one that was clear
and sharp was Ximenita, still a little girl, still waiting for her
mother's return.

"How stupid!" Ximena mumbled, wondering at the crazy
combinations, yet she didn't try to decipher the meaning of
what she saw; she only sat and brooded. It was during those
nights that her father returned; his image more vivid than ever,
his words still burning her, reminding her that a woman was like
fine crystal made worthless when handled by men.

She thought of the lovers, and the powerful urges that
compelled her to do it. She thought of her mother, and of her
sisters and brothers, all lost to her.

Without fail, the procession turned most painful when she
caught sight of Concha Urrutia, her image so transparent that it
was hard for Ximena to make it out, and next to Concha stood
Camilo Ibarra, his head still bloodied from the bullet wound she
had pressured her lover to deliver. It was here, at this instant,
that Ximena's memories became a torment. Of all her deeds
and misdeeds, of everything she had done to reach what her
ambition, pride and vanity had compelled her to do, it was
her act of revenge that returned to torture what was left of her
conscience.

It was the reappearance of Concha and Camilo that forced
Ximena to reflect on her decision to choose revenge instead of
forgiveness. She fought off the impulse to regret what she had
done: it had been her decision and, given the chance, she would
do it over again.

"I'd do it again." Ximena understood that she had gained

emptiness, that the satisfaction she had expected was false and meaningless, and was nothing but a crazy delusion,. Still, it had been her choice. Remembering the lessons on sin, penance and absolution taught to her as a child by the nuns, Ximena looked down at her hands, their fingers clasped as if in prayer, and she thought, *For me, there's only sin and penance. It's too late for remorse and absolution. That's all that's left.*

Those nightly visions and recriminations were Ximena's only contact with other beings, and they left her haggard and worn out to face the next day. Yet she felt that she deserved that punishment; that if she suffered it was because she had caused her own torment.

Her wretchedness, however, would end soon because one morning Ximena's musings came to an abrupt end just as the apparitions vanished, and an unrecognized rattle suddenly jarred her from her musings.

Startled, she looked around trying to identify the noise, and she saw that it was coming from the tin cup bouncing on the rickety shelf above the hand basin. It was the toothbrush clanging against the cup. More noises followed. Squeaking, grinding, shifting, all of it combined into a soft low crunching murmur.

Then there was a short but powerful jolt, and in a split second, without warning, the ground began to heave and buck and rear like a wild animal trying to rid itself of an intolerable load. Up and down, sideways, around and around, the ground beneath Ximena quaked and rolled so violently that it flung her from the cot, forcing her to grab at whatever support she could reach.

She was terrified by the unnerving sounds, the din of mortar cracking, bricks scraping against one another as they crumbled, one by one, and then in slabs, until walls, ceilings and support beams crashed down flattening whatever was beneath. She instinctively crawled under the cot, but the thing was flimsy and useless; it could not give protection against the weight of concrete, wood and brick.

Although the earthquake lasted only seconds, for Ximena Godoy it seemed an eternity, and when she found herself pinned under the weight of debris, she fought to free herself. At the same time, she screamed for help, but it was no use because the roar of the crumbling building drowned out her howling.

Crushed under unbearable weight, her mouth hanging open, Ximena gasped and tried to breathe. But she only managed to suck in sand and dust. She coughed and gagged until she felt the air oozing out of her; only then did she stop struggling to murmur one last word: *Ximenita.*

Within hours, newspapers and radios flashed the news across the nation reporting that an earthquake, *The Great Tehachapi Quake,* had destroyed the small community by that name in California. The country was informed that the catastrophic convulsion struck at 4:52 a.m. on July 21, 1952, devastating property, including the Women's Prison. Among the dead was Ximena Godoy.

Acknowledgments

I'm deeply grateful to Peter Limón (Tío Lili) for much valuable information he shared with me in preparation of this novel. He brought back to life vivid images of Post World War II Los Angeles, and the people who inhabited those days. My conversations with Peter inspired images of that generation of men and women who survived the Great Depression, and later on the terrible years of the War. Peter's descriptions recreated the dress and style of the times, its music, dance gambling, as well as a world of movie stars and gangsters. Through him, the Los Angeles of my birth and childhood came back to life.

I'm also indebted to Robert Robles, cousin and family historian. His research provided me with photos, newspaper articles and, of course, invaluable family *chisme*.

Lastly and of immeasurable assistance, is Leticia Gómez, literary agent and creator of the new imprint, ***Café con Leche***. Thank you, Leticia, for your faith in my work, for your editing talents and insights into this novel that tells the story of the unconventional and untraditional Ximena Godoy.

gl